Advance praise f̶o̶ ̶ !

"Eddie Sarfaty's humor is never cruel—or only as cruel as life itself. Whereas most humorists are so broad, so exaggerated that no chapter is as funny as a single page and no page as funny as a sentence, Sarfaty doesn't deal in one-liners or cheap laughs. All his laughs are expensive—they call on deep reserves of observation, humanity and kindness. This is a book you will read in one sitting all the way to the end with a smile on your face and tears in your eyes."
—Edmund White, author of *A Boy's Own Story*

"In *Mental: Funny in the Head,* Sarfaty mixes the grotesque and the tender into a heartbreaking portrait of family, that most potent of touchstones. Sarfaty creates a world that echoes the poignant irony of David Sedaris and Augusten Burroughs but is, without question, entirely his own."
—Patrick Moore, author of *Tweaked*

"In this engaging and frequently hilarious collection, Eddie Sarfaty combines humor and poignancy as skillfully as he writes about being Jewish and gay. This book proves that in addition to being a talented stand-up comedian, Eddie's also a wonderful writer."
—Bob Smith, author of *Openly Bob* and *Selfish and Perverse*

"Eddie Sarfaty is a gifted stand-up comic, but his book is not just a collection of humorous sketches and clever one-liners. These are fully realized true-life stories, fresh and well-observed, expertly crafted and naturally funny. Sarfaty uses comedy not to keep his people at arm's length but to bring us closer to them. He is not afraid to move us and he is not afraid to be smart. And he writes beautifully, like an angel with a wise heart and a wonderfully foul mouth."
—Christopher Bram, author of *Gods & Monsters*

"Anyone who reads this book and doesn't fall in love with Eddie Sarfaty is an idiot."
—Michael Thomas Ford, author of *Last Summer*

MENTAL

funny in the head

EDDIE SARFATY

KENSINGTON BOOKS

http://www.kensingtonbooks.com

KENSINGTON BOOKS are published by

Kensington Publishing Corp.
119 West 40th Street
New York, NY 10018

All Kensington titles, imprints, and distributed lines are available at special quantity discounts for bulk purchases for sales promotion, premiums, fund-raising, educational, or institutional use.

Special book excerpts or customized printings can also be created to fit specific needs. For details, write or phone the office of the Kensington Special Sales Manager: Kensington Publishing Corp., 119 West 40th Street, New York, NY 10018. Attn. Special Sales Department. Phone: 1-800-221-2647.

Kensington and the K logo Reg. U.S. Pat. & TM Off.

ISBN-13: 978-0-7582-2255-8
ISBN-10: 0-7582-2255-6

First Kensington Trade Paperback Printing: July 2009
10   9   8   7   6   5   4   3   2   1

Printed in the United States of America

For Mom and Michael

Contents

MENTAL

Second-Guessing Grandma

I make my grandmother cry.

I come out to her and her fists close and her eyes fill up. She is silent for the longest moment and then, speaking through the tears, she astonishes me.

"It's that gym where you go, that's where they all are!"

Her assertion makes me laugh inside. How could she possibly know that? She's never been to my gym. How could my frail little grandma, a sheltered girl from an Orthodox family, a woman who has barely left the house for the past thirty years, have any kind of insight on the subject?

The conversation continues with her becoming progressively more and more upset. She's perched on the upholstered green rocker from JCPenney, a half-finished afghan in her lap, and I'm sitting Indian-style on the wall-to-wall carpet facing her. I'm peripherally aware of my mom and dad listening helplessly to the whole exchange as they pretend to wash dishes in the next room.

Though I came out to my parents after college, as a rule I managed to find a million nonsexual things to talk about when visiting them—a relief since when I was with my friends, sex was the only thing we ever seemed to talk about. But this time

Granny brings up the issue and continues pressing it until I have no choice but to come clean. She also confesses to having purposely avoided the subject of my sexuality until now, but has finally decided to take the leap:

"Well, I thought that you were, and I made up my mind I was gonna ask you!"

"Well, how do you feel?"

"It's a shock!"

She sheds more tears and my soothing accelerates to match her distress. I hand her a Kleenex and hold her hand. My mother, accustomed to taking charge in a crisis, takes advantage of my grandmother's poor hearing, tiptoes behind the rocker, shakes her head, and mouths to me, *"You shouldn't have told her, you shouldn't have told her."* It's a big help.

With an evil stare I send her back to the sink and continue my comforting. Two seconds later the phone rings. I hear my mother pick it up and can tell from her voice it's my brother Jack who's in grad school in Chicago. I turn my attention back to Granny as my mother calls from the kitchen,

"Ed, Ed, pick up the phone!"

Annoyed, I yell back, *"Not now, for God's sake."*

And then I hear my mother announcing, as if into a public address system, *"He can't come to the phone. He's telling Grandma that he's gay!"*

And so I'm outed to my brother and think, "One less call to make."

I spend the next hour or so quietly seated on the floor and then leave my grandmother to catch my train back to New York and the apartment I share with three other twentysome-things—all gay and in various stages of self-loathing. The incident's constantly on my mind the entire week. It's still on her mind too, when I call home two days later:

"Hi, Granny, how are you?"

"How do you think I am?"

(Pin drops.)

"What are you doing? Watching TV?"

"No, just thinking."

(Crickets.)

"Well, what are you thinking about?"

"What do you think I'm thinking about?"

Similar stressful exchanges occur on days three, four, and five.

Being the youngest, the favorite, and the only one who still lives close enough to visit regularly, I feel a special devotion to my grandmother. Our relationship is one of the most wonderful things in my life. She lived with us while I was growing up—my maturation coinciding with her decline. At the age of ninety-five (although she'll only admit to ninety-two), her mind is sharp but her body is brittle. As time passes I find myself more and more in the role of the adult—keeping her informed, preparing her meals, and helping her into bed. The possibility that the bond between us could be permanently damaged is crippling to me.

After almost two weeks of tense, awkward phone calls, I again go home for a visit. There's no reference to my revelation and the day passes more easily than I expect. It isn't until late evening when it even comes up. I'm tucking Granny in—gently rotating her fragile legs onto the bed while I cradle her back and slowly lower her onto the mattress. As I smooth out the covers, she brings up the subject that we've managed to avoid the entire day.

"So, you don't like a girl to get married?"

My body tenses. "No."

"You prefer a boy?"

I breathe deeply. "Yes."

She pauses and then says resolutely, "Well, then that'll be your life and you'll be happy that way."

"Yes."

My tension melts away but returns when she says, "But it's not like making love with a girl. What can you do?"

I see where this is leading and try to head it off.

"Well, Grandma, it isn't about sex. It's about who you love and who you care for."

She will not be deterred.

"Yes, yes, I know that. But it's not like with a girl. What can you do?"

I dodge the question.

She presses.

I parry.

She asks again.

I change the subject.

She changes it back.

And finally after the fifth "But what can you do?" I blurt out, "*Well, I have two hands!*"

"So what do you do, jerk each other off?"

I'm stunned, horrified, and amused all in a single moment.

"*Grandma!*"

She laughs to break the tension.

She continues, "You know, I hear that some of the boys use the behind!"

I laugh to break the tension.

I toy with a couple of comebacks: "Wow, Grandma, what a great idea!"

Or, "Yeah, some of us . . . er . . . some of them do," but settle for planting a simple kiss on her forehead and saying, "Good night."

After that our relationship is almost back to normal. She's totally accepting, but it isn't clear that she understands the specifics of the situation. She knows I'm gay but appears hopeful whenever I even mention a woman by name. She repeatedly asks my brother, "What made him that way?" and confides to my mother her worries that I'm destined to become a prostitute—a proposition that, given my precarious finances, occasionally worries me too. My mother, who joined PFLAG immediately after I came out, suggests giving my grandmother a copy of *Now That You Know,* a book the group recommends and that I cynically refer to as *Everything You Always Wanted to Know about Homosexuality but Were Afraid to Hear.*

I pick up a copy for Granny.

Two weeks later I'm home for a visit and to do some laundry. I see the book lying on the nightstand; the wrinkled spine and folded corners tell me it's been read. I turn to Granny, who's busily working on yet another afghan.

"Hey, Granny, did you read that book?"

The crochet hook stops, she looks up and says point-blank, "Yes, and it's disgusting!"

My heart sinks and my guard goes up. "Disgusting?"

"Yes, it's disgusting! It says that some of the parents don't love their children anymore."

She makes me cry.

Lactose Intolerant

"Hello?"

"Hiya, Edwood."

"Just a minute."

I hold the kitchen phone up in the air and call to my mother.

"Ma, it's for you."

"Who is it?"

I immediately launch into a high-pitched coyote yowl.

"Yahhh-woooo!"

From the den my father echoes the call, and Ginger our retriever joins in from her favorite corner by the pantry. Although we do this every time Jen Wolfberg calls, and have for as long as I can remember, my mother is still irritated. She covers the receiver with her free hand and shushes us, as if after all these years, Jen's still unaware that it isn't just the dog howling.

"Hi, Jen . . . Oh, it's nothing; she probably heard a car. Listen, you gotta hear; you'll love this! My son, 'Mr. Actor' . . ."

My mom's been dying to tell Jen all about my latest "fiasco," as she calls it; she just can't resist garnering laughs at my expense.

". . . Yes, he was the number-one salesman but his brilliant scheme backfired . . ."

My mother's relish as she continues relating the story causes my sphincter to tighten.

"No, but they're subtracting the cancelled orders from his paycheck, and this week he owes them nine dollars . . . Oh, he's all right. I told Rita, and she nearly choked on a bear claw . . . I did call you first, but Barry said you were busy dusting your statues . . . Right, Lladrós. I tell you, *I had Rita wetting herself!*"

I join my dad in the den, but even with the TV blaring, my ears are assaulted by Jen's nasal laughter pouring out of the receiver. Ginger hears it too, and growls suspiciously. Since she was a puppy, she's regarded Jen as an intruder. Years later, her reaction will seem tame compared to the rabid grunts Jen will elicit from my father after dementia destroys his frontal lobe and he can no longer mask his emotional reaction toward her.

My mother continues. "No, we're not gonna let him quit! He's gotta pay it back! He's working full time and *still* accruing debt . . . I know, I know. Rita said he's practically an indentured servant!"

My mother explodes into laughter. Jen erupts too, and her abrasive honking causes Ginger to go mental. On one hand it seems unbelievable that a voice coming over the phone could provoke that reaction from such a sweet-tempered animal, and on the other it wouldn't surprise me to learn that field biologists were at that moment studying Jen's effect on dingoes in Australia.

Truthfully, I don't really care what Jen thinks. What's upsetting is that she laughs at everything. That's bad news. My mother getting a few chuckles for telling a story is like a compulsive gambler hitting the jackpot on the first pull of the slot machine; she'll continue to retell the anecdote to poor response in an effort to recapture the initial high of that first laugh. Like a gambler, she'll eventually lose some friends.

My mom continues. "Listen, doll, I have to go. What time do you want me to pick you up for the cemetery? . . . That's early—

she's dead, she's not going anywhere . . . Don't worry; I know where it is—section five, row seventeen—next to Goldclang."

Every Saturday, Jen and my mom visit Mt. Golda cemetery, where their friend Lucille is buried. They've had trouble locating the grave among the waves of gray granite ever since the groundskeeper removed the pastel wind sock and Day-Glo pinwheels Jen placed there as markers.

As I listen I feel sorry for Lucille, who probably thought that succumbing to the cancer would at least rescue her from Jen's grating voice.

"Okay, Jen . . . Okay . . . Okay . . . I will . . . Okay . . . Bye."

My mother enters the den and falls into a wing chair—exhausted but elated by Jen's response to the story.

"I had Jen hysterical!"

My father shrugs at me as I storm into the kitchen. It doesn't even occur to my mother that she's done anything wrong.

It's 1985, the summer before my junior year at Vassar, and I'm stuck at home on Long Island. Although I've been out at college for two semesters, I still haven't told my parents that I'm gay. I've spent the entire vacation rerouting my sexual energies into grueling morning workouts at the gym, then sabotaging myself by eating crap from lunch until bedtime.

Irritated by my mother's ridicule, I rip open a package of Oreos that she's attempted to hide behind the lettuce. I keep count while I eat them, and after knocking off an entire row, I don't trust myself to stop and throw the remainder in the garbage. I even spray the leftover cookies with Lemon Pledge to avoid the temptation of retrieving them from the trash later on.

Back in the den I flop down on the couch. On TV a delicious guy on a razor commercial directs all of my frustrations into my crotch. I contemplate a trip to my room for half an hour but decide to stay put because I don't want my mother claiming the couch for the rest of the evening. Also, I've been masturbating several times a day and am finding the frequency worrisome. At times, I've even considered spraying my cock with Lemon Pledge.

The summer started off well enough—actually better than I'd anticipated. Utilizing two years of college theatrical training to spectacular effect, I became the most successful telephone salesperson that *New York Newsday* has ever had.

A born salesman! The king of the phone banks! I was certain I'd have no problem talking someone into Scientology or depositing money into a Nigerian bank account. Unfortunately, my stint at the newspaper would be the only practical application of my drama degree until I attempted stand-up comedy ten years later.

Techniques I mastered in Drama 101—Introduction to the Actor's Art—allowed me to manipulate my cadence and timbre as I notified the suckers on my call list that they'd been selected to receive the paper at *almost* no cost. Modulating my instrument (that's theater lingo for voice), I simulated unbridled excitement as I congratulated them and took their credit card numbers. Of course I was creative with semantics; I never actually used words like "win." And I never divulged that the elite pool of those selected was limited to people in the 516 area code. Everything backfired six weeks later when the invoices went out and the suckers complained. The cancelled subscriptions were now being deducted from my paycheck. There will even be several weeks where I wish I owed *Newsday* only nine dollars.

My success was making the barely bearable job fun. Now the windowless office full of college students, single mothers, and retirees depresses me. All of them read the boring sales script in a droning monotone that makes the room sound like a beehive.

"Hi, Mr./Ms._____! This is_____ at *Newsday*! How are you today? (Wait for answer) Great! Listen, the reason

I'm calling is to let you know about an exciting new offer here at *New York Newsday*, New York's favorite newzzzzzzzzz . . ."

Despite my mother's mocking, I'm content to be home after my evening shift, lying on the lumpy couch watching TV with my parents. We're watching a rerun of *The Mary Tyler Moore Show*—arguably the greatest sitcom of all time. It's the brilliant episode where Chuckles the Clown, dressed as a peanut, is killed by a rogue elephant. It is without a doubt the best thirty minutes of the series.

Ten minutes into the program my father gets up to make coffee. He doesn't care at all for Mary—or Lucy—or Maude. He finds Carol Burnett unwatchable and *The Golden Girls* beyond endurance. It crosses my mind that his aversion to funny women hasn't prevented him from loving my mother so much. I place an order for iced tea and my mother asks for a cup of decaf Sanka—which for some reason she doesn't find redundant.

Returning with our beverages, he delicately breaks the news to her.

"Honey, we're out of milk."

"For God's sake! I told you to buy an extra quart! What in the world am I supposed to do now?"

It's a calamity of immense proportions understandable only to someone who's had to drink Sanka black.

I'm irritated before the words leave her lips.

"Oh, Ed?"

"What?"

"Would you mind?"

"Sure, right after the show."

"I need you to go now. They close at eleven."

My shifts at *Newsday* are exhausting and the remnants of my top salesman's ego heighten my annoyance. Plus it's over ninety degrees outside, and my car has no air-conditioning and a broken window handle on the driver's side.

"Oh, Ma, can't you drink it plain?"

Her eyes remain focused on me as her head changes from full front to three-quarter view. I don't stand a chance.

"Yeah, all right, I'll go—do we need anything else?"

"No, just the milk."

I get up muttering that I'm going to miss Chuckles's funeral. As I scan the cluttered kitchen for my keys, I spy a few packets of Cremora Non-Dairy Creamer on the counter. I call to my mom in the den.

"Ma, you know you have some Cremora right here?"

"I don't like the fake creamer—it makes the Sanka taste fake."

The irony is lost on her.

"Then why'd you buy it?"

"I didn't. I took it from the diner."

"What for?"

"You don't know when it might come in handy."

What was I saying about irony?

Under a stack of coupons, I locate my Farrah Fawcett key ring. Looking back, I marvel at how naïve I was to think that a key chain could serve as my beard. Oh, occasionally someone would notice it and I felt like one of the boys. But they probably knew that the engine was the only thing she ever got revved up.

I hop into my car, a 1969 Oldsmobile Delta 88—a vehicle almost as massive as a Delta 747—and lumber through the quiet town toward the only supermarket with evening hours. The market is fifteen minutes away but it feels like thirty if you factor in the humidity. I won't even get back in time for Chuckles's eulogy; by the time I return he'll be moldering in his grave.

The market's isolated and the drive there is eerie at night. It's located on a piece of wooded land about three miles square, which always strikes me as the perfect place to dump a body. The rest of the parcel had also been slated for commercial development, but construction was halted when a high

school biology class discovered an endangered species of salamander. The street lamps are kept off since artificial lighting
may have a detrimental effect on amphibian breeding behavior. Apparently the salamanders have poor body images and
will only have sex in the dark.

The supermarket glows conspicuously, allowing me to guide
the Delta like a ship around a lighthouse. I dock in a handi-
capped space and feel a twinge of guilt even though there are
only two other cars in the lot and plenty of empty spaces. I pull
the handicapped-parking tag down from the visor and hang it
from the mirror. My mother has renewed my grandfather's permit every year since his death to avoid walking an extra twenty
feet each time she goes to the store. She justifies depriving
someone in a wheelchair of the spot, claiming she needs to
minimizes the wear and tear on her expensive nine-and-a-half
double-A shoes with the high arch that she has to special order
through a catalogue.

I jump ship and sprint to the door. It's locked. In the far corner of the store I see the fluorescent fixtures starting to go dark
one by one. I bang on the window, and the darkness stops its
advance midway across the ceiling. A guy with curly hair
emerges from an aisle and I wave my arms frantically like an
idiot in the background of a TV news report.

As he walks toward me, his face comes into view under a
spray-painted sign for infant formula. "Handsome!" I think,
noticing his strawberry locks tinged with carefully placed Sun-
In highlights and the Aerosmith T-shirt under his polyester
smock. His nametag says Tommy. He's the kind of guy I would
have been slightly afraid of in high school. As Tommy points to
his watch and mouths, *"We're closed,"* I notice the dark blond fur
on his forearm. I smile, shrug, and hold up a finger to indicate
that I only need one item.

He smiles back, relents, and loosens the lock at the top of
the door. He motions me in, and it crosses my mind that he

looks a lot like Christopher Atkins from *The Blue Lagoon*. Thanking him profusely, I think that he would indeed look pretty excellent in a loincloth.

I sprint the perimeter of the store. At the end of the produce section, I turn right at the bakery and nearly slam into the dairy case. I grab a carton of skim milk on purpose, because I know my mom prefers the two-percent and I'm still pissed off about missing Mary Tyler Moore.

I arrive at the express line out of breath. Tommy looks down at the milk.

"No cookies?"

"Yeah, cookies!"

"Aisle three."

"One second."

"Take your time."

I bolt down the aisle and return with a package of Hydrox.

"Excellent choice."

"Yeah, much better than Oreos."

"Most people don't know what's good."

"I do."

When I get home, it's almost twelve-thirty. Before I can turn the knob, my mother opens the door.

"Oh, thank God you're back. I was ready to call the police!"

"I don't think they'll bring you milk."

"Don't get smart with me! Where have you been?"

"You won't believe what happened."

"I'm listening . . ."

And so even though I know I'll never live it down, and the story will be one that she can't wait to share with anyone who'll listen, I fess up.

". . . The guy follows me out of the store and shuts the security gate . . ."

"Have a good night. Enjoy the Hydrox," he says before he hops into his car and drives off.

As I walk to my car, I'm agitated by the cyclic cricket song. The chirping augments the awkward absence of foreground noise—as if God just told a really bad joke and no one is laughing. There seem to be millions of crickets; the salamanders must be eating like kings—or at least like frog princes.

The parking lot's completely empty now except for a tiny foreign job. I reach my car and put the milk on the roof. The carton's sweating through the brown paper bag and I wonder if fat-free milk, like a thinner person, perspires less than heavy cream.

Sliding my hand into my right pocket, I feel some change, some Chiclets, and a Chapstick, but no keys.

I stop breathing, then start again.

I check my left pocket—more coins and, of all things, a Monopoly house—but no keys. My back pocket yields a pay stub, and the pocket on my polo shirt, where I know that my keys most certainly are not, yields nothing. I look in the bag, on the ground, and under the car. As I pick my head up, I catch a glimpse of Farrah hanging from the ignition.

I stop breathing, then start again.

I peer into the car to check the locks. All the buttons are down.

It's about eight miles back to my house. There are no pay phones—just posts installed before construction was interrupted. (And of course there are no cell phones; it'll be years before I'll have to suffer Jen's nails-on-chalkboard voice anyplace but at home.)

I try to relax. I repeat Chuckles the Clown's credo in my head—"A little song, a little dance, a little seltzer down your pants"—but I can't calm down. I'm angry with my mom, the keys, the fucking salamanders. Looking at the milk, I think, "Sanka is for losers."

The heat is aggravating, and the crickets won't shut up.

Stressed, I pull myself up onto the hood, rip open the cookies, and aggressively scarf down an entire row. Disgusted, I fling the rest of the package into the woods as dessert for the salamanders.

After the rage and gluttony, but before sloth takes control of my insulin-soaked brain, I try to formulate a plan. A long, thin piece of wood on the ground catches my eye. Skillfully cramming it between the window and frame, I attempt to lift the button and unlock the door. After a few minutes I'm sweating profusely. I stop for a swig of milk and decide that skim really does suck. Sweating, stopping, and swigging, I continue in vain. Eventually, using all of my strength, I wedge the stick in so tightly that I can no longer move it at all. It would be easier extracting the sword Excalibur from the stone.

The air's humid and the mosquitoes, attracted by my sucrose-infused blood, are tapping me like a sugar maple. I down another mouthful of milk, breathe deeply, and resolve to give it one more try before I give up and start the long trek home.

I grab the stick and am making another attempt to dislodge it when I'm nearly scared out of my skin by a raspy Darth Vader voice, only inches from my ear.

"Looks like you got yourself a problem."

I let out a girl-on-a-roller-coaster scream, turn, and come face-to-face with an incredibly creepy guy who seems to have just faded in from the darkness. He's tall and gawky, with a tangle of stringy hair that occludes his right eye. His posture is so poor that if he were an old woman, he'd be described as having dowager's hump. He's spooky as hell, and for a moment I imagine him as the Lord of the Salamander People. I'm reluctant to engage him, but I'm in need of assistance and reason that given his spinal curvature, I could outrun him if need be. I explain my predicament to his visible eye, and he professes expertise at opening locked cars. For some reason, he seems like someone who would know a great deal about such things.

I watch his assuredness fade, however, as he too is unable to dislodge the stick and then spends fifteen minutes attempting the same maneuver with a piece of wire that we find nearby. Perspiration sparkles on his earlobes, and his hump looks even more pronounced through his sweat-drenched shirt. He throws the wire to the ground in disgust.

"It's these old cars—they're a lot sturdier than the crap they churn out today."

He offers to give me a ride. Though I'm tempted, there's still something eerie about him. Besides, he's not hot at all.

Not wanting to be perceived as rude, I assert that I don't want to trouble him any further and am adamant that he shouldn't go out of his way. We agree that he'll call my house when he gets home. As I tell him my number—4,9,9,6,3,9,2—I get a goose-bumpy vision of him leaving my parents an anonymous message detailing the locations of my trunk, head, and limbs.

He says the number aloud several times, "4996392, 4996392, 499 . . ." and walks away chanting it in time to the cricket's chirping. Repeating the number automatically, he stops to think, and either forgets it or loses confidence that he has it right. He turns and heads back toward me to confirm but stops before I can answer. Wiping the forelock out of his eye, he squints, bends forward, and says, "Hey, buddy, your passenger window is open."

My mother snorts and yells to my father in the den, "Mike, your son's a genius!"

Then she turns back to me. "I'm so glad we've gone into debt sending you to college!"

She goes into the den to relay the details to my father, but by the grace of God, the phone rings. At this time of night the caller can only be Jen Wolfberg. I call to my mother and hold the phone out.

"Yahhh-wooo!"

She grabs the receiver and smacks me on the shoulder.

"Hi, doll . . . Oh, nothing. They're watching *Wild Kingdom* . . . I know, it must be a rerun . . . Anyway, you'll get a kick out of this. My son, I send him out for milk . . . blah, blah, blah . . ."

So as I predicted, the story has become one of her favorites. It follows on the heels of my introduction to folks at her office, she pulls it out of mothballs at family birthdays and weddings, and uses it to regale her replacement friends. Once I even heard her tell it to a stranger on the checkout line at that very supermarket.

But unlike some of my mom's other stories, this one always gets a chuckle from the listener. Sometimes they find the story funny, but other times it's because she cracks herself up as she tells it—and they find it too uncomfortable not to laugh along. Occasionally someone will shoot me an apologetic look for being entertained at my expense and are surprised to see me laughing too.

I can't help it. I find my mother's enthusiasm for this story hysterical—especially since the entire thing was fabricated to account for the hour and a half I spent getting stoned and having sex with Tommy the supermarket guy.

Helter Shelter

I close the door to the tiny office, muting the clatter of the elevated train above the busy Brooklyn street. The podgy Midwestern woman at the desk behind the counter looks up from her crocheting and greets me in a saccharine, Bible-study tone.

"May I help you?"

"Yes, I'd like to find out about adopting . . ."

I'm cut off by the shrill *brrrrrring* of the rotary phone on her desk. She holds up her index finger and winks at me as she answers the call.

"A Pound of Love, Claire speaking."

The sight of her frosted lips against the dirty, flesh-colored mouthpiece has a disturbing pornographic quality.

"Yes, we have several pit bulls in need of good homes."

As she listens, she impatiently clicks her baby-pink nails against her cloisonné sweater clip.

"Uh-hum."

She rolls her eyes.

"Yes . . . Yes . . . There's a fifty-dollar adoption fee . . . Uh-hum. And you do understand that there's an extensive background check including police records . . . No, I'm afraid it's mandatory . . . Hello . . . Hello . . ."

She slams down the lipstick-smeared receiver, mutters, *"Ass-hole!"* and glares at the phone for a moment. Then letting go of her anger with a deep breath, she turns to me refreshed.

"I'm so very sorry."

"No problem."

"Welcome to A Pound of Love. How can I help you?"

"Well I'd like to find out . . ."

She interrupts me with a traffic-stopping palm.

"Before you continue—I know kittens and puppies are adorable—but I do hope you'll consider adopting an older animal."

"Actually, I was looking for an adult cat."

"Excellent! If you'll fill out the top section of this application, we can get started."

I take the clipboard that she holds out, write my name and address on the form, and hand it back to her. She looks it over.

"Thanks, Edward, I'm Claire. I only have a few questions right now. We can finish the rest later if you see a cat you're interested in."

"Okay."

"First of all, do you have a gender preference?"

A smirk appears involuntarily on my flushing face.

"No."

Claire waits a beat before continuing. I can tell she has a fag hag's fine-tuned gaydar and can easily spot any homo except the one she's currently in love with.

"Do you have any other pets?"

"No."

"Children?"

"No."

"I didn't think so."

She looks up from the clipboard and winks at me. "We insist that any cats placed by A Pound of Love be kept indoors."

"This is New York City. Who lets their cat outside?"

"You'd be surprised."

"That's terrible!"

I can see that my concern scores points.

"You don't have any intention of declawing, do you?"

I think of the new corduroy chair that my boyfriend Jeffrey and I just bought from Pottery Barn. It's our first joint purchase and my way of baby-stepping toward us eventually living together. I'd hate to see it used as a scratching post but know from Claire's tone that there's only one answer to her question. "Certainly not, declawing's barbaric!"

"Very good! Now, if for any unforeseen reason you need to give up custody—such as health or financial circumstances—do you agree to return the animal here to A Pound of Love?"

"That's not gonna happen."

"We just have to make sure."

"Yes."

"The fifty-dollar adoption fee is tax deductible and includes spaying, vaccinations, and a kitty-care kit. We do a complete background check—landlord, employment, criminal, credit, and personal. We'll notify you of approval within forty-eight hours."

"Okay."

"May I ask why you're looking to adopt?"

"I need the unconditional love."

"Of course."

"I'm kidding."

Although I'm briefly irritated by my failed joke, I like Claire. She has a Jane Goodallishness about her, and I sense her to be someone with limited tolerance for people because she prefers the company of creatures incapable of masking their emotions or manipulating others.

I like that she so nonchalantly hits the nail on the head. "Of course!"

Of course, don't we all want unconditional love and acceptance? I do. It's 1996, and after eight years of being on my own in New York, I'm worn out trying to feel worthy in a city where everyone graduated at the top of their class, has an Olympian physique, and manages to read, see, and hear everything before it's published, released, or recorded. I'm exhausted from trying to battle my way into—or defend my position in—the hearts of men by changing, pretending, or tolerating. I want something in my life whose love doesn't depend on me going to the gym or clubbing, feigning an interest in sports or opera, having a thirty-two-inch waist, a six-figure salary, or a doorman building. I want to be accepted without having to suffer boorish in-laws or arrogant friends, or to drink, drug, keep kosher, count carbs, get hair plugs, or shave my balls.

Claire tucks the clipboard under her arm, heads out the front door, and motions for me to follow her. As I turn to exit, I come face-to-face with "The Wall." The wall is covered with hundreds of snapshots and cards detailing successful adoption stories. It seems impossible to me that I didn't notice it when I came in.

There are portraits of tabbies in Santa hats, calicos asleep in bathroom sinks, and kittens mesmerized by goldfish. There are cats burrowing through laundry, asleep in bassinettes, and even a photo of two Siamese curled up next to a woman in an oxygen tent. The picture's stapled to a mass card with handwriting in the margin that reads:

> AUNT ELIZABETH LEFT US ON APRIL 28TH
> WITH HER BELOVED ANNA AND LADY THANG BY HER SIDE.
> GOD BLESS YOU A POUND OF LOVE!

At the top of the wall is a sign with changeable numbers that reads: OVER 53913 POUNDS OF LOVE ADOPTED. I immediately recognize the numbers as the ZIP code for Baraboo, Wisconsin, home of Ringling Bros. Circus. I've always had a fascination with the big top, and play with the idea of a clown motif for the glossy photo of me and my new darling on the front of the Rosh Hashanah card that I'll send to Claire for inclusion on the wall.

We leave the cluttered office, and Claire leads me around the outside of the building toward the cat house. To get there we pass through an alley lined with two rows of kennels. The dogs are packed in three and four to a cage and go berserk as soon as they catch sight of us. Again Claire's sweet demeanor vanishes and she shouts at the poor animals, *"Goddammit! Shut up, you filthy things, or it's the needle for all of you!"*

She catches the look of shocked amusement on my face. "Sorry—I'm really more of a cat person."

"I can see that."

At the far end of the alley sits a small one-story structure painted the same shade of pink as Claire's fingernails. A Hello Kitty doormat welcomes us. As she reaches for the door handle, Claire turns to me. "If we can't find suitable homes for them, these cats live out their lives here. At A Pound of Love, we never destroy an animal unless it's sick and there's no hope."

As she opens the door, I'm almost knocked down by the acrid blast of ammonia that singes my eyes. I cover my nose and mouth with my forearm.

"Whoa!"

"I'm sorry, the air conditioner's broken."

"It's worse than the L train."

"You'll get used to it."

I doubt it. The fumes distort the air like the heat on the Serengeti and I feel like we should be looking for cheetahs instead of house cats. The one-room building houses over two hundred felines, who lounge on trees fashioned out of carpet-covered lumber. One of the walls is lined with upholstered cubbyholes, and there are dozens of disemboweled stuffed mice hanging from the ceiling and tree branches for the cats to swat.

The cats are stirred up by Claire's entrance and at least thirty of them head directly for us. Claire greets them in baby talk. "Oh yes, it's time for din-din, isn't it? Yes, I think it is! It's time for din-din! Shall we see what's for supper? Shall we see what's for supper?"

She removes the lid of a galvanized garbage can near the door, and the remaining kitties respond to the metallic sound of their dinner bell. As Claire begins ladling Cat Chow directly onto the floor, the pack descends on her. I half expect that after the feeding frenzy only a few fake fingernails, some dental work, and a sweater clip will remain.

After the animals disperse I realize just how disgusting the place is. While on a philosophical level each pound of love is arguably a precious living thing and one of the Lord's unique creations, an entire ton of love is undeniably unsanitary, a vector for disease, the potential epicenter of a cholera epidemic. From my vantage point near the door, I can count over twenty litter boxes—which aren't anywhere near enough, because I can count almost twice as many places where the cats have soiled the black-and-white tiled floor, making it look as if there's a big, revolting chess match in progress.

Aside from the stench and squalor, the innocent Hello Kitty doormat is misleading because the three remaining walls are decorated with provocative images. One wall's hung with a giant cutout of Eartha Kitt as Catwoman seductively beckoning the viewer with her outstretched claws. The opposite end of the room features a film poster of a sultry Ann-Margret in *Kitten with a Whip,* and on the long wall opposite the cubbyholes is painted a movie-screen-sized mural of the three estrogen-driven murderesses from the Russ Meyer cult classic, *Faster Pussycat! Kill! Kill!* The steamy film images, the uninhibited animal sounds, and the disorienting shadows cast by red Chinese lanterns hung at irregular intervals seem completely appropriate for a cat house.

Claire strides right into the room, and without once looking down, somehow manages to avoid every piece of cat shit. She signals me to follow, and I gingerly tiptoe across the gritty floor as if through a minefield. It's disgusting, but I tell myself I'll be doing a good deed by rescuing an innocent creature from the noxious fumes and constant struggle for survival in this walk-in litter box, which I dub the Helter Shelter.

In a far corner, a spindly Indian woman wrapped in a frayed red sweater is busy scraping clumps of stinky saturated clay from the sides of an overwhelmed litter pan. The sight of her— frail and uncomplaining—in the center of the feces-covered floor reminds me of the wretched, unsanitary villages in those Save the Children commercials with Sally Struthers. I chastise my inner racist for thinking that this poor creature must have been imported illegally and sold into servitude, because it'd be near impossible to find an American willing to do such a disgusting job.

Claire and I approach a buxom blond woman in her early fifties. She's wearing a lab coat and swearing in some Slavic tongue while attempting to administer medication from a dropper to an orange tabby hiding behind a jumbo bag of kibble. The cat's fierce in its opposition to the remedy, and the poor woman's hand and forearm are covered with deep scratches. Blood runs down her fingers and splatters onto one of the few unsoiled white floor tiles.

Claire introduces the woman as Frumka, the veterinarian, who's quick to qualify her credentials. "In Ukraine I manage three cow herds before Chernobyl. Now I mind pussycats."

Claire reassures her, "We're very lucky to have someone with Frumka's experience." She then extends her hand in my direction. "This is Eddie. He's looking to adopt an adult cat."

Frumka looks me over. "You have children?"

Apparently this is a big issue; I can't decide if it's a general question or if she's concerned about the vicious tabby committing infanticide. I'm about to say no, but Claire interrupts. "Eddie's single and lives alone."

The subtext is obviously that I'm gay, and the cheerfulness with which Claire offers the information makes me believe that it'll be to Frumka's liking. Frumka grins and accents her look of pleasure with a staccato nod. "Is excellent! This pussycat will be your child."

I am taken aback at the suggestion that I adopt the ferocious Morris. Claire jumps in. "I think we can find a more suitable match for you. Do you have a specific breed in mind?"

Frumka gestures to the open room. "We have many fancy cats, some with papers." She picks up a cream-colored fluff ball and thrusts it into my arms. "This one, one hundred percent Angora!"

"Oh, I'm not interested in a pedigree. It upsets me that people go out and buy purebreds when there are so many affectionate animals that desperately need homes. Intrinsically one cat isn't any more valuable than another."

I score big points with both women, but I'm not just working my audience. I believe my own words. I'd been less than enthusiastic when my friends Kevin and Fernando spent two thousand dollars on a purebred bichon frise puppy (who turned out to have a meat allergy) instead of rescuing a lovable mutt from death row at their local shelter. I was even more judgmental two years later, when they jumped through every conceivable emotional, financial, and medical hoop in order to have a designer baby who began life in a Lalique petri dish instead of giving a home to a needy kid from foster care.

I playfully rub the Angora under its chin and feel its whiskers brush against my cheek. It seems completely indifferent to me. For a moment before I release it I wonder if there's a part of me afraid of having a fancy cat. I've had a hard enough time feeling deserving when I've dated guys with more money, better bodies, or superior educations. Perhaps the idea that I'd lose my heart to a blue-blood Himalayan or some other aristocat that might not find me up to par is a possibility I don't want to face.

I also find it unconscionable when people adoption shop for their pets, kids, and sperm donors by looks—even though that's historically been my preferred method for choosing potential boyfriends—which might explain some of my more spectacular relationship failures. Somehow, I guess I think that if I browse the cat house searching for an animal based on personality, I can make up for some of the men I've regrettably passed over with my shallow husband-hunting strategy.

And so I tiptoe through the cat house in search of the perfect companion. I maneuver around the doody and become only slightly accustomed to the toxic air. I pass over two elegant Abyssinians and purposely ignore a beautiful Russian Blue in search of the misfits and oddballs—scrawny cats with torn ears and tubby cats with tiny heads. I browse the room while Claire follows behind clacking her nails against her sweater clip. Occasionally she gestures toward a particular candidate, and I stop to let the animal sniff or mark me with its scent but keep moving if it seems too eager. (Another unfortunate method I employ in my manhunts.)

After being scratched by a feeble-looking tuxedo cat that I'm on the verge of choosing, I scan the place and lay my eyes on her: a plump gray tabby with no neck lying in the dim far corner. On her side with her head on the floor and her front legs tucked under her ample body, she looks like a seal. She lifts her head as I approach, and I see that she has a black Adolf Hitler mustache. As I crouch down at her side, she smells the air and lets out a simple—and what seems to be a friendly—meow.

She has the cautious air of a fat girl on the playground wary of unsolicited kindness, and the painful social history I conjure up for her melts my heart. I'll do my best to make her feel beautiful and loved—to make up for her time alone in the corner. I'm determined to gain her trust and form an unbreakable bond. This cat will be my fag hag! She'll finish my ice cream so I don't get fat, have veto power over the men in my life (unless of course, they're really hot), and she'll be constantly assured of her importance every time I don't have better plans.

She allows me to pet her, and I let my hand linger on her rump to see if I can gain her confidence. It excites me when she begins to purr, and I ascribe a loving nature to her when she gently licks the scratch made by the skittish tuxedo. It doesn't occur to me that she could simply have a taste for blood.

Naïvely I look up at Claire, who's gripping the cloisonné clip at her throat and seems to be holding back tears. There's an expression of knowing satisfaction on her face. I breathe calmly, "I think this is the one."

"I think it is."

She offers her hand to help me up. "Come with me. We'll go to the office and find Giselle's file."

I burst out laughing. Giselle is anything but graceful; in the ballet world she would most closely resemble one of the tutu-clad hippopotami in Disney's *Fantasia*. But there's something tragically silly about the assignment of such a dainty name to a creature so bulky, and I find myself even more drawn to her.

I thank Frumka and follow Claire to the exit. Outside, I'm astonished by just how fresh the sooty air under the train tracks can smell and feel after the stinky cat house. When we pass the dog kennels the mutts again go wild, and again Claire loses it. *"Shut up, you beasts, or I'll get the cleaver and haul you off to the Korean's."* Again she punctuates her outburst with an apologetic smile.

Back in the cramped office, Claire searches for Giselle's file while I browse the wall and choose a spot for the photo I'm styling in my head. From her records I learn that Giselle's believed to be approximately four years old and has been at the Helter Shelter for a little over three years. She'd been rescued from euthanasia at a city-run facility that needed to make room for the never-ending stream of strays that struggle for survival in the streets and alleys of New York.

The file contains a photo of Giselle, a veterinary certificate detailing the dates of her vaccinations, and a brochure extolling the fine work done by the good folks at A Pound of Love—along with a donation envelope.

When I'm done looking over the file, Claire slips it out of my hands. "I'll need your social security and driver's license numbers so we can access your legal and financial records, and I'll also need two personal references from nonrelatives who've known you at least ten years."

"No DNA sample?"

"I know it seems like a lot, but we want to make sure Giselle's going to a good home."

"I totally understand."

As I hand Claire my documents, I think, "As if they're ever going to find anybody else to adopt this mieskite animal!"

She continues, "The background check typically takes two days. I don't foresee a problem unless there's something you'd like to tell me before we go forward. If there is, this is the time."

I'm too embarrassed to mention my overnight incarceration for turnstile jumping seven years earlier and assure Claire that everything's fine. "There are no skeletons in my closet."

"Oh, I'm sure your closet's empty. Now, I just need your signature at the bottom."

Claire hands me the application and a pen. I look it over, and as I sign my name, it occurs to me that the promise of unconditional love seems to come with a lot of conditions.

I exit A Pound of Love and walk up the stairs to the elevated train. As I push through the turnstile, I start to obsess that my prison record will prevent Giselle and me from being together.

I want to prove myself a responsible pet owner, and so set about cleaning my apartment thoroughly. I spray my plants with cat repellent and give a poisonous dieffenbachia to my downstairs neighbor, David. I even hide my porn just in case a social worker pops in for a spot inspection. Over the next two days, I prepare the house for the new arrival like an expectant parent. Although I grew up in a family that considers it bad luck to purchase anything for a new baby before it's been safely delivered, I take a chance and buy a sparkly collar hoping there won't be a miscarriage of justice if my conviction should come to light.

After trudging home from the pet store with a twenty-five-pound bag of Cat Chow slung over my shoulder, I find a message on my machine from Claire saying that I've been approved. I raise my fists in the air, shout *"YES!"* and fall to my knees like a victorious marathon runner. It hurts a lot.

The following day I call in sick to the Eton Club where my boyfriend Jeffrey and I both work. Denny, the general manager, is pissed off when I tell him I'll be out for a few days, but I need time to bond with Giselle. Plus, it's an excellent way to exact my revenge for all the times I've covered for him while he slept off one of his three-day coke binges.

When I enter the office at A Pound of Love, Claire greets me with a big Jesus-loves-you grin. "It's lovely to see you again, Eddie. I'm so pleased we've found a suitable home for Giselle."

"Great, so no red flags?"

"There was one glitch, but I think everyone deserves a second chance."

I blush and am searching for something to say when Claire sweeps her arm toward the door. "Here she is now."

The spindly Indian woman comes in holding Giselle, and I can feel my face light up. Claire gestures to a chipped enamel baby scale in the corner.

"Nell, will you please weigh the cat?"

Nell puts the cat down and slides the weight along the bar until it's level.

"Seventeen pounds even."

"Seventeen pounds. Thank you, Nell."

Claire reaches for a pencil to add seventeen to the total pounds of love adopted, but I'm already doing the arithmetic in my head. When I check the kitty meter at the top of the wall, however, I notice that the numbers have changed since my last visit. It now reads 53936—a ZIP code I'm not familiar with. Trying to imagine which lucky feline's found a new home, I turn back to Claire. "You've had an adoption!"

"Several."

"Several?"

"Yes—all kittens."

"Oh."

Nell puts the cat in my arms, like a newborn, while Claire snaps a Polaroid. We watch the photograph develop, and I'm pleased at how good Giselle and I look together. Claire tapes it to the wall. "I just need a check," she says.

"Oh, sure."

I hand off Giselle to Nell, who gently coaxes her into a cardboard carrying case before leaving us to return to the cat house.

I pull out my checkbook. "Fifty dollars, right?"

"Well, the fifty dollars covers the basics, but you're free to write a check for any amount."

I can tell from her tone that my check better be for more than fifty dollars, so I add an additional fifty as a donation.

"Well, I guess it's official," I say, handing her the check.

"Not quite."

She fingernails through the papers in Giselle's file and pulls out a faux-parchment certificate stamped with a gold seal.

this to certify that on the 28th day of september 1997, a relationship of unconditional love was entered into by edward j. sarfaty and giselle

The document's been tea stained and the edges singed to give it an antique look. It's signed in a flourish of hot-pink magic marker by Claire Halverson, Adoption Supervisor, and in neat, careful penmanship by Frumka Osyczka, Veterinarian, who's used a basic blue ballpoint. I thank Claire and she smiles modestly. "I hope you like it."

"It's suitable for framing."

"I did it myself."

"The calligraphy's beautiful."

"I took a course at the Learning Annex."

"It shows."

I put the certificate and other paperwork in the manila envelope that Claire provides. She reaches her finger through an air hole in Giselle's box to say good-bye and then gives me a maternal hug before walking me to the door.

Giselle growls with fright the entire subway ride back to Manhattan. I open the box so I can pet and comfort her, and nearly lose half my ring finger when she snaps defensively. I suck in air and let out a list of expletives, which amuses the stoned junior-high kids sitting across from me and shocks an older woman to my right. I assure them, "She's just stressed."

At home I leave Giselle in the box and set it down in the center of the apartment so she can get used to the sounds and scents of her surroundings before being released into the strange environment. When I bend down to pet her through the air holes, the box spasms violently, causing me to flinch. With my heart pounding I make several more attempts to approach, but each time the box jerks and twitches as if a poltergeist is in residence. I wait several hours for her to calm down, but finally—when it seems too cruel to keep her locked up any longer—I, like a modern-day Pandora unprepared for the evil I'm about to unleash on Apt. 2C, open the box.

Giselle makes a run for the safety of my closet and I decide to leave her alone and let her venture out when she's ready. In the meantime, I browse through guidebooks for the trip to Europe my parents have asked me to accompany them on. Except for occasional hisses and growls, the next few hours pass relatively uneventfully.

At dinnertime my boyfriend Jeffrey comes over to meet her.

"Where's the bundle of joy?"

"She's hiding in the closet. I don't think she's having an easy adjustment."

"That's what you get for adopting a problem child."

"That's not funny. She was probably abused and neglected."

Jeffrey pounds on the closet door. "Come out! Come out!"

"Stop, you're going to scare her even more. She'll come out when she's ready."

"Okay, I'll leave her alone. What's for dinner? I'm starving to death."

Jeffrey's never just hungry; he's always "starving to death."

Unfortunately, while I've completely stocked up on Cat Chow and kitty litter, I've neglected to buy anything that we might make a meal of.

"I've been so busy, I haven't even thought about shopping."

Jeffrey points to the huge bag on the counter. "You remembered to buy cat food."

"I'm sorry."

"It's okay; I've been replaced in your affections."

"Hardly."

"That's what you say now—but never mind, I knew one day I'd be tossed aside. Is there anything in the fridge?"

I open the door. There's half a cantaloupe, a jar of anchovies, some condiments, and an open container of cottage cheese. I check the date and sniff it.

"Expired?" he asks.

"Yeah, but it smells okay to me."

I hand him the container, and he swirls it under his nose like a glass of merlot. "I can work with that."

Jeffrey's an excellent cook, and I've seen him whip up unbelievably delicious meals using combinations even more bizarre than the hodgepodge in my refrigerator. He loves trying exotic foods, and his willingness to explore the culinary unknown has introduced us to some fantastic new flavors. He's always looking for new recipe ideas and unorthodox food combinations and has thrown several killer dinner parties featuring fusion cuisines of his own invention such as Peruvian-Welsh, Czech-Cajun, and Malaysian-Lapp. But even though I've just donated the month's grocery money to A Pound of Love, the idea of anchovies mixed with anything holds no appeal.

"Let's just order in."

"What are you hungry for?"

"You pick."

That's all I have to say. The neighborhood where I live is one of the most ethnically diverse in all of New York, and new restaurants are opening all the time. If left to my own devices I'd order the same chicken Caesar salad from the same Greek diner every day, but to Jeffrey the variety is irresistible.

"Where are the menus?"

"Behind the cookie jar."

He quickly shuffles through the pile of take-out menus that

have found their way under my apartment door. I see him discard the majority and begin scanning some I don't recognize.

"Narrow it down?" I ask.

"Yes. Khmer or Estonian?"

"Surprise me."

He orders in from the new Estonian restaurant around the corner. The brown bread that comes with dinner is delicious, but the meal's a nightmare (or likely to induce one) and we have plenty left over, including an entire order of some jellied meat that even Jeffrey's adventurous palate won't hazard.

Though neither of us has the least bit of interest in it, the smell of the repulsive dish brings Giselle out of hiding, and I wonder if it's reminiscent of some Ukrainian peasant fare that Frumka packs in her lunch. The cat lets out a hungry meow that startles Jeffrey. I make the introduction.

"Look who's here! Jeffrey, meet Giselle."

"Giselle?"

"She came with it."

"You have to change her name."

"Too gay?"

"Are you kidding?"

"Any suggestions?"

"Let me think."

Giselle emits a second meow, throatier and more desperate sounding than the first. Jeffrey scoops up a glob of the jellied crap with a soupspoon and holds it out to her. She licks the spoon voraciously, as if it has a Tootsie Roll center. When she's done, she sniffs the air and meows again.

I affect my best English orphan. "Please, sir, may I have some more?"

Jeffrey follows my lead and looks down haughtily at the hungry animal, like the master in a Dickensian workhouse. *"MORE? You want MORE?"*

Giselle meows pleadingly, and I put down the dish of slime, which she greedily attacks.

"How about Oliver?" I suggest.

"She's hardly a waif."

"True, she looks pretty hardy."

"Yeah, Oliver Hardy."

"That's perfect—especially with that mustache."

"Oliver's a boy's name."

"Don't worry—we'll make her live as a tom for a year and undergo intense psychotherapy before we get her the penile implant."

Jeffrey leaves right after dinner to work a late shift at the Eton Club, and Oliver retreats to the closet. The quiet evening of bonding I've imagined never materializes, and I fall asleep to a rerun of *Designing Women*.

The next morning the apartment's silent with no visible signs of life. The only clue that the biomass of the place has increased is a horrible smell that nudges me out of my slumber. As I stumble down the ladder from my sleeping loft, the stench grows stronger and I feel as if I'm descending into a sulfur mine.

Now after indulging Oliver with the Estonian meat by-product, I'm prepared for an unpleasant kitty litter experience, but the real horror is finding that she prefers the privacy of my closet to the publicly situated litter box. I patiently clean up the mess and use the opportunity to discard some ancient porn—and a pair of saddle shoes, which Jeffrey swears will be coming back into style. I assume the incident is just part of the normal adjustment period and that the learning curve won't be too steep. I'm right: it takes only three more tries before my training's complete, and I no longer forget to shut the closet door.

A few days later, after there couldn't possibly be any of the gelatinous goo left in her system, I realize that the nauseating Baltic fare really had very little effect on Oliver's digestion. Her gastrointestinal tract processes everything the same way. I go through six different brands of supermarket cat food and several varieties available only through pet shops. I try special products I have to mail order, and even recipes I have to prepare myself. At first I'm convinced she just needs the right diet but then begin to suspect that her duodenum secretes an enzyme capable of melting igneous rock.

The smell is awful. I try every air freshener sold, but the light flowery fragrances are no match for Oliver. It's like trying to quell the stench of a landfill with a spritz of Chanel No. 5. The brand that proves most effective is an industrial product called Alpine Meadow, but even then the scent only mixes with the stink. Instead of suggesting an idyllic *Sound of Music* setting, it brings to mind an image of Julie Andrews singing on an Austrian hillside befouled by ten thousand dairy cows.

For the next few days the stealth bombing continues; I never catch Oliver in the act. I hardly see her at all—except at meals. The rest of the time I have to get down on my knees and lift the dust ruffle just to get a view of her under the daybed that doubles as a sofa. I try coaxing her out with toys, treats, kind words, music. Nothing works. Every attempt at handling her is met with scratches and bites. I know Denny and Carl the coat-check guy at the Eton Club, both huge animal lovers, are expecting to see pictures, but the best shot I can get is of two radioactive yellow eyes in the dark surrounded by dust bunnies.

The following weeks aren't any better. Oliver's aggression escalates and my fingers are always covered with Band-Aids. At work customers question my wounds and I laugh them off, fabricating a ridiculous anecdote about getting caught up in a very moving episode of *The Waltons* while grating a wedge of Parmesan.

Denny in particular isn't buying my story. He teases me that he's going to call social services and arrange an intervention.

Wendell Briar, a self-described middle-aged queen who disapproves of any animal that can't be found on a menu or on a rack at Barneys, joins in. Mocking the tone of a battered wife making excuses for a drunken husband, he assures everyone who asks that "Eddie walked into a door, but he's fine—and anyway the cat is very, very sorry and swears she'll never do it again."

I'd dreamed of returning from work each day to find Oliver eagerly waiting for me, but now I dread the foul game of hide-and-seek as she finds new and inconvenient places to soil. The smell I could handle—if only she'd use the box. Once she's barred from my closet she relieves herself in the bathtub, an open drawer, and even in an end table I leave overturned after repairing one of the legs. Her refusal to use the litter box causes me to think she must have been a participant in the nauseating chess game in progress at A Pound of Love (from the messes she makes, she was likely the defending champ). Jeffrey's amazed by Oliver's inventiveness at avoiding the toilet and nicknames her the Artful Dodger.

Over the next few weeks I consult friends with cats and follow their recommendations. I read *Cat Fancy* magazine and books from the pet store. I try every available kind of cat box filler—traditional, clumping, super-clumping, scented, unscented, nontracking. I switch from clay to wood shavings to sawdust to washable plastic pellets to litter made from recycled paper. I add baking soda, chlorophyll, and catnip. And I even move the box to the site of her last offense so she'll associate the location with the activity.

Eventually the combination of egregious smells and sacks of rejected litter piled up by the door is the only way anyone would know that a cat lives there. Oliver only shows herself at mealtimes; the sound of the can opener or the rattle of a box of Friskies causes her to come charging like a rodeo bull. Jeffrey, who grew up in rural Idaho and is great with animals, tries tirelessly to make friends with her, but after one too many scratches renames her once more. The new moniker, "You Fucking Cunt!" sticks.

Steadfastly believing that the way to her heart is through her stomach, I make excuses for her. "She's just cranky because her tummy's upset. I'm sure once I find the right diet for her everything will be fine."

"Please, Eddie, she's a 'C. U. Next Tuesday!' And by the way, I think all this shitting in every nook and cranny is just out of spite."

"Cats don't have the memory span required to hold a grudge and exact revenge cold. Besides, I've done nothing but treat her well."

"Well then, you're paying for something that happened in one of her previous eight lives. Maybe we should call the pet psychic."

"Who?"

"You know, that flaky blond woman from TV."

"The one who looks like Mrs. Howell from *Gilligan's Island?*"

"Yeah, at least you'll get some idea of how this is going to turn out."

"Please, you don't have to be psychic to know that. Basically all pets have the same future." I put two fingers to my forehead and speak in a trance like a carnival clairvoyant. "I see an illness, an overly expensive illness . . . and a needle . . ."

"No illness could cost more than what you've already spent on litter and food."

"At least she's eating."

"But it's all going right through her."

"Actually, I think she's been putting on weight."

"It's the stripes, they're very unflattering."

"Those aren't stripes, they're stretch marks! But I don't care if she's fat, as long as she's happy. And if she's not happy being fat, I'll be there at her bedside when she wakes up from her gastric bypass."

The situation continues, and I cough up a hundred dollars for an electronic self-cleaning litter box. We're thrilled when Oliver decides to use the new contraption for an entire week. The success helps me convince Jeffrey to spend the night— something he's been reluctant to do because the barnyard smell's been a real mood killer.

A few nights of undistracted sex increase our optimism, but it soon becomes apparent to me that hope can be the most evil thing in Pandora's Box when Jeffrey inadvertently leaves the closet door ajar and Oliver has a relapse. Regrettably, after that she shows no further interest in the expensive device. On his way to pee one night, Jeffrey discovers one of Oliver's stink bombs with his bare foot and explodes. He refuses to sleep at my place again.

For the next week, I go to bed alone and discouraged. When Oliver, finally appearing to sense my sadness, comes out of hiding to cuddle up next to me, I'm elated. Her display of sympathy, however, further fucks with my hopefulness. She lets me pet her for eight whole strokes—a record—then sinks her talons into my wrist, inflicting scratches too shallow to be mistaken for a suicide attempt, but too deep to be dismissed as a pathetic cry for attention.

The stress in our relationship escalates when I get an irate phone call from Jeffrey accusing me of cheating and giving him crabs. I vehemently deny playing around behind his back and we have a huge fight—not our first, but our biggest. He challenges me to explain the bites all over his crotch. "Eddie, if you didn't give them to me, then where did they come from?"

"I don't know."

"Well, you're the only one I've slept with."

"Well, are you sure you've got crabs?"

"What else could it be?"

I don't want to push his most sensitive button and refrain from remarking that he could have a case of mice and not be able to see them through the mat of fur that coats his body.

"Why don't you get out the electric clippers and do some manscaping so you can get a better look."

"I can't, I'm on my way to the doctor's."

He hangs up abruptly but calls back an hour later.

"They're flea bites."

The source is unquestionable. I feel awful about Jeffrey's situation, but my initial response to his discovery is selfish and insensitive:

"God, no wonder Oliver's cranky—who wouldn't be, all itchy and irritable?"

Relieved to learn that her horrible behavior has nothing to do with anything I've done, I continue, "I knew it wasn't me—it's the fleas! The poor misunderstood thing! She's like the panic-stricken Europeans who turned their terror of the Black Plague into violence against the continent's Jews. Her hatred isn't personal. It's misplaced anti-Semitism caused by tiny parasites nobody thought to look for!"

"I'm so glad you're happy."

"Sorry, I didn't mean to be a dick. Thanks for your patience—you've been great. It's just such a relief to finally get to the cause of her problem."

"Oh, Eddie, she's got more than one problem."

"But this could very well be the root of them all."

"It better be."

"You'll see, everything will be fine."

"Well, at least I know you weren't cheating. I'm sorry I said what I said."

"No apology necessary."

I ring up Dr. Barker, who not only has a great name for a vet, but interestingly also has a black poodle, a black cat, and a black boyfriend. He sets up an appointment at his animal clinic/spa on the fashionable Upper East Side.

In the waiting room decorated with framed photographs of all the recognized cat breeds, I admire the graceful lines of the Cornish Rex and the luxuriousness of the Norwegian Forest Cat. The other owners have their ribbon winners on their laps and are petting them gently while I hide my scabby fingers and try to ignore the Tasmanian devil screeching in the carrier under my seat. I feel superior to them and their patrician pets. I've done a selfless thing by adopting a special-needs child, and I pay no attention to the nip/tucked woman seated to my right who looks down her expensive Fifth Avenue nose at us.

Doc Barker and two techs attempt to extricate Oliver from her carrier, but she's so ferocious that they finally give up. He administers a shot of ketamine through an airhole, and we wait a few minutes for the party drug to subdue her. As he slides her out of the case, she's startled out of her K-hole and sinks her fangs into his hand.

"Oh, you Fucking Cunt!" he screams, and then catches himself. "Sorry."

"It's okay; it's my boyfriend's pet name for her."

A few minutes more and Oliver settles down and passes out. Although she seems tranquilized, Doc Barker isn't taking any chances and pokes her cautiously with a surgical clamp before donning a pair of oven mitts and attempting to handle her again.

I ask, "How long will it take to get rid of the fleas?"

"Usually one application suffices. She should be ready tomorrow evening. You can pay the receptionist on your way out."

He glances at the shelf in the corner and I know he's remembering my old cat, Regina, whose ashes he wouldn't release until I scrounged up the money to pay off the cost of her cremation.

I make out a check for eighty-five dollars and head home to write an even bigger one for the exterminator who's coming to de-flea my apartment. His fee is greater than my bank balance, and I resort to rolling the spare change in the cookie tin on my dresser to make up the difference. Jeffrey's apartment also needs to be sprayed, and I have to ask him to cover the cost until I can pick up some extra shifts at the Eton Club. It's the cause of our next fight.

I sleep peacefully despite the relationship unrest and the worry that the pesticide from the flea bomb will cause the pigeons on my sill to produce eggs with thin shells. I'm alone sans boyfriend and sans pet, but rest assured that once Oliver's vermin free, all will be right and the unconditional loving will finally begin.

The next day I return to Doc Barker's where I'm informed that Oliver's going to need another dip—the fleas are out of control. He can't even keep her in the office and has had to quarantine her, lest she infect all the Park Avenue pussycats. He's got worse news too. "Her stool's so vile that I checked for parasites—she's got the nastiest case of roundworms I've ever seen; I'm surprised she's not severely undernourished. Plus, she's also got a major ear mite problem."

"Is that all?"

"I'd recommend a full set of shots as well."

"She's had all her vaccinations. I have a health certificate from A Pound of Love."

"Given her parasite situation, I wouldn't put much stock in it."

"How much is this going to cost?"

I'm disgusted that I sound like my ex, Doug the Cheapskate, who used to refer to Regina as "our little money pit."

"I haven't added it up, but it's a nice chunk of change. Frankly, Eddie, I think you should consider putting her down—she's far too antisocial to ever make a good pet."

I'm appalled! Who does he think he is? A hardened beat cop writing off some neglected ghetto kid who's had a bad start? I'm determined to prove him wrong. I'll get through to her. There may be struggles, and I may have to resort to tough love, but there'll be a breakthrough—like the dramatic turning point in an interracial-adoption movie starring Cheryl Ladd on Lifetime: Television for Women.

"Doc, can I use your phone? I'm going to ask my mom to send you a check."

I hate going to my mommy for money but dial her, sure that Oliver's character defects will be removed along with the fleas, mites, and worms. She'll be deloused in every sense of the word. Luckily Chanukah is early that year, and my mom agrees to give the receptionist her Visa number over the phone. Doc Barker keeps Oliver for an extra week.

My mood is hopeful and I set aside my customary annoyance with the holidays, letting Jeffrey decorate my apartment. The live tree he puts up and the spruce garlands with which he adorns the doorways, windows, and toilet tank add a gentile warmth to the place, and I agree to invite friends over to sample the traditional Ecuadorian Christmas recipes that he's been dying to try. I use the week of Oliver's convalescence to thoroughly scour the apartment after my downstairs neighbor David complains about the scent of urine seeping through the ceiling above his sleeping loft. His grievance annoys me, especially since I've never once said a word about the four-in-the-morning screams and chemical smells that emanate from his pad when he hosts S&M parties as Dungeon Master Dave after his day job managing a Crabtree & Evelyn.

I purchase four bottles of a product called Piss Off and a black light that can detect any urine or vomit that might have escaped my notice. I scan every crevice, corner, and textile for traces of feline product like a detective looking for blood spatters and fingerprints at the scene of a homicide. During my survey I realize just how much damage Oliver's done to the new corduroy chair, and I rearrange the furniture hoping Jeffrey won't notice the destruction she's wrought on our purchase. When he questions the new configuration, I tell him it's so we can have a better view of ourselves in the mirror when I fuck him on it.

Jeffrey thinks my explanation's hot, and finding ourselves alone in a clean-smelling apartment for the first time in weeks, we dive into each other. I'm whispering filth into his ear, and we're having a great time breaking in the matching ottoman when he notices the shredded fabric on the bottom. He lets out a scream, and I immediately stop thrusting thinking I've gotten a little too vigorous.

A fight's avoided when I assure him, still in a seductive whisper, that one of the interior designers at the Eton Club will surely reupholster it inexpensively given all the free Stolichnaya we've poured for them over the years.

I go to fetch Oliver from Doc Barker's, naïvely expecting to return home with the sweet-natured waif she's named for. But real life doesn't work like nineteenth-century fiction, with everything neatly wrapped up and everyone content with their lot. Oliver's as miserable a creature as ever. And since I subsequently develop a level-four skin reaction to her flea medication, I couldn't pet her even if she'd let me.

Besides, I couldn't catch her if I wanted to. Now that she's parasite free she's got a lot more energy. Every crystal icicle and colored ball on Jeffrey's Christmas tree becomes a cat toy, and we're awakened several times a night by the sound of breaking glass. Her assault on the furniture continues with a new vigor, and within three days the throw rugs are shredded. When I pass through the tattered drapes that block off the alcove kitchen, I feel like I'm exiting a car wash.

And still I make excuses for her and refuse to give up. "Oh, she's acting out because she's misunderstood."

I let my relationship go to hell because of the special-needs child. And not just my love life, but my financial, physical, and emotional health are all suffering. Oliver's drained my bank account and put me into debt. I'm not sleeping, so I'm eating more to keep up my energy. I'm getting fat, but I'm too tired to exercise, even if I did have the time—which I don't because I'm putting in extra shifts at work. But at least she's healthy, and seems to have finally given her approval to a new litter called Dump & Clump.

Once more, however, hope shows its ugly side. Jeffrey freaks out when he discovers me switching litter brands yet again.

"What are you doing? She likes that one!"

"Yeah, but read this." I hand him an article torn from my latest issue of *Cat Fancy*, outlining the controversy about the new clumping litters. "Apparently cats breathe in the dust when they scratch. It congeals in their lungs and chokes them to death."

"At least it'll save me the trouble."

"And they lick it off their paws, which can cause a fatal blockage in their intestines."

"Please, Eddie, *nothing* is blocking that cat's intestines."

"I'm sure she'll be better now that she's worm free."

"Fine! But one more mess, and I'm out of here. Just because Christmas is coming doesn't mean it has to smell like a manger."

Our hot encounter in front of the mirror has opened the floodgates and Jeffrey's awash in testosterone; he's intent on exploring as many positions on the new chair as possible. Although the exhaustion and weight gain have made me crabby, I'm determined not to be a Scrooge and force myself into some humbuggery. We spend an entire Tuesday testing the chair's springs and unfortunately manage to add a rip or two of our own. We're trying a complicated new move that Jeffrey saw in a video, and from the syncopated rhythm of his breath and light moaning I know he's enjoying himself big-time. I close my eyes to take in the sensations throughout my body when suddenly a bloodcurdling scream pierces the air. At first I think Jeffrey's climaxing, but he jumps up swearing and grabbing his crotch. Oliver's apparently mistaken his scrotum for a Christmas ornament and hooked her claws deep into his sac. Jeffrey's lightning-fast response in pulling away rips the delicate skin even further. There's blood everywhere. As he drops to the floor in agony, he upsets a bottle of Orange Crush on the coffee table and sprays us both with sticky soda.

The intense pain triggers a wave of nausea in Jeffrey, and I hurry him into the bathroom. As he falls to his knees in front of the toilet, he upsets Oliver's litter box, showering himself with particles and dust that stick to his Crush-and-blood-coated body. I try to stop the bleeding with a bath towel, but it's out of control due to his healthy-heart aspirin regimen. I run to dial 911, but he refuses to let me call an ambulance for such an embarrassing injury. So, knowing he's had some experience with S&M scenes that have gotten out of hand, I phone Dungeon Master Dave to take a look at Jeffrey's balls. Dave shows up wearing a harness and chaps and carrying an army medic's bag. He tries applying direct pressure but Jeffrey lets out a wail like a banshee; apparently there's a limit to the pounds per square inch you can put on someone's genitals. Dave turns to me, panicked, "This is really serious, Eddie. He needs to go to a hospital."

Jeffrey refuses. *"No way, Dave!"*

"Well, it's either that, or I apply a tourniquet to your nuts—and I've never done that to someone with an actual injury before."

Jeffrey clenches his jaw. "Okay."

I throw on jeans and a sweatshirt. Pants seem impossible for Jeffrey, so I wrap him in his bathrobe and help him on with his shoes. As we're heading out the door, he screams at Oliver. *"I don't care if I have to kill you myself—you're outta here!"* Her ears flicker in response to his volume and then she resumes calmly licking the orange sticky off her tail.

"Eddie, she's gotta go! It's her or me!"

I nod silently and close the door.

The Dungeon Master hails us a cab, and we head downtown to the emergency room at St. Vincent's. Although St. Luke's is closer, Dave assures us that the staff downtown is much less judgmental about sexually related emergencies.

The choice proves to be the wrong one when we approach the volunteer at the reception desk who greets us in a mocking falsetto. "Well, look what the cat dragged in!"

I'd laugh at the accuracy of the expression if she wasn't somebody we know—and intensely dislike. It's Abraham, one of the cocktail waiters at the Eton Club, who volunteers at St. Vincent's dressed as a candy striper—named Candy Striper.

Jeffery's disgusted. "Fuck!"

Abraham glances down at the blood-soaked terry cloth at his groin. "Goodness! What seems to be the problem?"

"He needs to see a doctor."

"Have a seat; someone will be with you shortly."

"Now, Abraham!"

"It's Candi, Candi with an 'i'."

"Just get us a doctor."

She calls across the crowded waiting room. *"Oh, Dr. Brewer, we need you right away—we have a terrible teabagging accident here."*

She snickers, does a runway turn, and pushes her pill cart down the hall with her overly powdered nose in the air. Jeffrey pounds his fist on the counter. "Shit, she's gonna tell everybody."

"I know, I guess the cat's out of the bag."

"Not funny."

"Sorry."

Luckily it isn't Dr. Brewer's first scrotum. He patches Jeffrey up in minutes, and we're in a cab heading back to my place in Hell's Kitchen in under an hour.

The two of us spend the next morning trying to get Oliver into her cat carrier, but she won't come out from under the daybed. She backs away from our snow-gloved hands and dodges the broom and mop with which we attempt to force her out of hiding. I open a can of tuna hoping that the smell and the *zzzzz* of the electric opener will lure her out, but she senses something's up. After an hour I'm ready to order some of the Estonian goop when Jeffrey has an idea. He pulls my ancient Hoover out from under the miscellaneous no-place-else-to-store-it-in-a-Manhattan-apartment pile beneath the loft ladder. The noise frightens Oliver, but the bulky vacuum won't reach far enough under the furniture to flush her out. As she retreats farther into the corner under the daybed, I can see her terrified meows register on Jeffrey's face. His look of relish is disturbing yet sexy. I stop him a little after I know I should.

"JEFF, TURN OFF THE VACUUM, SHE'S TOO FAR BACK."

"I KNOW."

"SHE'S NOT GOING TO COME OUT; IT'S QUIETER UNDER THERE."

"I KNOW."

"YOU'RE JUST SCARING HER MORE."

"I KNOW!"

Jeffrey turns off the Hoover and Oliver's screams cease. He then disappears through the car-wash curtains and returns from the kitchen with the blender, which he plugs in and pushes under the end of the daybed where Oliver's cowering. "This should do it!"

He hits "Mix" and Oliver lets out a grisly sound like a goat being slaughtered.

"YOU DON'T LIKE THAT, DO YOU?"

He looks up at me. "READY? HERE SHE COMES!" And with

a satisfying grunt of revenge, he forcefully jams his thumb down on the button marked "Frappe." The dreadful racket panics the cat, and in a blur she dashes from under the bed directly into the carrier. I slam the door shut and turn the lock.

We're leaving the apartment just as the mail arrives. Ironically, on top of the pile of bills and Christmas cards is an envelope from A Pound of Love. It's a standard nonprofit, junk-mail plea for money—but Claire's written a personal note in the margin. I read it to Jeffrey: " *Eddie, Merry Xmas! I just want to let you know that we have a beautiful cat with a very sweet disposition that'll make a perfect playmate for Giselle. Give me a ring. Claire.*' "

"As if!"

"It's in pink ink and the 'i' is dotted with a smiley face."

"Jesus."

I hesitate outside the entrance to A Pound of Love. It's painful for Jeffrey to stand for long, and he can barely mask his impatience to get back home.

"Eddie, what's the matter?"

"I know this is the best thing but I feel so guilty, like I'm turning Anne Frank over to the Nazis."

"Think of it more like giving Eva Braun a lift home."

He holds the door open and waves me through ahead of him. As I enter the office, I put the cat carrier behind my back and grasp it with both hands. Claire's overjoyed to see me. She puts down her crochet hook and smoothes out her reindeer sweater as she steps out from behind the counter. "Well, hello there!"

"Hi, Claire."

"I'm thrilled you've come! And this must be your other half?"

"Yes. Jeffrey, Claire."

Claire extends her newly manicured hand to Jeffrey, "It's lovely to meet you," and then turns to me. "He's gorgeous!"

Jeffrey blushes. "Nice to meet you too."

Claire rushes on excitedly. "Did you get my note? Frumka will be so happy to see you! You're going to adore this new cat. She takes a bit of warming up to, but she'll make a marvelous pet and I think th—"

I'm a little overwhelmed by her enthusiasm. Jeffrey's not and interrupts her.

"Actually, we're not here to adopt another cat. We've come to return Oliver."

"Oliver?"

I take the carrying case out from behind my back. "He means Giselle."

"Oh, I see."

I want to lie and say that we're moving to a new building that doesn't allow pets, or that Jeffrey's developed an allergy, but I know Claire's probably heard it all before.

"I'm sorry, but it just isn't working out, and I wanted to honor the contract and bring her back here."

I feel like a jerk, like I'm breaking up with a boyfriend who's gained a few pounds or been diagnosed with a serious illness. Claire plants her hands on her hips, adopts a defensive pose, and drops her love-thy-neighbor tone. All of a sudden I'm on trial at Nuremberg. "Okay, what's the problem?"

Her demeanor intimidates me. "Well, it isn't just one thing. You see . . ."

Jeffrey steps in. "She's an absolute nightmare!"

Claire looks to me for confirmation.

"It's true."

I present Claire with a blue canvas binder containing the cat's medical records, a spreadsheet of expenses I've incurred, and receipts from the vet, the exterminator, and the pet store. I've included Polaroids of the damaged furniture and close-ups of my flea bites and allergic reaction. I've also enclosed a copy of Jeffrey's hospital treatment form but have tastefully refrained from attaching a snapshot of his scarred scrotum. I narrate as Claire looks detachedly through the book. I try hard to hit home the point that the Oliver I'm returning is in far better condition than the Giselle I took away so hopefully almost three months before.

Claire snaps the book shut and tosses it on the counter, her face completely changed. "Well?"

I try to discern just what it is she's expecting. I take a stab. "I'd like to make a donation to make up for your inconvenience."

"Fine! You know, I don't know why I'm surprised by this. You boys have such a hard time with commitment; the first sign of a problem and you're out the door."

From the venom in her voice I can tell this isn't the first time a gay guy's disappointed her, and I picture her sobbing into a wrist corsage, still a virgin the day after the prom. She gestures at Jeffrey dismissively with her head and stares me down. "I suppose you've found the unconditional love you were seeking someplace else. I presume he knows about your police record?"

"Police record?" Jeffrey asks.

"It's nothing, I'll tell you later."

Claire turns to him. "Be careful, sweetie! If a man can't keep his commitment to a pet, it doesn't bode well for you! For your sake, I hope you're less trouble than a little kitty!"

Jeffrey won't have it. *Shut up. You don't know what you're talking about—he's worked his ass off taking care of that monster. Anybody else would've drowned her in the Hudson!*

The anger in his voice gives me an erection.

"Eddie, we're out of here!"

As we turn to go, Claire rushes to the wall and tears down my adoption-day picture. "Here, don't forget this!"

I reach for it, but she rips it up and throws it in my face. I explode. *"You're crazy! You know that? Forget about that check!"*

"Oh, big fucking deal! Get the hell out of here!"

"My pleasure!"

Out on the street I'm shaking with anger. "I hate confrontation!"

"Fuck her! You did the right thing—and you better not give them a cent, I mean it. Come on, let's go home. We still have a few moves we haven't tried out on the chair."

The entire experience brings Jeffrey and me closer, and his display of strength and support makes me realize how much I really love him. His balls heal remarkably fast and over the holidays we repeatedly test the chair's sturdiness and versatility. Despite the rips and the corduroy burns we get, we're quite pleased with our purchase. We decide to take the next step and move in together. We debate what piece of furniture we should buy and break in next and, reasoning that the number of possible sexual positions will be doubled, we order a convertible sofa.

A week after New Year's I receive another plea for money from the Helter Shelter. I'm irritated that Claire hasn't taken me off their mailing list. I'm sure it's intentional—that she's trying to exploit my guilt.

And as hard as I try not to, I still can't help feeling a little guilty. How else can I feel when confronted with pictures of sad-eyed puppies and helpless kittens? I contemplate sending a donation for the animals' sake—but don't want to give Claire the satisfaction. So instead, I write a big check to the ASPCA and send a photocopy to A Pound of Love. On the back of the envelope—in hot-pink Magic Marker—I scrawl "Happy New Year, Claire! C. U. Next Tuesday!" and dot the "i" in her name with a smiley.

My Tale of Two Cities

Part I: Paris

"The French hate the Jews."

"What?"

"Ask your grandmother—she'll tell you."

"Grandma, do the French hate the Jews?"

"And how!"

My grandmother makes the assertion with authority. Apparently, being teased by some Quebecois children in 1914 Montreal is concrete proof that all French hate all Jews.

I turn back to my mother. "She's exaggerating."

"You wait and see how they treat us in Paris."

"We'll be fine; we just won't wear our yellow stars."

"Don't be smart."

"If they hate us so much, why are we going?"

"I thought it'd be nice for your father."

I glance over at my dad, who's watching a show about the bubonic plague on PBS. Even though he has dementia, and I'm sure is unable to follow the narrative, he sits mesmerized. He's fascinated by "educational television" and will focus intently on everything from reruns of *Mutual of Omaha's Wild Kingdom* to footage of the Battle of the Bulge. After a lifetime of appearing younger than his years, his age has caught up with him. He's seventy-one and looks it—on a good day.

My mom continues, "Besides, the London/Paris package wasn't much more money than London alone."

She slips the faded travel brochures out of the fruit bowl on the sideboard where they've been cushioning the bananas for the last six years. My parents originally planned this once-in-a-lifetime trip to Europe for their thirty-fifth anniversary in 1991, but were forced to cancel it when my father was hospitalized with kidney stones. He had stones half a dozen times when I was a kid, and the unearthly screams coming from the bathroom terrified me. Since stones tend to run in families, I worry excessively and drink gallons of water every day to avoid developing them. Heaven forbid I should just follow my doctor's orders and cut down on calcium, but ice cream is the mortar in my food pyramid.

Luckily my parents' second honeymoon was insured, and they didn't lose their deposit. They've rescheduled the trip more than once, but each time "something" has come up and they've cancelled. Many people find travel stressful and it's obvious that, to my mom, the idea of a European vacation is far more appealing than the reality of one. I suspect that if she could simply convince her friends of the wonderful time she had in Gay Paree by listening to some Edith Piaf and reading *France for Dummies*, she would do so. When my father developed dementia, however, my mother realized that if they didn't go soon, they'd never be able to go.

My father has Pick's disease, which is often misdiagnosed as Alzheimer's. In addition to Alzheimer's it has components of Lou Gehrig's disease and Parkinson's as well. It's kind of like winning the neurological trifecta.

As the disease progresses, my father—never much of a talker to begin with—is speaking less and less. And my mom—who can't stand silence—feels compelled to fill the air. All in all it's not too different from the way things have always been between them. In fact, when my mother first began describing changes in my dad's behavior, my brother and I didn't really pay much attention.

"I'm telling you: There's something wrong with your father! He doesn't listen! It's like talking to a wall!"

"So?"

We just assumed he was selectively tuning her out the way husbands do, but it soon became evident something wasn't right. My father developed the habit of constantly biting the middle knuckle on his index finger. Usually he just teethes gently without exerting a lot of pressure, but he also uses the movement to express emotions he no longer has the words for. His displays, sometimes joyful, sometimes angry, are always heartbreaking. When overwhelmed by feelings he can't verbalize, he sinks his teeth into his knuckle and shakes and grunts uncontrollably. Even though he's been prescribed medication to calm him, the episodes nevertheless occur in certain stressful situations. By far the biggest outbursts are provoked by my mother's best friend Jen Wolfberg. After half a dozen disturbing incidents in which the sight of her sent my father into paroxysms of rage, Jen started avoiding my parents socially and now will only speak to my mother on the phone. My mother, though understanding, is heartbroken. She's at a loss to explain my father's behavior.

"Why do you do that to Jen?"

"I don't like her."

My brother Jack and I think it's hysterical when my parents return from a visit to my father's neurologist.

"I told the doctor what your father said about Jen."

"And?"

"She said, 'Maybe he never liked her.'"

Jack and I shrug in disbelief. When she walks into the kitchen, we explode in laughter. We've known for thirty years that my father can't stand Jen.

To her credit, my mother handles my father's illness well; she skips right over the standard stages of grief—shock, denial, bargaining, etc.—and moves right to acceptance, adopting the motto, "Lower your expectations and every day's a plus." She is, however, quite nervous about being alone with my impaired father on foreign soil. So, before she finalizes their reservations, she asks if I'll accompany them. I haven't spent more than two consecutive days with my parents since I graduated from college, and two uninterrupted weeks with them seems like a crushing proposition. But I'm grateful to be able do this for them, and since this is their last chance to go, I agree. My gratitude quickly turns to anxiety, however, when my mother informs me, "Daddy and I've decided we're not going to take the tour; you'll be with us, and you'll know what to do."

I'm not surprised that my mother would put this responsibility on me. Both of my parents are acutely aware that their children are better educated than they are (and I'm sure it doesn't help that I'm rarely able to quash my obnoxious impulses to show off the bits of useless trivia that accumulate in my head). My dad's a very bright guy, but his self-image has been damaged by the fact that he grew up with a learning disability at a time when there was no such thing as a learning disability; there was only stupid. So, when he worked hard to poor results, he (and everyone else) drew the only available conclusion. He humbly defers to my brother and me on any academic subject. My mom, also extremely bright, works with numbers and grows uncomfortable discussing questions of art or literature that don't have concrete answers. As a result, she has a peculiar habit of distancing herself from her own opinions. During my four years as a college thespian, my endeavors were always met with encouraging remarks like, "Oh, you were wonderful! I thoroughly enjoyed the show! Of course, I don't know a thing about theater, but I thought you were great."

Her qualified compliments have been invaluable in forming my sense of self-esteem.

I ask my mother to reaffirm her decision to put me in charge of our itinerary.

"Are you sure you want to rely on me? I've never been to London or Paris before."

"But you've done quite a bit of traveling."

"Quite a bit" means that I've actually been out of the country—once. She doesn't know that my one trip abroad ended disastrously, with me covered in blood and sobbing uncontrollably in a Portuguese emergency room. In any case, to her, who'd obsess about which vaccinations she needed to visit the Canadian side of Niagara Falls, I'm a globetrotter.

"Okay, I'll get some guidebooks and see what there is to see."

I'm actually relieved that I'm not going to be trapped on some cookie-cutter tour with sixty sexagenarians complaining about their boxed lunches and viewing the Tower of London from a bus seat while some chatty tour guide disseminates misinformation about Lady Jane Grey, which I'd feel compelled to challenge.

I spend a week poring over travel guides and street maps planning our schedule. I present my mother with an itinerary that I think will give us a well-rounded experience of the two capitals. Because of her Francophobia, I start with my recommendations for London.

"There's this great exhibit on historical London at the Guildhall Library. I think it'll give us a fantastic overview of the city's past."

She passive-aggressively dismisses my suggestion.

"Oh, I don't think your father would care for that."

"Okay, well what about this show at the Victoria & Albert? It chronicles the museum's growth and features highlights from the various collections."

"That doesn't really sound like his thing."

The disease has claimed most of my dad's words and therefore most of his opinions, but my mother is able to express his supposed dislikes with such authority that she could almost convince me he wouldn't care for a schedule filled with lap dances and hand jobs.

After she nixes the majority of events, exhibits, and entertainments I propose, I'm at a loss.

"Fine, then you decide!"

"Me? I don't know too much about English history."

"Then at least give me a clue. What kinds of things do you think Daddy would like?"

"I don't know—maybe something famous—like Madame Tussauds."

"You want to go to Madame Tussauds?"

"I think he'd like that."

I'm tempted to point out that all of the head shops and porn theaters are being cleared out of Times Square to build a New York branch of Madam Tussauds only an hour from their home. But, remembering that this trip isn't about me (and to avoid an argument), I revise the schedule to suit her tastes, reasoning that at least on a tour I could have fun stumping the guide with arcane trivia about the Plantagenets or William of Orange.

I'm sure that my recommendations for Paris include even more that "your father wouldn't care for," so before I present it to her, I alter my proposed itinerary to include only places and things I know she's heard of and that aren't too difficult to pronounce.

The weather's beautiful when we arrive in Paris, and we decide to go out walking to get a feel for the metropolis. We stroll about for hours, my mother and I taking turns holding my dad's hand and pointing out the major sites—the Arc de Triomphe, the Eiffel Tower, Notre Dame—as well as the ornate details on buildings, fences, and lampposts. In addition to taking in the architectural confections, we're also devouring the real ones. Each of the three of us has a sweet tooth (and the dental work to go with it), and since my dad's illness hasn't stripped him of his ability to enjoy sugar, we stop at every patisserie that we come across so he can get his just desserts. As he eats his treats, my mom lets him amble along in front of us under her vigilant eye. I keep tabs on him too, secretly hoping he'll forget to finish his cookies.

When my father first got sick, my friend Joe said to me, "When people lose their minds they become more themselves." It's true: senility doesn't make old people nasty, it makes nasty people old. Pick's disease has simply turned my sweet-natured dad back into the sweet-natured boy he'd been. As my mother watches him looking up at the buildings with a madeleine in each of his hands, I can see her remembering the past.

We spend the last hour of daylight on a bench in the Luxembourg Gardens watching some boys trying to sink a sailboat in a fountain. As the sun disappears, my mother picks apart a millefeuille and licks the cream off her fingers. She hands me a piece.

"You have to taste this, it's absolutely luscious."

"Thanks. I think my father's enjoying himself."

"He is."

Leaving the gardens, we step into the street and head off for our first dinner in the City of Light. The concierge at our hotel has recommended a little place in the Marais, and even though the night's warm and the restaurant doesn't look too far away on the map, my mother notifies me that my father's tired, so we opt to take the metro rather than walk.

She's confused by the automated ticket machine in the station, but a handsome man nearby comes to her assistance. He cannot get it to work, but offers to sell her some extras tickets that he has.

"Thank you, sir! I really appreciate it. Merci! Merci!"

Five minutes later, when the tickets prove bogus, she's furious. *"Goddamn it! We're not here one day, and the trip is ruined!"*

She takes a deep breath to collect herself and catches sight of the gold Star of David hanging from the chain around her neck.

"Arrgh! Your mother's an idiot! Stupid, stupid, stupid!"

My stifled laugh comes out as a sigh.

"Don't start."

"I didn't say a word."

"I should've listened to your grandmother."

I squash my impulse to point out that while the French may hate the Jews, they love gullible Americans.

Just then the train comes tearing down the track. The racket, combined with my mother's distress, triggers a reaction from my father, who's already overloaded by the frenetic atmosphere of the station. He begins to shake and shout unintelligibly. My mother quickly sits him down, wraps her arms around him, and whispers soothingly in his ear. But he can't stop. His wordless cries, like those of an animal caught in a spring trap, tear at my heart. I can see the terror on my mother's face as she fends off her own embarrassment and reassures the platform full of people who are trying not to stare. "He's okay. It's all right, it's all right."

I take my dad's head in my hands and look in his face. "Shush, Dad, shush, shush, shush, shush, shush . . ."

It takes a full ten minutes for us to calm him down and then five more before we feel comfortable moving him.

"Are you okay, Dad? Ready to go and eat?"

He doesn't answer but rises to his feet.

"Then let's go."

My mother shoots me a look of helplessness, stoically takes

his arm, and together we lead him back up the stairs to the street.

The restaurant's decor is an excellent example of art nouveau, and the waiter's exceedingly patient as I fumble through my pocket phrase book attempting to order the meal. My mom, pathologically cautious of "exotic" foods, orders the *saumon*— the only word on the menu that she's able to decipher. Unfortunately when her entree arrives it looks nothing like the reheated frozen fillet she's used to getting at the Applebee's back home. After carefully wiping off the béchamel sauce and declaring that the fish isn't done enough, she makes it perfectly clear that she's not going to spend a week eating in restaurants where the menu isn't in English. I'm appalled.

"France without French food? We might as well write a guidebook called *Paris on Ten Calories a Day!*"

My mother counters my sarcasm with a "What? I didn't have enough with the subway?" look that makes me feel guilty about giving her a hard time. I'm on my best behavior the rest of the evening.

I attempt to start the next morning on an upbeat note and propose that we take in the collection at the Musée d'Orsay. At first my mom agrees but makes a face when she finds out the museum's in a converted railway terminal.

"I think your father's had enough train stations."

"There aren't any trains there now."

"Do you really want to risk it?"

From her tone it's clear that I don't. So I make an alternative suggestion.

"Then why don't we go to Versailles today?"

"Is there a train involved?"

"I think there's a bus."

"Perfect! But first I have a few things that I need to pick up. Let's get that out of the way."

"What do you need?"

"I promised Jen I'd see what kind of money they get for Lladrós over here."

"Did you tell her that Lladrós are from Spain?"

"She knows that but she thinks since Spain is right next door, they'll be cheaper here than at home. I also want to buy some Shalimar while we're here. It'll only take an hour or two, and the exercise will be good for your father."

I'm not up for an argument, plus I'm open to anything that'll burn off the box of profiteroles I've eaten for breakfast.

Shalimar's the only perfume my mom wears, and she's intent on bringing some home. Our search for Guerlain's flagship store takes way longer than expected, slowed down as we are by our limited language skills and my father's pace. Finally, after hours in the broiling sun we get there—sweating and in need of perfume.

My mother, expecting to find the fragrance cheaper in Paris, is stunned by the price and argues with the bewildered shop-girl. Unfortunately the poor girl only speaks French, and my mother tries to bridge the language barrier with volume. "I CAN GET IT FOR LESS THAN THAT IN BLOOMINGDALE'S!" She turns to me. "Do you believe this?"

"It's not that much money. If you need it, get it."

"That's not the point."

"Then let's go."

"You're right, let's go. I'll pick up a bottle at the mall when we get home. Come on, Mike."

On the way out she spots the tester bottle, sprays on way too much of the signature scent, sniffs her wrist, and makes a face. "Feh."

"Something wrong?"

"No, it's fine. I don't know; I guess for some reason I ex-pected it to smell different over here."

The discovery reinforces her decision to forgo the purchase, but she leaves the store resentful that the next time someone compliments her perfume, she won't to be able to say, "Oh, I picked it up it in Paris."

Outside, my mom holds her forearm up to my father's nose. He lights up for an instant, and I can see her make a mental note. Later, when he's in the nursing home, she'll give herself a spritz whenever we visit. She'll watch the scent take him back to a time when he's no longer an old man alone in a hospital bed, but at home sleeping wrapped around her for one of the thousands of nights of their life together.

After a quick dash into a china shop, so my mother can honestly say to Jen Wolfberg, "I told you there was absolutely no point in shipping Lladrós from France," we stop for more profiteroles and then head to Versailles.

The palace is packed with tourists, and even though most people are paying attention to the tour guide, whispers and crinkling candy wrappers echo through the cavernous rooms. My dad looks up at the elaborately painted ceilings with the wonder of a child whose balloon has escaped. My mother and I are mobilized in case he gets spooked.

"Nice place, huh, Dad?"

He nods. I turn to my mom. "Think you'd like living here?"

"I wouldn't want to clean it."

From room to room my mother continues to speculate on the upkeep of the royal residence, contemplating the number of servants necessary and the hours of vacuuming required. In each boudoir and salon she despairingly points out the impossible task of keeping all the gold polished. I find the obsession with housework ironic coming from a woman whose idea of preparing her own house for company consists of simply putting all the junk in neater piles.

We enter the famous Hall of Mirrors—a spectacular room that's a nightmare for anyone insecure about their appearance. Who can fully appreciate the intricate carving and gilded bronze when everyone can see your cold sore, bald spot, and fat ass all at the same time? I ask a British woman to take a photo of us while my mother uses her currency calculator to estimate how many francs the French government shells out for Windex each year.

Suddenly, my father catches sight of himself. He's distressed by his appearance and bites his finger threateningly at the old man in the glass, his animal noises reverberating throughout the hall. We immediately jump into action and whisk him out of the place, all the while shielding him from the reflections of his reflections.

He's much better once we get him outside, and we decide to forgo the rest of the palace and instead spend the beautiful day strolling through the gardens. Countless fountains later, we end our visit in the Petit Hameau, the fake little village where Marie Antoinette escaped reality and where we too can forget for an hour that anything's wrong.

Over the next few days we take things easy, spending a lot of time outdoors and avoiding the major tourist attractions during the busiest times. My mother and I prod my dad with questions, looking for assurance that he understands where we are and what he's looking at. Most of the time it's not clear whether he's aware or simply parroting what we say.

We walk the Paris streets at a leisurely speed and do a lot of sitting. A *lot* of sitting—for long stretches in the delicate shadows of the leaded windows in Sainte-Chapelle, on a bench at the Stravinsky Fountain, in front of Monet's water lilies at the Musée de l'Orangerie, and in countless cafes eating countless petits fours. After all the sitting and sweets, I can't wait to hear my mother brag to her friends about the new chin she picked up in Paris.

Though we're getting a feel for the city, our relaxed pace necessitates passing up many things I'm curious to see. Of course I know that even if we weren't accommodating my father's disease, the list of places I hope to explore doesn't coincide with my parents' interests. Unlike me, they don't have a penchant for the dismal. So I scrap my plans to visit the catacombs and Père-Lachaise, and even though I know my mom would take perverse delight in a place that helps prove her point about the French hating the Jews, I accept that I'll have to wait to cross the concentration camp at Drancy off my wish list.

But no matter your itinerary, when in the French capital an excursion to the Louvre is mandatory. Wary, however, of the way my father might react to the crowds at the museum, my mother's put off our visit until our last day. Luckily, it appears that it's the noise of the crowds—rather than the crowds themselves—that sets my father off; he seems quite at ease in the respectful silence at the Louvre. We begin our tour of the highlights—the Venus de Milo, the Winged Victory, and *Liberty Leading the People*—without incident.

When we enter the gallery where the *Mona Lisa* is hanging, my mother can't suppress her annoyance at the small size of da Vinci's masterpiece and at how many people are crowding around it. She'll not have my timid father denied a look and pushes her way through the mob so he can get a close-up view.

"Look, Mike, do you know who that is?"

His reaction to the painting takes us by surprise. He snarls viciously at the portrait and then suddenly lets loose with string of expletives that shocks the other visitors and almost makes Mona blush. He then clamps his teeth down so hard on his knuckle that he draws blood. Still on guard after the metro and mirror incidents, I immediately leap into action and pull him away from the crowd. In an instant I have him sitting in a quiet corner. The episode has been nipped in the bud, and a few minutes later he's calm as can be. I look at my mom. "What the hell was that about?"

"I'll have to tell Jen."

"Tell her she's in good company, that he only growls at women who have classic beauty."

"She'll like that."

"Or who look five hundred years old."

"Cute. Let's go."

"Do you want to go, Dad?"

"No."

I respond with assurance to the look of frustration my mother shoots me.

"He'll be fine, I promise. We'll just stick to parts of the museum that aren't so crowded."

"All right, but if he starts again that's it. Come on, Mike."

I nod in agreement and follow as she leads him off into a sparsely populated side gallery.

There's a certain sense of urgency whenever I go to a museum in a strange city. Aware it's unlikely that I'll be there again anytime soon, if ever, I feel compelled to cram as much into my visit as possible. I stop to take in every painting, sculpture, artifact, and installation. I carefully read the placard beside each display, and I study the exhibition guide as if there's to be an exam. Inevitably, overloading my brain with so much information blows a fuse, and I forget everything almost immediately. My memory of my trip to the Prado two years earlier is a complete blur, and my boyfriend Jeffrey and I once had a huge fight about whether we'd ever been to the Gulbenkian in Lisbon until he showed me a photo that he snapped of the delicious security guard's ass.

At home in New York, my museum time's much more relaxed. I can walk around the Met anytime and so don't feel pressured to digest the entire inventory in an afternoon. Taking in a special exhibit on a single painter like Matisse or Courbet, I come away with a better understanding of the artist and his time. Alternately, I enjoy mindlessly ambling around to see where chance might lead me, moving from a gallery of ancient Greek amphorae to a room of sixteenth-century Flemish drawings to a display of Mughal carpets. With no constraint on my time, I can choose to contemplate a single painting for as long as I like and, studying evidence of its decay, appreciate how fortunate I am to see it before it's inevitably lost to time. I can marvel at the artist's technique and, at the same time, speculate about which soft drink's advertising campaign the genius in question would be sacrificing his talent to if he were alive today.

Even without a time restriction, the Louvre is overwhelming. The number of baby Jesus paintings alone is staggering. And I imagine God as the annoying new papa, ready to pull a hundred canvases out of his wallet and bore anyone unwittingly congratulating him on the new arrival. After several hours I can't concentrate any longer; the art is going in one eye and out the other.

"Ma, I think I've had enough of the Madonna. How about you?"

"Eh—she's not so much to look at. Come on, Mike."

He follows unquestioningly as our feet instinctively take us to the gift shop.

Museum shops fascinate me, and I always end up spending a disturbingly large proportion of my visits leafing through books of the exhibit I've just seen. Of course a tiny reproduction of a great painting in a coffee-table volume can't compare to the original, but focusing on a book lets me block out all the people, other artwork, and dead air competing for my attention. My mother finds the same escape and cultural experience browsing through silk scarves printed with Victorian angels and enamel pill boxes lidded with Delacroix battle scenes.

Even though the shop's bustling with tourists, I'm able to tune out the polyglot crowd around me and get drawn into a volume of Renaissance works. I'm captivated by the very same information I was unable to process in the galleries, and on page after page I'm intrigued by paintings we've just seen but of which I have only the vaguest recollection. A quarter of the way through the color plates I come across a mother and child composition that seems completely new to me. It's beautiful.

"Hey, Mom, do you remember seeing this painting with the infant on the green pillow? I want to go check it . . ."

They're gone.

I know I should put the book down and search them out, but frankly, I'm happy to be rid of them for a while. This week is the most time I've spent with my parents in over ten years, and these few minutes in the Louvre's gift shop are the longest I've been alone since we left the tarmac at JFK. I turn my attention back to the book, figuring that they'll come and get me when she's bored looking at museum-quality reproductions.

Fifteen minutes later, my reading's interrupted by my mother's panicky voice.

"Where's your father?"

"What do you mean? I thought he was with you."

"I told you to watch him while I went to the ladies' room."

"You did?"

"I did."

"I don't think you did."

"Don't tell me I didn't. I did!"

"Okay, you did, you did. Let's just find him."

We frantically search the shop and then scour the nearby galleries for almost half an hour. My mom's beside herself and is ready to call the police, but the museum staff assures her that it's not necessary. A few minutes later, a docent spots my father sitting quietly on a bench in front of a large oil of St. Michael vanquishing the devil. My mother lets out a cry that echoes through the hush-hush rooms and draws the attention of everyone in sight. *"Goddamn it, Mike!"*

Ignoring the spectators, she kneels down next to him, takes his hand, and kisses him on the cheek. Her voice is equal parts anger and relief.

"You can't wander off like that! I was worried something happened to you."

I sit down on the other side of him. "Are you okay, Dad?"

He doesn't say a word, just points at the colorful image of Satan facedown on the ground, crushed under the winged saint's foot. Our eyes follow his finger to the painting and then scan back up his arm to his face. From the way his eyes are focused, it's crystal clear that he isn't just staring blankly. He's not quite in the present but he's definitely aware, almost as if he's listening to something. My mother, fixed on his profile, asks, "You like that, honey?"

He nods.

"What do you like about it? Is it the angel? Is it the—"

I cut off her questions. "Ma, let's just sit."

My dad's intellect is shot, but the image is touching him even if he doesn't have the words to say how. In a way, he's like an animal with limited mental capacity but with a full complement of emotions—a combination that I, who habitually undermine my happiness with bombardments of ingenious "logic," almost find enviable. Unfortunately, unlike an animal, he hasn't been deprived of shame. The disease is cruel; it's taken away his abilities but not the awareness that he used to have them. I can tell that expecting him to speak will only fuel the unfathomable frustration he must feel, and I'm happy to let him look as long as he likes.

My dad's always been emphatically opposed to religion. He once told a Jehovah's Witness on a subway platform, "I'm sorry, but my covenant is with Lucifer." The idea that he, who found no connection to Judaism except when cursing God for smiting him with kidney stones, is finding serenity in this Catholic icon seems preposterous. But here he is, his mind somehow put at ease by Raphael's colorful angel. The tranquility on his face is contagious, and for the first time since we left home my mom's eyes aren't darting around like those of a prey animal. I know that no matter her thoughts on, or experience with, the French, she'll be forever grateful for this moment in the Louvre. We sit calmly with my dad pulled into the painting and my mother and I pulled into him. He barely moves, his hands, chapped from constant teething, gently folded in his lap. Finally he starts to tire and my mother, sensing that he's begun to slip away, breaks the silence. "Mike, should we look more? Or do you want to eat lunch?"

"Eat lunch."

She questions me. "Lunch?"

"Lunch."

"Come on, Mike."

She helps my dad up. As she's kneeling down to tie his shoe, he turns to the painting.

"Bye."

My mom turns her head to see who he's talking to and then looks up into his face. It's a moment of devastating intimacy and lasts just long enough for me to feel as if I'm spying on them.

"Let's go," she says.

I take a last look at St. Michael as they walk toward the exit. Outside, we skirt the busy crowd and begin our search for a substandard restaurant.

Part II: London

On the taxi ride from Heathrow, my mom strikes up a conversation with the driver.

"When do you think they're going to switch driving to the right side of the street?"

"Dunno, ma'am, but I hope they give us plenty of time to practice up."

I'm annoyed by her question but even more annoyed by the cabbie's affable response. I hope he really hates American ethnocentricity as much as I do and merely doesn't want to jeopardize his tip.

As she engages the driver, I study my father's profile and can somewhat gauge the level of pleasure he's getting from the sights outside his window.

"You having a good time, Dad?"

His eyes acknowledge me, but he can't access the language to make himself understood. In frustration he bites the knuckle of his index finger as he watches the strange city go by.

We check into our hotel. I'm all for lying down but my mother presses her agenda.

"Your father must be hungry. You're hungry, aren't you, Mike?"

He responds with an acquiescent nod.

Still partly under the illusion that I'm in charge of our plans, I suggest, "Okay, why don't we go to a traditional English pub and experience some of the local flavor?"

"Oh, that would be lovely!"

I ask the hotel clerk for a recommendation, and he directs us down the street to a neighborhood institution called the Pig & Piper.

The place is charming with blown-glass windows and wood paneling. Inside, some locals are playing darts and drinking ale. Outside, the bill of fare is written on a slate. My mother takes one look at the words "kidney pie" and quickly redirects my father, who's instinctively heading toward the door.

"Oh, no, Mike, no!"

"What's wrong, Mom?"

"Your father can't eat the food here."

"What are you talking about?"

"He has a very sensitive stomach."

"He eats horseradish out of the jar."

"Let's keep looking."

We meander through the adjoining streets and arrive at another amiable establishment called the Cock & Crown. My mother quickly scans their slate, which includes exotic items such as toad in the hole and spotted dick.

"Mike, don't you think we can do better?"

Again he nods and we're off.

Our search for "something better" continues, and after forty-five minutes of my mother turning up my dad's nose at the Cup & Ale and looking down his nose at the Bear & Crow, we find ourselves back in front of the Pig & Piper. My mother's distraught.

"Again?"

I point out that the shepherd's pie sounds nice but she makes a fussy face, and I imagine her as a finicky child refusing to eat off a plate where the vegetables, meat, and potatoes are all touching each other. We end up having our first English meal in a Cantonese restaurant.

"Isn't it interesting the way they make the chow mein here?" she remarks.

"Yeah, it's like we're in a completely different country."

"You're funny."

My mom claims to adore Chinese food but only ever orders wonton soup, spareribs, and chow mein. She won't even try anything else. I doubt she ever has, and I resent that she's exempted herself from her own "You at least have to taste it" rule that she instituted when we were kids refusing to eat the recipes she garnered from Campbell's soup labels and the back of the Ritz cracker box.

We all feel calm after eating and enjoy the stroll back to the hotel during which we encounter posters for productions of *King Lear, A Doll's House,* and Sophocles' *Electra.* After four years of studying drama in college, I'm ecstatic at the prospect of seeing the classics brought to life—especially of seeing Shakespeare on his home turf. Of course, in the back of my mind, I know that my father "wouldn't care for" anything as serious as eye gouging or matricide, but I hope we'll at least be able to take in a lighter classic such as *A Midsummer Night's Dream* or *The Comedy of Errors.* Ironically, I'm even more excited when I read a tepid review of *Midsummer*. Ever since feeling jealous of my best friend Jill in high school because her family regularly attended the Broadway theater, I've fantasized about casually bursting the bubble of some braggart who'd gone on and on about the strings he pulled to get tickets to the hot new British import: "Oh, it's not so great—I saw it in *London*."

As I watch my dad's face light up in reaction to the colorful posters, I feel grateful to be a comfort to my parents on this trip—even though I'm not always sure how to help them. My dad is easily excited in strange environments, and it's hard for him to communicate what he's feeling. He expresses himself in a mixture of partial sentences, guttural noises, and spastic movements—a kind of emotional hieroglyphics that are difficult to decipher. My excitement over our first outing in the Theater District is dampened when my mother, the self-appointed Rosetta Stone, translates my father's mumbling, grunting, and finger biting as "I'd prefer to skip Shakespeare and see *The Mousetrap*."

It takes awhile to let go of my resentment, but I reason that *The Mousetrap*, a murder mystery by Agatha Christie and the longest-running show in history, is a theatrical landmark. Coming to London and not seeing it would be like a trip to New York without a visit to the Statue of Liberty.

Like the statue, which inside is nothing more than a grimy, narrow staircase, the play is much better in theory, and I relish being able to tell people back home firsthand just how mediocre it is.

The next morning my mother insists that, before we head off to see the sights, we go shopping for gifts and souvenirs.

"I don't want to run around like a lunatic shopping last minute."

"But if we wait until the last day, it'll only take one day. This way it's going to take all week."

"Don't be cute."

I know there's no arguing with her.

"Okay, what do we need to get?"

"Not much—just something nice for Grandma and your brother, some knickknacks for the girls at the office, and a few items I promised to pick up for Jen."

"I hope it's not more of those dreadful Lladrós."

She fingers through her handbag and pulls out a list of Princess Diana memorabilia that Jen's requested. I look it over. "Give me a break! Tell me you're not going to make us schlep all over London for this junk?"

"I feel guilty about the way your father's been reacting to her."

"What's she going to do with all of this anyway? Her house is overflowing with kitsch as it is."

"She's putting it away for the grandkids. It'll be worth a lot someday."

"She better hope they don't knock her off early."

"That's not funny."

"You're right. They'll probably keep her on life support indefinitely just to avoid inheriting this crap."

She ignores the remark and turns to my father, "Come on, Mike, get your jacket, it's time to go. Ed, help him will you?"

I comb my dad's hair and zipper his jacket. He accepts my help without any fuss. He's the world's biggest kindergartner.

"Ready, Dad?"

"Where are we going?"

"To buy stuff for Jen."

A round of knuckle biting ensues.

"What's the matter?"

"I don't like her."

My mother gets annoyed with me. "You had to start?"

"I didn't say anything."

A few years later, after Diana's death in a Paris tunnel, I'll begrudge Jen's good fortune when she makes a killing selling all of the schlock at a huge profit on eBay.

During the following few days, we take in the typical attractions—the Changing of the Guard, Buckingham Palace, Westminster Abbey, etc. We stop for tea at Harrods, where we plow through two plates of scones and clotted cream while my mother spies on a woman she's convinced is the Duchess of York consuming way more than her allotted number of Weight Watchers points. Afterward, walking along the streets, my mother snaps photos nonstop, and my dad holds my hand and looks with wonder at the buildings and monuments that I point out. For him, it's literally the trip of a lifetime.

For three nights in a row we go to see musicals, two of which are quite good and one of which is terrible—but which I'll at least be able to brag about having seen in the West End. I know that my mother, too, can't wait to tell her friends on Long Island all about her theatrical outings—not only that she's previewed the shows abroad but that she saw them for *sooo* much less.

After a fourth musical comedy at a matinee, my resentment is building, and I start to feel that if I don't see a play where someone uses the word "forsooth" soon, I'm going to indulge in some eye gouging and matricide of my own. The next morning I suggest that maybe we should take in something with a little more substance.

"I'd really love it if we could see *King Lear* tonight."

"I think your father would have trouble understanding the language."

She has a point.

"Well, what about *A Doll's House*? Janet McTeer is supposed to be fantastic."

"That's Ibsen, isn't it?"

"Yes?"

"You see, your mother knows something."

I laugh. "Well then, let's get tickets."

"I don't think it's for him."

"Oh for God's sake! Why don't you—"

"What? His life isn't painful enough that I should make him sit through two hours of miserable Norwegians? I want him to see happy things."

I feel like an asshole. She's absolutely right.

That night we pass over the musicals and purchase tickets to a wild English farce (I can't remember the name) with lots of physical comedy—people running in and out of doors, mistaken identities, men in drag, etc. But even though my dad can't follow the absurdly convoluted plot, he's delighted by the frenetic pace and broad humor, his uninhibited laughter infecting everyone around us.

Our last day in England has been reserved for the Tower of London and Madame Tussauds. The mystique of the Tower fascinates me—the beheaded queens, the murdered princes, the ravens. The Crown Jewels fascinate my mother. My dad, like the ravens, responds to anything shiny.

As we file past the collection, a guide in a Beefeater uniform details the provenance of each bracelet and bejeweled dagger. The other visitors listen intently to the glamorous history, but I can't help thinking about the starving populace who actually paid for this obscene display of wealth. My mother points out a huge sapphire and says to my dad, "Mike, how come you never buy me anything like that?"

He unhesitatingly reaches for his wallet, and I know he'd purchase it for her without a second thought. As he begins to pull out the few dollars we let him carry around, she stops him.

"No, sweetheart, put that away. I'm kidding. I don't need that. Where would I wear it?"

She kisses him on the cheek and whispers something in his ear that coaxes his mouth into a crooked grin. When their heads separate, her eyes are moist, and for an instant I can see the two of them forty years earlier, she tenderly reassuring the shy young man who took months to summon the courage to ask for her phone number. I know that later, when my father's gone and I've finished my seven stages of grief, I'll recall this image and think that if it were the only memory I had of my parents, it would be enough for me.

After seeing where Anne Boleyn was imprisoned and I'm yelled at by another Beefeater for trying to put my head on the chopping block, we leave the Tower and head for Madame Tussauds.

Now, I can appreciate that using eighteenth-century techniques to create lifelike wax figures was a grand achievement in a time before plastics, but in this age of mass reproduction it seems absurd to get excited over a mannequin of Isaac Newton. But my mother loves it. Her expressions of delight are punctuated with my father's nods. My first thought is that his agreement is reflexive—the result of endeavoring to keep the peace for the past thirty-odd years. But having witnessed the moment in the Jewel House, I start to wonder if maybe it's simply that when she's happy, he's happy.

We take time after Madame Tussauds for one last walk around London before dark. The plan is to have a final night at the theater before we head home to New York in the morning. It's too late to go back to our hotel, so we kill time in a small café before going to buy tickets. We're faced with the decision between seeing *Martin Guerre*—an award-winning new musical by the creators of *Les Misérables*—or *The Buddy Holly Story*. For my mother the choice is easy.

"*Guerre?* That's French!"

"So's that éclair you're eating."

"Oh, you're so smart. Wipe the icing off your father's face."

I'm not only disappointed that we haven't seen any Shakespeare but am appalled that we've schlepped all the way to England to see someone impersonate a dead American. On the way to the theater, though I retain an outward calm, inside I want to claw my face off in frustration. But I don't utter a word for fear of exploding. The only way I can drag my ass up the stairs to the mezzanine is to remind myself that the story's going to end in a fiery plane crash.

I sit through the first two numbers with my shoulders knotted and a puss on my face. I fucking hate it. I hate it because it's good; it's very good, and I don't want to admit it. Perhaps it's a case of lowered expectations making something a plus, but the show's undeniably entertaining. The actor playing Buddy Holly is perfect for the part, and the energizing music's infectious. My father, sitting between us, is tapping his feet and bopping his head. My mother leans across him and whispers to me, "He's having a grand old time."

The joy on his face softens me.

The first act is great, but the second act is unmemorable— not because it sucks, but because the intermission's fantastic!

As we walk to the lobby, my father's humming along to a recording of the real Buddy Holly singing "Peggy Sue." My mother takes his hand in hers.

"You remember this song, Mike?"

"They played it at the Nevele."

She's almost knocked off her feet. She cautiously prods him, "You remember going to the Nevele?"

He nods assuredly. She continues, "Do you remember who we went there with?"

"Harold and Beverly. She had to go to the hospital."

"That's right."

I exchange a look with my mother. "Dad, why did she go to the hospital?"

"She had gallstones. Harold was sore he didn't get to eat his drumstick."

"Are you serious?"

"He blamed her for ruining their vacation."

"He did not."

My mother assures me, "He could be a real pain in the ass."

My father laughs. "He used to make a rubber face like Sid Caesar."

I can see that my mother, too full of emotion, doesn't know what to do. So I continue prompting my father. "What else did he do, Dad?"

"Pinched Jen."

"Jen Wolfberg! Really?"

"She was a looker."

"Really?"

"When she kept quiet."

My mother suppresses a laugh. "Oh jeez!"

"Didn't Barry get mad?"

"He didn't mind."

My mother turns to me. "Ask him what else happened that weekend."

"Dad, do you remember what else happened?"

He looks at me blankly.

My mother takes over. "Come on, what else happened, Mike?"

He can't recall and starts to lift his knuckle to his mouth. My mother grabs hold of his hand. "No, sweetie. What else happened? What did I tell you at the Nevele?"

"The baby."

"That's right, the baby. What's the baby's name?"

"Jackie."

"And who is he named after?"

"Pop."

She points to me. "And who's that?"

"Jackie."

"No, not Jackie. You know who that is."

"Edward?"

"Yes, that's Edward."

I well up when I hear my father say my name. I know it won't be long before he doesn't know who I am.

For the next fifteen minutes, until the chimes ring to signal the start of the second act, I hang on to every word as my father recalls details of my parents' trip to the Catskills almost forty years earlier. Even though we're feeding him questions, he's not grunting or just bluntly blurting out reactions, but actually having a conversation. He's maintaining eye contact and cracking jokes about a Thanksgiving weekend in 1959. With Pick's disease, as with Alzheimer's, the oldest memories are often the last to succumb as the illness invades the brain, but somehow Buddy Holly's music has worked its way down into cells the disease hasn't yet bored deep enough to obliterate. That the vibrations of the drums, bass, and guitar could affect my father so profoundly makes sense to me. I suspect that memories associated with sound, the only sensory information that can really penetrate the womb, are preserved in a primal part of the brain.

I squirm through the rest of the show; I can't wait to see what else the rock and roll has uncovered. But when the curtain comes down, my dad—like an aging Olivier who's pulled his Hamlet out of mothballs for a final command performance—is too exhausted to entertain further, and so we head back to the hotel. He quietly stares into the tunnel as the three of us share a bar of Cadbury chocolate on the tube platform at Charing Cross.

His cameo at *The Buddy Holly Story* is the last real public appearance of my father. I'm grateful to the music for releasing those memories; I know the illness won't take too much longer to completely destroy that part of him.

At Heathrow the next morning, I keep my dad focused on

my new book of Gainsborough portraits—a gift from my mother to apologize for making me skip the National Gallery. Satisfied that the colored plates are keeping him calm in the bustling airport, she excuses herself to shop for some duty-free Shalimar.

Aboard the plane my mom gives my dad the window seat. I offer to sit in the middle, but she refuses. "No, Ed, you have long legs, you take the aisle."

I don't argue with her since most of our legroom's been sacrificed to the Princess of Wales tea set jammed under the seats in front of us. I buckle my seat belt and sigh. My mother studies my face. "You're ready to go home," she says as she pats my knee.

"Kind of."

"Thank you for coming. I know this wasn't the easiest trip."

"I think Dad had a good time."

"He did—and I appreciate it."

I squeeze her hand and she smiles, then leans her head back, and closes her eyes. As I reach for the Sky Mall catalogue in the seat pocket in front of me, I catch my dad as he abruptly swings his hand up to his mouth and sinks his teeth deep into the knuckle of his index finger.

"No, Dad!"

Startled, my mom jerks forward and grabs his hand. "Mike, what is it? What's wrong?"

He responds by shaking violently and letting loose with a string of disturbingly loud growls. Pulling him forward so that they're forehead to forehead, she whispers comfortingly, "It's okay, baby. It's okay. It's okay."

When I turn to assure our fellow passengers that everything's all right, I catch sight of the stewardess making her way down the aisle toward us.

"Oh, no!" I cry.

My mom looks up. *"What?"*

"Look!"

With my chin I point up the aisle. I can see the tension spread across my mother's face as it registers that the woman looks more than a little like Jen Wolfberg.

Can I Tell You Something?

"Hey! Come to my fucking show!"

The lesbian laughs. "Sorry, hon, I can't."

"What do you mean, 'I can't'? What's so important?"

"It's bedtime."

"Bedtime? At eight-thirty? What are you, ninety?"

My sarcasm works and she laughs again. I'm glad. I need her to think I'm funny. With her thumb she points over her shoulder to another lesbian with a toddler in a stroller. "Not my bedtime. His."

"Oh, him? The show's only an hour. You can leave him parked in front of the club. What could possibly happen to a child in Provincetown?"

Both women laugh. The second one hands back the flyer I've given her.

"Another time. Great flyer, though."

"Thanks, ladies. Have a good night."

I look down at the full-color postcard promoting my stand-up act. After six years of hawking my show on Commercial Street, or "flyering" as it's known to the performers in Provincetown, I've stumbled upon a brilliant idea. I've entitled my 2004 show *Come to My F#@&ing Show*. The name's a big hit and allows me to get a laugh while legitimately cursing at people who are rude or blowing me off.

My bitterness doesn't only stem from constantly having to lure folks into my show at the Crown & Anchor; all the acts are working the street, including Broadway veterans and local legends. I'm also resentful that I've got to compete for an audience with a dozen drag queens who're ready to pounce on anyone who looks like they might have twenty bucks to spend. Now, most of these impersonators are quite talented, but each summer there are always a few guys who think they're stars simply because they've waxed their chests and donned a ball gown.

This summer the usual stress I feel trying to get noticed on a street full of gender illusionists (or delusion-ists, as the case may be) is heightened by the necessity of also vying for attention with a guy in a turkey suit (roasted, not feathered) and a troupe of towel-clad gym boys who march through town to the sound of a trombone. They're the cast of *Naked Boys Singing*, and their show is not only selling out every night but also has every lecherous queen on Cape Cod shelling out ten extra dollars to check out the man-meat from the front row. The challenge of being a regular guy in a T-shirt competing with the constant parade of flesh and taffeta is compounded even further by Commercial Street, itself rife with distractions—cute guys, windows full of rainbow crap, adorable dogs of every breed, and disgusting amounts of ice cream, fudge, and saltwater taffy.

Rick, the owner of the Crown & Anchor, has suggested that I flyer in a costume, but a costume isn't part of my act. Stand-up is all about being who you are, which is why the rejection is so personal. Early on in my comedy career, when I'd have a bad set and lament that an audience hated me, my mom would attempt to cheer me up by telling me: "It's none of your business what other people think of you." The problem, of course, is that that's *exactly* my business. My friend Patrick believes I'd get more attention if I worked the street shirtless, which wouldn't be a bad idea if I were able to stay away from the fudge and taffy myself.

Flyering is nothing if not a humbling experience—especially when you're over forty. I often feel like a loser and think I might as well be handing out coupons for dry-cleaning or mini storage. But then again I do net eighty percent of each ticket and get to spend Memorial Day through Columbus Day in a resort that thousands of people scrimp and save to visit for one short week each year.

I'm lucky that this week my guest star, Danny McWilliams, is helping me. We've worked together several summers in Ptown performing in *Funny Gay Males* with our good friends Bob Smith and Jaffe Cohen. I've been privileged to work with these three pioneering comics for several seasons, but this year I'm working solo. Danny's here in Ptown visiting friends and has agreed to do an opening spot on my show. He's the funniest person I know. With a turn of his head or the arch of an eyebrow, he can imitate anyone or anything: Robert DeNiro, Bette Davis, a Hoover upright.

I approach a young gay couple and hold out a flyer.

"Hey, guys, looking for a show?"

The guy closest to me takes the postcard as they pass, but the other snatches it from his boyfriend's hand. *"Do we look like we're looking for a fucking show?"* He tosses it over his shoulder as they walk away.

I bend down to pick it up, and as I'm wiping off the card I say to Danny, "Do you believe that schmuck?"

"What a fuckhole! He should have his left nut hacked off with a SARS-infected meat cleaver and used as a golf ball by a bunch of cunt-less dykes!"

I adore Danny. He can snap like a twig when something angers him or over the mere mention of someone he detests. Say the name George W. Bush, and a Niagara of filth comes pouring out of his mouth: *"That piss-soaked cumbag! He should be fisted by Freddie Krueger! I'd love to kill his mother, dig her up from the grave, bring her back to life, and then kill her again. I'd staple her pussy shut, so in her next life no more turds like him come out of it."*

He curses in sentences, sometimes in paragraphs, and his venom is so specific it's disturbingly poetic. On the page—or related secondhand—his rants are shocking, but his Tourette-like eruptions are so uncensored that they have an inexplicable innocence. I love that he lets his anger out as needed instead of letting it fester. A moment after one of his outbursts he's as calm as can be, and I know that he'll never die from anything stress related. I sigh. "I'm wiped out."

"Me too. I need more coffee."

Danny does *not* need more coffee. I do, however. The show is a breeze compared to working the street, and we still have three hours of flyering ahead of us.

"I'll get us some."

I fetch two large coffees, each with a double shot of espresso. As I exit the coffee shop, I'm accosted by a local drag performer named Tina Casserole who is as good at hiding her talent as her genitalia.

"I see you're charging up, Eddie."

"It's been a long day so far."

"Oh, I know, it's all soooo exhausting. If I don't caffeinate, I run out of steam halfway through my show. I get *soooo* over-heated in that crinoline. I'm envious that you boys can just throw on any old thing to flyer. You're *soooo* lucky you don't have to wear a costume."

I'd love to respond to her condescension with a Dannyesque tirade, or at least tell her to shut up while I point out that wearing a costume makes promoting yourself a lot easier. It doesn't take much effort to attract a crowd when you're three hundred pounds and dressed like Scarlett O'Hara. But "Hell hath no fury like a man dressed as a woman scorned," and I hold my tongue.

"Yeah, Tina, I'm *soooo* glad I don't have to deal with all of that."

"Be grateful that your show is just talking."

"You're right, it's just talking."

I cannot wait to relate Tina's remark to Danny. I know he'll explode like an H-bomb, and I'll wish I had a school desk to hide under.

"Just talking! That fat twat-fister! Her wig has more talent than she does! I hope she gets herpes from rimming Don Knotts and drowns in a pool of her own yeast-riddled snatch juice. No, no wait: I hope she gets egg-sized hemorrhoids and leaves a greasy shit stain dragging her ass across the stage like a wormy schnauzer."

I take out a Kleenex and wipe off the coffee that's spurted out of my nose. "Are you done?"

"That'll do for now."

"Okay."

"Just talking! I'd like to see what kind of crowd she'd attract without the wig and dress."

"I've seen her without the wig and dress—it's not pretty."

"Anyway, I bet her act sucks."

"You've never seen it?"

"No. Is it any good?"

"Can I Tell You Something?"

Danny howls. He loves the expression "Can I Tell You Something?" We both do. It's an inside joke for the Funny Gay Males. The four of us use it to describe awful people, places, and things.

Sometimes we use the phrase as an adjective:

"Hey, Bob, how was your date?"

"Dinner was okay, but the sex was so Can I Tell You Something."

And sometimes as a noun:

"Is Tina talented?"

"No, she's a big, fat, obnoxious Can I Tell You Something."

Although we employ the phrase privately for our own amusement, occasionally, when we're appalled but keeping our disgust to ourselves seems prudent, we utilize it to covertly insult someone:

"Eddie, do you like my new outfit?"

"Oh, Tina, Can I Tell You Something? Wow!"

By far our most common—and important—use of "Can I Tell You Something?" is when we're consulting each other creatively. As comedians we all have pretty thick skins—nobody could possibly stay in the business for very long without developing one. And as friends we've grown to trust each other to tell the truth. Every comic, no matter how successful, writes bad jokes—you have to in order to write the good ones. And every comic, no matter how successful, also bombs occasionally. I've seen Margaret Cho suck, Bill Maher flatline, and Drew Carey leave the stage with his tail between his legs. On more than a few occasions "Can I Tell You Something?" has been Jaffe's response to a new bit I'm working on, and it's not uncommon to find "CITYS" scribbled in the margins of an essay that I've asked Bob to take a look at. "Can I Tell You Something?" is a reminder of the standard we hold each other—and ourselves—to.

I first heard the story of the phrase's origin one night when the four of us were hanging out after our show. Bob, Jaffe, and Danny were sharing a joint and talking. As usual, I was the designated listener.

Every week while he was in college, Danny would read *Back Stage*—a showbiz trade paper. There, in every issue among the casting notices was the same ad for comics, singers, novelty acts, etc. Danny would staple his resume to his headshot and take the A train to Times Square. In a dingy building in the Theater District was a casting agency with its name on a glass door like the offices of Bialystock & Bloom in Mel Brooks's *The Producers*.

I don't know the real name of the agency, but Danny always refers to it as Ointz & Shmointz.

At eighteen, Danny was just getting his feet wet doing stand-up and hadn't yet realized he was supposed to do original material. So he prepared for Ointz & Shmointz's auditions by memorizing old Phyllis Diller routines—a smart move since he wasn't out of the closet and was desperate to avoid getting pigeon-holed.

Now, I cannot imagine anything funnier than sweet-faced, Catholic-schooled Danny McWilliams from Ozone Park, Queens, doing a butched-up impression of Phyllis Diller, but apparently Ointz & Shmointz were not so enthusiastic. Ointz, a nebbishy little man, would listen for the obligatory three minutes and then politely cut Danny off. "Thanks, but it's not quite what we're looking for right now. Come back in a few weeks." Shmointz, a big mound of a guy, would say nothing and just flip through the pile to the next resume.

This went on for over a year and Danny, despite his youthful optimism, continued to call on Ointz & Shmointz with little expectation that their responses would be any different. During his last visit to the grimy office, Danny delivers a performance that would crack up Phyllis Diller herself. Ointz thanks him with his usual "It's not what we're looking for" speech and Danny turns to go. As Danny reaches down to pick up his knapsack, the sullen Shmointz calls out, "Hey!"

Thinking that his dead-on impersonation has finally gotten its due notice, Danny whips around hopefully. "Yes?"

"Can I tell you something?"

"Sure."

"You stink!"

Ointz jumps in. "Hey, what are you doing? That's not nice! Don't say that!" but his partner will not be silenced.

"No, no, no! HE STINKS!"

Ointz apologetically shrugs, says, "Thank you," and Danny, the wind knocked out of his sails, runs teary eyed through the crowd of ventriloquists, contortionists, and jugglers eagerly waiting their turns.

Now Danny is the first to admit that Shmointz was right.

"I sucked! They should've gotten Phyllis Diller to beat me with a two-by-four."

Even so, I hate the thought of anyone hurting Danny. I've often wished his foul mouth had come to his own defense that day, but at eighteen his skill as a four-letter wordsmith wasn't sufficiently developed. Actually, I suspect that traumatic incident laid the foundation on which his filthy prose is built. Despite acknowledging his poor performance, Danny still lets loose whenever Bob, Jaffe, or I mention Shmointz.

"He's the plague-ridden flea on the dingle-berried asshole of an amputee's stump-fucked wife."

Danny and I laugh at Tina Casserole's expense and continue working the street. Our effort pays off, and we have a nice-size audience in the Crown & Anchor's cabaret room.

The show couldn't go better; my job's a cinch after Danny's primed the crowd. Like Don Rickles, he can get away with being caustic because the warmth that radiates from him highlights the good-natured silliness behind his foul mouth. The audience eats it up; I wouldn't even attempt to go where he does.

After the show Danny and I stand at the door and thank everyone for coming. When the last audience member exits, I head home and Danny takes off on his bike to smoke a bowl and stargaze from the breakwater. As I walk past the restaurant next to the cabaret room, I hear, "Hey! Can I tell you something?"

The phrase startles me. I turn on a dime, half expecting to see Ointz & Shmointz sitting there eating lobster rolls, but the two guys having dinner look anything but sullen.

"Who, me?"

"Yeah, you were great tonight."

"Oh, thanks. I'm glad you had a good time."

I always make sure I stop and show my gratitude when someone takes the time to compliment my performance. It sounds clichéd, but unless you're in it for the rejection, erratic employment, or disapproving family, the only reason to do stand-up is the audience's response.

The guys invite me for a drink. I'm a little guarded at first but accept their invitation once I realize that they're just being friendly. When you're a gay comedian there are always guys who pay attention to you, guys who don't pay attention to you, and guys who don't pay attention to you at first but somehow end up at your show. Comedy is all about the emotional connection with the audience, and if you have a good set, their interest is piqued and suddenly otherwise uninterested men want to get into your pants. My friend, a very talented comedian named Mark Davis, refers to them as chucklefuckers.

It turns out that the guys, Arn and David, aren't chucklefuckers but drama queens who run a small theater school in Washington, DC, called It's Just A Stage, with a large variety of courses for kids as well as adults. In addition to acting, directing. and playwriting, It's Just A Stage boasts offerings such as Ad-Libbing for Townsfolk, Relationship Histrionics, and the Children's Strindberg Workshop. Arn asks if I'd consider coming to DC to teach a stand-up class in the fall.

Stand-up is daunting to begin with, and making the leap from doing it as a hobby to doing it for a living was extremely scary. The idea that I'd actually be telling others how to do it is beyond terrifying to me. My first impulse is to turn down Arn's offer, but then I remember something my friend Becky, a successful actress, once told me: "Say yes to everything! If the job demands a skill you don't have, lie, and figure it out later." In the years I've known her, she's bullshitted her way into roles that required her to play the oboe, speak Gaelic, hurl a shot put, and geek a chicken.

I accept their proposal, and we agree that we'll work out the specifics the following week when Arn and David return to DC. Continuing down Commercial Street, I calm myself with the thought that if vegan Becky can overcome her revulsion to slaughtering poultry, I can certainly conquer my insecurity. Besides, I reason that, after years of stage time, I must know more about the nuts and bolts of stand-up than people who don't know anything. I am definitely qualified to give advice to a room full of Can I Tell You Somethings.

As the summer winds down I, like everyone in Ptown who is sick and tired of dealing with vacationers, have a terrible case of Augustitis. I can't wait for my f#@&ing show to be over. No amount of caffeine can get me energized, and by the last day of flyering I don't even care if I have an audience. I'm not even pushing people to buy tickets anymore but just handing them postcards and asking, "Could you please throw this out for me?" while directing them to the nearest trash can.

Autumn always provides a much-needed break after Ptown. This September, however, my performing schedule is a little too light, and the minimal income the comedy class will bring in will make a huge difference. Even though I'm nervous about teaching, I'm glad I listened to the Becky in my head.

In DC, I crash with my cousin Elliot, his wife Mindy, and their two school-age daughters, Rachel and Jody. I have a very small family; the girls are the first children since I was born, and I'm glad to have a reason to spend time with them. Elliot and Mindy, while socially liberal, are also observant Jews. They are shomer shabbos, which means they take it literally that God rested on the seventh day. From sundown Friday to sundown Saturday they won't write, turn on the stove, drive a car, or even flick on a light switch. I find it a little bit much. Although I went to Hebrew school and had a Bar Mitzvah, I'm not a fan of organized religion. I believe that edicts of faith are written by men, not God, and I strongly suspect that the prohibition against lifting a finger on the Sabbath was the idea of some lazy rabbi trying to get out of mowing the lawn. Besides, forgoing the use of modern work-saving conveniences seems to go against the spirit of things. It's hard for me to imagine the Almighty on his day off, sitting in the dark eating cold soup, when there's a Knicks game on ESPN and a freezer full of Pillsbury Toaster Strudel.

Like me, neither Mindy nor Elliot grew up in particularly observant families, and to their credit they don't require me to follow their rules, even though I'm staying under their roof. They do, however, try to set a good example for the kids. Mindy is consistent about adhering to the rules, but Elliot gets irritated by the restrictions from time to time. He approaches me as I'm sitting in the den getting ready for my class, which meets on Saturday at four in the afternoon.

"You know, Eddie, just because we can't turn on the television it doesn't mean you can't. I wouldn't mind if you want to watch an episode of *Star Trek* before you go out."

"Thanks. What time is it on?"

"Three o'clock."

I look at my watch. It's a few minutes before the hour. "Perfect."

Although I'm judgmental about Elliot breaking the Sabbath and using the guise of tolerance as a tool to circumvent the fourth commandment, I turn the set on. I have my motives.

The kids come running as soon as they hear the TV and plop themselves down on the carpet. Rachel asks, "Can we watch *Harry Potter* on video?"

Elliot is irritated. "You've seen it four times. Eddie's watching *Star Trek*."

"Eddie, can we pleeeease watch Harry Potter?"

Elliot cannot stand whining and gets short with her. *"Don't you have some Torah to read?"*

To me, a product of the TV generation, the idea of spending a Saturday studying the Old Testament seems pretty grim, and I feel bad for the kids. I pick up the remote, and quickly machine-gunning through the channels, surf right past *Star Trek's* opening credits. I shush Elliot's objection and keep going until I reach channel sixty-eight, Comedy Central. A set I've recorded is being rerun, and it's important to me that Rachel and Jody see it. I don't want them growing up thinking that I'm just some crazy uncle type who sleeps on an air mattress in the family room from time to time.

There's no picture on sixty-eight. I turn to Elliot. "Isn't sixty-eight Comedy Central?"

"We don't get Comedy Central."

"You get over a hundred channels."

"I know, but we don't get Comedy Central."

"You should call your cable company."

"I can't. They'll find out we're not paying for service."

"You're stealing cable?"

"We're not stealing it. We didn't *do* anything. When the woman downstairs ordered it, we got it too for some reason. I don't want to mess it up."

It cracks me up that the eighth commandment is being passively broken as well, and I wonder if Elliot's logic applies to all of the Lord's directives. Would he really be breaking commandment number seven, "Thou Shall Not Commit Adultery," if he just lay there while someone else did all the work?

I rise to my feet.

Elliot asks, "Don't you want to watch *Star Trek?*"

"I have to go."

I reach for the remote, but he waves me off. "Don't worry about it. I won't be angry if you leave it on."

I bend down, and as I hit the power button on the set, I wink at the kids and say to him, "Don't you have some Torah to read?"

Rachel and Jody crack up. Their laughter nourishes me and reaffirms how important it is to me that people think I'm funny—even two little girls whose humor consists of knock-knock jokes and fart noises.

I head to my class.

I start to obsess that in my nervousness about teaching I've overprepared for the first session. It seems ironic. In the years I've been performing stand-up, I've always fluctuated between feeling that it's impossible to prepare enough and feeling that it's impossible to prepare at all. You have to believe you're funny when you grab the microphone—or at least be able to act as if you believe it.

The class, Comedy Boot Camp, meets for three hours every Saturday for six weeks. The students have been asked to come to the first session prepared with a joke or humorous anecdote. The six weeks of writing and refining jokes is supposed to culminate with a field trip to a local open mike where the students can try out their material for the first time. They're encouraged to invite their friends, families, and coworkers for moral support and so that someone will laugh if they suck.

I start things simply. Going around the room, I have everyone introduce themselves and tell the group why they've decided to take the class. I'm fascinated by the range of characters and by the diverse reasons they give. What really amazes me is how many of them clearly have no idea what a comedian does. Even if you've never actually been to a comedy club, it seems fair to assume that you've seen *Letterman* or *The Tonight Show* or *Showtime at the Apollo* or *Last Comic Standing* or a comedian on a black channel, a gay channel, a Spanish channel, or one of the hundreds of stand-up artists on Comedy Central. Apparently, though, it's not just Elliot and Mindy who aren't paying for cable.

Because of this, few of the students seem to have the appropriate amount of anxiety for the situation. It freaks me out that

they don't realize the enormity of trying to go from zero to Se-
infeld in six short sessions. I'm caught even more off guard by
their willingness to trust me. But after fielding questions about
my few short television spots, I realize that even in this age of
mass media where everyone can indeed be famous for fifteen
minutes, once you're on TV, you command a certain amount of
respect. It's true. I only have to remind myself of the deference
I've seen people give to a total asshole who goes to my gym just
because he sells Christmas ornaments on the Home Shopping
Network.

I'm determined that my students won't regret trusting me. I
will not give them a false experience. Back when I wanted to get
my first taste of doing stand-up, I enrolled in a course with a
similar format. The instructor was very supportive; he constantly
told everyone what a great job they were doing. His disservice
did nothing to instill confidence. No matter how worthy anyone was of the praise he lavished on them, they saw him constantly lying through his teeth to people who bit the big one. If
only he'd been honest with the Can I Tell You Somethings, then
the rest of us with potential could have developed a lot more
poise. In my class I'll be kind, but I'll tell it like it is.

I start off by informing the students of two simple truths.

Number one: "This is going to be way harder than you think."

And number two: "Ninety-five percent of everything you do
in here is going to suck."

After my encouraging remarks, the students take the stage
one by one and present their best attempts at delivering material. The idea is that this will give me some notion of what they
find funny and how comfortable they are speaking in front of
an audience.

As I expect, the majority of the enrollees are water-cooler
comics, former class clowns, and the lives of the party—all of
whom will fall by the wayside on the journey to opening night.
Unfortunately, success in those situations isn't necessarily a

good indicator of how well someone is going to fare in front of a crowd at Manny's Ha-Ha Hacienda or the Maison de Laughs. After all, it isn't that hard to feel witty and brilliant entertaining commiserating coworkers, bored classmates, or inebriated friends.

Also among those who'll crash and burn before the six weeks are over are several who have enrolled for specific reasons that have nothing to do with an inaccurate self-assessment of their own funniness. Three single women are taking the class in the hope of meeting a man with a sense of humor. Once they realize, however, that most of the men in the class are Can I Tell You Somethings, and that those who are funny are not so because their lives are anywhere near perfect, the women disappear and head back to the Internet. There's a painfully shy man who's registered because his therapist recommended stand-up as a good confidence-building exercise—an obvious ploy by the shrink to set back the poor guy's recovery and keep the cash flowing. It works. In two weeks the introvert is out of the class and booking extra sessions on the couch. In a similar vein, there's a dynamic face-your-fears-and-cross-them-off-your-life-list woman who, just previous to the class, has walked on hot coals, confronted her birth mother, and had her first anal erotic experience. She lasts four sessions before fear gets the best of her, and instead of braving the mic, decides to drive across the Great Plains on a Vespa chasing tornadoes. Three people in the class—one from Brazil and two from Kyrgyzstan—are there desperate to improve their English. Their incomplete grasp of the American idiom, although at times hilarious, is heartbreaking.

Also among the group who go missing in action is a retired puppeteer who's spent a fortune on plastic surgery to prepare for a longed-for career in front of the curtain. The combination of his nipped face and the Lamb Chop voice he affects makes him disturbingly puppetlike, and it occurs to me that he'd probably be far more successful as a ventriloquist with his hand jammed up his own ass. He lasts four weeks. One woman, Lorraine, a devout Christian Scientist, makes it all the way to the fifth session before she bails out. Week after week I do my best to help her punch up the three painful minutes she's written on Mary Baker Eddy, her church's founder, but she meets my suggestions with accusations that I'm trying to subvert her beliefs. It finally becomes clear to me that her religion, with its prohibitions against surgery and modern pharmacology, also strictly forbids laughter—the best medicine. I leave her in the hands of God—the only one who can help her.

Of the five folks who stick it out to the end—Spencer, Bev, Helen, Chuck, and Maggie—some are good writers, some are good performers, some are both, and some are neither but have confidence anyway.

Eleven-year-old Spencer Penn is an only child. He's one of those obnoxiously precocious kids whose self-assurance can be attributed to the doting of his anally attentive mother who has literally put all her eggs in one basket.

On the first day of class he takes the microphone out of the stand, and with a nod of assurance from his mommy in the back of the classroom, launches into the monologue she's helped him rehearse. The jokes are decently structured, and the premise—a sixth grader mocking his aromatherapist—is novel. It's obvious, however, that the kid's got no clue what he's talking about—he might as well be riffing on menopause. Spencer's first three jokes, all painfully CITYS, fall flat despite him punctuating them with silly faces that I'm certain kill at the dinner table. Used only to unconditional positive reinforcement, he starts to crumble. I can see him, in desperation, trying harder, but the only tricks he knows are useless. His puerile mugging receives only forced laughter from most of the adults, and a put-upon smile from Helen, who spends eight hours a day up to her kneesocks in preteens at St. Ursula's school for girls. He's caught way off guard when grandmotherly Bev, everybody's idea of a sweet little old lady, jumps up and lets loose.

"What the hellaya doin', kid?" she demands, making a sweeping gesture toward the rest of the class. *"You're losin' 'em! You're losin' 'em!"*

We're all stunned, but Spencer doesn't miss a beat and throws it right back at her. *"Don't blame me, lady, my mother wrote this crap."*

Bev—along with the rest of us—busts a gut.

"Good save, Spencer!" I say simultaneously to him and his mother, who's taking notes. "Keep that line ready. Okay, who's next?"

Bev Grimes, one of the two senior citizens in the class, is a diminutive woman with white hair, and eyeglasses on a chain. Imagining that by her late seventies, she's racked up enough humorous (or at least interesting) material to fill three minutes of stage time, I've been looking forward to what she has to say. I'm prepared for typical women's stuff appropriate for some-one her age—ill-behaved grandchildren, estrogen replacement therapy, the dearth of eligible men, etc. But after her reaction to Spencer, I'm not exactly sure what to expect. When she opens her mouth, she's filthy!

"My snatch hair is *sooo* white . . ."

The class is aghast—except for Spencer, who innocently calls out, "How white is it?"

"Thanks, kiddo! It's so white my husband calls me Santa Clit!"

I'm horrified, but Spencer thinks she's hilarious, and the rest of the class, taking their cue from him, erupts.

A lot of comedians look down on using filth to get a laugh, and I personally hate toilet humor and gratuitous sex talk. I emphatically discourage its use unless you're playing to a room full of eleven-year-olds. I do, however, believe it's possible to work blue *and* be brilliant. Bev, however, is not brilliant. She continues, "My pussy is *sooo* loose . . ."

This time everyone responds, "How loose is it?"

"It's so loose, I have to use Dentu-Grip to keep my husband's schlong from falling out."

Feeding off the laughter, Bev continues. She gets fouler and fouler, going into far too much detail about the toll her ongoing battle with flatulence has taken on her relationships *and* her upholstery. It's all I can do to keep her from putting the microphone below her waist and making fart noises. I wish that I Could Tell Her Something, but the class's enthusiastic response is evidence of a basic fact of comedy that I can't dispute: no matter how disgusting the material, the majority of any audience will laugh at old people talking dirty.

Chuck Marro, the other senior citizen, is an attorney who still practices part time. He's in his late sixties with skin so tan and hair so white that he looks like a negative. His whole routine revolves around the idea that he's not planned responsibly for his golden years. Unable to live on his meager social security benefits, he's been forced to move in with his parents at their retirement village. Complicating the cramped living situation is Beatrice—his parents' African Grey parrot—an ancient, gregarious bird that continually blurts out embarrassing things like "Enough with the spit!" and "Pinch them harder, Elaine!" and a host of other even more inappropriate comments overheard in their bedroom during the past sixty years. Despite the absurdity of his premise, Chuck's skills of persuasion, honed through years in the courtroom, are so finely tuned that I find myself forgetting it's an act.

Helen Buchbinder, a Jew worn down by thirty years of teaching in a Catholic school, walks timidly to the front of the room.

"Eddie, I don't know what to say—I don't feel particularly funny."

"It's okay, we all have days like that."

"I mean ever."

"Ever?"

"My friends at the school think I'm hilarious when I'm angry."

"Okay, then let's start there. What gets you angry?"

"Well, it's 2004 and kids are still asking me why the Jews killed Christ."

"Whadya say?"

"I point to the crucifix and tell them, *'If you think what we did to him was bad, wait and see what I'm gonna do to you if you don't sit down!'*"

"That's a pretty funny start. Keep it. What else makes you angry?"

"My mother."

"What about your mother?"

"She doesn't speak to me."

"How come?"

"I tried to kill myself once; I slashed my wrists. She's Orthodox; she thinks it's a sin."

"Why? Did you use a dairy knife?"

I laugh at my own joke and Helen cracks a smile. "Write that down," I say.

Maggie Wasilewski, resentful of the expectations put upon her as mother, breadwinner, and lover, is handling things innovatively. She avoids unfulfilling sex with her potbellied husband by zapping him with a Taser at bedtime, then convincing him in the morning that he zonked out after a mind-blowing orgasm. She also sells her kids' organs on eBay to finance their education (and well-deserved spa treatments for herself). She commits to her premises so effortlessly that I wouldn't be surprised if her children showed up in the audience with IVs and their kidney recipients. She is hands down the funniest one in the group.

I'm not very familiar with the stand-up scene in DC, so I

speak to a few comic friends of mine, who inform me that there are two regularly scheduled open mikes on Friday nights—the only night that fits everyone's schedule. One is at the Sit & Steep Tea House in Dupont Circle, where patrons can enjoy the class's comedic stylings over a pot of freshly brewed Darjeeling; the other is at a gay club in Adams Morgan with a luau night featuring two-for-one mai tais and a pig roast. It's a no-brainer. Dinah, the emcee from the Sand Bar, responds to my e-mail almost immediately and graciously offers to host the class. I'm relieved that we're not going to have to try and entertain at the tea house where people will either be overcaffeinated or falling asleep in their chamomile.

On open-mike night I arrive at the Sand Bar about ten minutes before showtime. From the noise emanating from inside and the number of people smoking on the sidewalk, the club appears crowded. Before I enter, I ask the bearish bouncer to point out Dinah. He smirks.

"Don't worry, you can't miss her."

I step inside. The beach-themed Sand Bar is tackily decorated with plastic flamingoes, painted coconuts, neon palm trees, and giant drink umbrellas. It's like walking directly into a piña colada. The place is mood lit by faux tiki torches, and the male waiters are dressed as characters from *Gilligan's Island.* There's a festive seediness to it, and I half expect that upon pulling back the beaded curtain to the kitchen, I'll find the Skipper blowing Mary Ann. I wave to my students, who are all in a corner rehearsing their lines. Watching the five of them pacing back and forth mumbling to themselves reminds me of inmates in a Victorian madhouse.

"Eddie?"

I turn to find myself face-to-sternum with a gargantuan drag queen.

"Hello, dahling, I'm Dinah Sores. Welcome to the Gayman Islands. You're here just in time; we're about to start."

"It's nice to meet you. Thanks for helping me out."

"My pleasure."

Her name couldn't be more appropriate. Not only is she the size of a megalasaurus, but her skin looks as if it's been battered by the elements for millennia. She's dressed all in baby-girl pink. Offsetting her Jurassic face is a platinum blond wig in a low-rise bouffant. By far the most noticeable thing about Dinah is the fact that she doesn't tuck, her ample endowment turning her A-line dress into an A+.

She takes a compact out of her bag and checks her makeup.

"Am I presentable?"

"You look great but . . ."

"But what?"

"You might want to . . ."

I gesture sheepishly to her crotch.

"Oh no, sweetie! No, no, no, no, no! Just because I'm in drag doesn't mean I'm not a man. I want the audience to see all of me and then some."

She has a point. Stand-up comedy is all about being who you are.

"Good for you."

"Are your students prepared?"

"They're freaked out but they're as ready as they'll ever be."

"Then on with the show!"

I pride myself on not prejudging people, but Dinah has "Can I Tell You Something?" written all over her.

It's Friday night, and the Sand Bar is pretty busy to begin with. The students' friends, families, and colleagues have swelled it to overflowing. I worry that some of their guests might feel uncomfortable in a gay bar, but my fear dissolves when I notice just how large the cocktails are. I'm glad that the audience members are lubricating themselves. As much as my students think it's they that need a drink to brace themselves, it's the audience that needs the fortification. Nothing is more torturous than watching bad comedy. If you're dying up there, the audience is envious.

Dinah steps onto the stage and Oh Boy, Can I Tell You Something! She has a decent personality but opens her set with a slew of tasteless jokes about rectal itching, female circumcision, and an endless, hacky story about Catherine the Great's first date with Francis the Talking Mule. Old ladies talking dirty are funny; old drag queens talking dirty are not. The students and their guests laugh politely, but as the groaners mount up the regulars get boisterous.

When the first Jell-O shot hits the stage, Dinah is prepared. In a flash, she opens her parasol and continues undaunted. I watch in astonishment as she handily deflects over ninety percent of the olives, cherries, coconuts, and other projectiles with which she's mercilessly pelted. Although her act is terrible, I'm impressed that she continues without missing a beat. When someone does score a direct hit, the spectators toast and chug. Apparently this is a weekly tradition at the Sand Bar. I pan the room to check the reaction of the students. I can see that they're shocked, but I signal them not to worry. I know the crowd is just getting energized. Anyway, the audience is packed with supportive people. Their friends will applaud and compliment them (I suspect using their own equivalents of CITYS). I want them to enjoy their first experience at the microphone. If they continue in this endeavor they'll often not have a crowd, and if they do, it almost certainly will not be sympathetic.

Miraculously, Dinah turns the tide and begins to win the room over by applying her cesspool vocabulary to President Bush. Of course, her anti-Republican tirade goes over big-time in a gay bar. I'm annoyed that it isn't very smart and that there aren't any jokes per se, just a stream of mundane profanities. If only Danny McWilliams were here to show her how it's done.

One by one the students take the stage.

Due to his bedtime and an early-morning Cub Scout meeting, Spencer is up first. Of course he does well. How could he not? He's cute, he's smart, and he's eleven riffing on the benefits of sandalwood as an aphrodisiac in a room full of homo- and metro-sexuals. He ends on his "My mother wrote this crap line," and gets a charitable round of applause—which he milks mercilessly by making campy bows à la Baby Jane Hudson.

Dinah Sores, arching an overplucked eyebrow at the boy's curtseys, snidely remarks, "Thanks, Spencer, I'm sure it won't be long before you're a regular here at the Sand Bar."

As I expect, Chuck does well. His old-school, grandfatherly appeal is a hit in more ways than one, and he's the recipient not only of generous applause but Mr. Howell's phone number. Although he's not gay, I can see that he loves the attention, and I imagine him taking the guy home, getting chucklefucked, and explaining to his parents why the parrot is suddenly saying things like, "I'm not gay; I just like it up the ass once in a while." His parents, both well into their nineties, are actually there downing margaritas with the boys. I find the look of parental adoration on their faces charming and creepy at the same time.

Bev proves my point: a sweet-looking granny with a gutter mouth can get away with murder. She starts out demurely, but about a minute into her set she turns raunchy. Dinah, alarmed by the direction Bev is going in, pokes her head out from backstage and graciously extends her parasol. Bev winks at her. "Leave it closed, honey. I'll use it like that!" She then grabs the parasol, and making a pucker sound, pops it under her skirt and gesturing obscenely with it. I'm appalled, but the crowd goes crazy.

After Bev's vulgarity, Helen's thoughtful, dark persona is a welcome change. Her material is a great blend of sarcasm, self-deprecation, and absurdity. That she never smiles adds gravity to what she's saying, and her deadpan punch lines blindside the crowd. In addition, she has just the right amount of nervousness for them to sense—yet not be turned off by. Gays love rooting for the underdog, and throughout her set she gains momentum that she's obviously bewildered by. The standing ovation she gets is nothing less than miraculous, and I think perhaps Elliot and Mindy are right—Jews *are* the Chosen People.

I've told Dinah to put Maggie on last. Her soccer mom gone wrong shocks her friends and delights the gays. She's got that abrasive warmth that made Joan Rivers a star. As I look around the room at the cheering crowd, I notice the only ones not laughing are her kids, who are either at that age where they're perpetually embarrassed by their parents, or who are so run down from operating on one kidney that they're too weak to clap.

Finally, it's my turn. I'm nervous—very nervous. These people have trusted me for six weeks. They've put themselves on the line with the belief that I know what I'm doing. Bombing the first time they see me take the stage would not only be a nightmare for me but would likely undermine any confidence they've been able to cultivate in six short lessons.

My worries are compounded by the homosexuals. Sometimes an audience of gay men can be exceedingly hard to please. Many of them, partly as a defense against a hostile world and partly through the joy of allowing themselves to be who they are, have developed wickedly sharp senses of humor. They can be hypercritical of another gay guy they think isn't any funnier than they are.

Out of the hundreds of hours I've logged at the mike, there have been only two other times that I've had this do-or-die feeling. The first was when my parents came to see me do stand-up for the first time. I dreaded having a bad set and being confronted backstage by my mother: *"Now will you think about grad school?"*

The second was when my boyfriend Jeffrey first came to see

me perform. It was a terrifying prospect, having months of intimacy and finely tuned sex flushed down the drain just because my timing was off that night. Let's be honest: if someone thinks you stink, they're not going to stick around for long. Who—with a heart or a conscience—is going to commit to a lifetime of "Can I Tell You Something?" Thank goodness that in both of those instances I knocked 'em dead.

Fortunately my set at the Sand Bar goes smoothly. I feel fantastic and congratulate myself for my ability to perform well under pressure. Not only do I slay the crowd and impress my students, I win over the boys. When I step off the stage, I find myself waist-deep in chucklefuckers.

After the show all of the students are being praised by their friends and families for their bravery. The ones that did exceptionally well are also getting complimented by strangers. Bev, in particular, is receiving a lot of attention. If I didn't know that most of her admirers are gay, I'd think she was a GILF (Granny I'd Like to Fuck).

Across the room I see Dinah Sores talking with the ursine bouncer. She's dabbing some club soda on her maraschino-stained dress. I go to her.

"Dinah, thanks again for everything."

She's not exhibiting her earlier warmth. "You're welcome."

The bouncer jumps in. "No, thank *you*! We didn't meet formally; I'm Lenny, one of the owners."

"Oh, hi! I'm glad you're pleased. Maybe we can do this again next semester."

Dinah is obviously annoyed by the suggestion.

"I'll have to check the schedule and get back to—"

Lenny interrupts. "Absolutely! We'd love to have you back. This was the best comedy night we've had since Dinah started it three years ago. When are you in town next?"

My eyes dart to Dinah's face. She's got the look of a creature facing extinction. Before I can divert my gaze, she catches me looking and excuses herself. "I better go clean the Jell-O off the drapes."

As she skulks away, I notice that she's either tucked or else her goodies have shrunken in shame. Lenny turns to me. "I have to go put the door money in the safe. Again, you did a great job. We'll be seeing you here again soon."

I remain at the Sand Bar schmoozing for another hour or so. I'm psyched to see the students enjoying their triumph. They have every right to be proud, and I sing their praises to their guests, making sure they understand how fearless their friends and family members actually are. The guests in turn give me, in unsolicited asides, their assessments of their loved ones' talents and prospects. I find it somewhat disturbing that despite the sixty-year difference in their sons' ages, I have almost identical conversations with Spencer's mother and with Chuck's.

Seeing Maggie and shy Helen being fawned over by a bunch of handsome men is wonderfully gratifying. I'm ecstatic that everyone seems to have had a good experience and find myself looking forward to the next semester. I leave the Sand Bar and head back to Elliot and Mindy's in such a great mood I decide the fourth commandment notwithstanding, I'm going to flip on the TV and let them watch *Harry Potter* with me and the kids.

A week later I get a call from Lenny, the owner, asking if I'd consider taking over as host of the Sand Bar's comedy night. When I inquire about Dinah, he jokes, "The tribe has spoken and she has been kicked off the island." Although my ego is always up for a stroke and I can certainly use the work, I don't want to repay Dinah's kindness by taking her job. I politely turn him down. Nothing can save Dinah, however; Lenny offers Maggie the job.

I'm proud of my decision to take the high road, but my good deed does not go unpunished. Dinah calls accusing me of fucking Lenny to get her job. I try to assure her that sleeping with

Lenny was not part of any plan to achieve stardom at the Sand Bar and joke that I only did it because I was too much of a cheapskate to pay eight dollars for a banana daiquiri. She isn't amused. The force and volume of the invective that comes spewing out of the receiver terrifies me. When I hang up the phone, I'm shaking.

Dinah continues to harass me for weeks. Every morning I'm awakened by a phone call lambasting me for my professional ethics. I try repeatedly to reason with her, but her rage is Vesuvian. If I didn't know how hard she was trying to look feminine, I'd swear she was abusing steroids. I stop answering her calls, but in addition to the shrieking messages she leaves, she clogs up my computer, phone, and mailbox with vitriolic e-mails, text messages, and letters containing such specific threats that I begin to seriously question my safety. I consider calling the police, but am far too embarrassed to report that my stalker is a seven-foot Zsa Zsa Gabor who's hung like a horse. Finally, after receiving a bedtime e-mail that contains the word "castrate" no less than six times, I feel I have no other choice but to retaliate. I can't wait for her a.m. call.

In the morning I pick up the phone on the first ring, wait a beat to make sure it's Dinah, and then calmly hand it to Danny. Not only is he the most loyal of friends, but any enemy of mine is instantly an enemy of his. I know that he'll defend me with a fervor I'd have trouble mustering myself.

I lean back, put my feet up, and watch his anger erupt with a jolt that's off the Richter scale. Dinah's volcanic rage is nothing compared to Danny's Big Bang. And as for her vocabulary, she's way out of her league. Danny puts the "pro" in profanity. He's the undisputed King of the Curse, and in this instant his language is so vile, it's unprintable (no, really!). I can practically hear the cascade of sweat pouring down from under Dinah's wig, and I'd give anything to see her cowering in terror under Danny's ruthless assault. After the carnage, Danny gently places the receiver on its cradle, smiles sweetly, and says, "Buy me breakfast."

Of course, Dinah's menacing ceases. Who'd want to risk incurring Danny McWilliams's wrath a second time? Although I teach again at It's Just A Stage for the spring semester, and make a few guest appearances at Maggie's show at the Sand Bar, I don't hear one word from or about Dinah. She doesn't even cross my mind until months later, when back in Provincetown, I again find myself competing for an audience with an army of six-foot-six bleached-blond Can I Tell You Somethings.

The Eton Club

"Jeffrey, it's me. I'm short a waiter . . . Abraham . . . I know, he's an asshole . . . I would, but the new bartender didn't show up either and I'm really stuck. I promise I'll make it up to you . . . However you want . . . God, you're such a pig . . . No, I love it . . . You're the best, I love you. I'll see you in a bit."

I hung up the phone, checked the time, and cursed the clock as I furiously stirred the Bloody Mary mix and fantasized that the tomato juice and horseradish were Abraham's blood and guts. It was almost time to open the doors of the Eton Club, and I was impatient for Denny the general manager to return from the dry cleaner's and help me set up. As I struggled to get the cap off of the Worcestershire sauce, a voice caught me off guard.

"Well, well, well . . . look who's minding the bar!"

My mouth spread into a smile that raised my ears half an inch, and I turned to see a Cheshire-Cat grin above a pair of folded hands resting on the back of a bar stool.

"Wendell, you're here early."

"That's a fine greeting!"

"I'm sorry; it's just unusual for you to make an appearance during amateur hour."

"I'm not staying. I just stopped by to inquire if you and Jeffrey were free to attend the ballet on Thursday evening."

"Sure, that sounds great! We'd love to go!"

"I'm pleased. We'll dine afterward at Café Grisette, if you approve."

"Anyplace is fine with me. I'm coming for the company."

"You charmer! You know exactly what to say."

"Would you like a cocktail, as long as you're here?"

"I could be persuaded."

I smiled at the understatement, knowing it would have been more difficult to persuade him to breathe.

Wendell took a seat as I poured a generous shot of Ketel One, added a splash of soda and a lemon wedge, and set it down on the marble counter. He raised the drink in my direction.

"To your health and prosperity!"

"To yours too, Wendell!"

The Eton Club was a gentlemen's bar located on East Fifty-sixth Street in Manhattan, its faux-Edwardian exterior wedged between an Indian restaurant and a locksmith. The older gay crowd it attracted carried calling cards engraved with hyphenated surnames and posed in ascots in front of the prints of the Yorkshire countryside that adorned the walls. Although there was an air of sophistication, the backdrop was about as real as the set of a high school drama-club production.

Wendell Briar fit in perfectly. It was as if a set decorator had selected him with the same care she'd used when choosing the hunting-horn wall sconces and flame-stitched armchairs. He was a slight man with a large head that eclipsed his dainty body, giving him a babyish look. His lipless mouth, turned up at the corners, projected to the eye of the beholder either an aura of judgmental calm or of creepy mischievousness. He had a subtly—yet perpetually—raised eyebrow that craved a monocle, and in his dark tailored suit and his stubborn starched collar,

he reminded me of Charlie McCarthy. There would be many
occasions when I'd be sorry nobody was controlling his mouth.

Looking at the ease with which Wendell took to the surroundings, I wondered if the Briar mansion had been similarly
decorated. Wendell was the last of an old, moneyed Brooklyn
family and a principal partner in a prestigious law firm, started
by his grandfather, specializing in estate planning for New York's
wealthy. There was a Briar Avenue somewhere near Prospect
Park, as well as a Briar rose named for Wendell's grandmother
at the Brooklyn Botanic Garden in Park Slope. On a bookshelf in
his apartment sat a framed letter from Thomas Dewey, the gov-
ernor of New York, welcoming Wendell to Brooklyn (and the
world) in 1943.

The club's oak and etched-glass doors rattled as Denny entered.

"Eddie, are you all set up?"

"Almost. What time is it?"

"Five of."

"Shit."

Wendell drained his drink, pulled a fifty from his wallet, and
slipped it under the empty glass. He winked at me. "I'll stop by
later."

He turned to Denny. "Dennis."

I picked up the tip. "Thank you, Wendell."

"You're welcome, my prince."

I blushed and laughed off the compliment as Wendell slipped
out past the funereal floral arrangements that graced the en-
tranceway.

I put the fifty in my pocket, grateful for Wendell's generosity
but angry at myself for growing so comfortable with the ease of
my financial situation. I'd responded to an ad for the position
of assistant manager at the Eton Club in 1995, after an ankle injury ended my career as an aerobics instructor and my unem-
ployment had run out. I thought the flexibility afforded by bar

work would enable me to pursue my career in stand-up comedy, but like a lot of the staff at the Eton Club, I became trapped. Before I knew it, five years had gone by.

Except for Abraham, who was a career waiter (and bitter about it), the crew at the Eton Club consisted of the usual assortment of actors, artists, and writers who'd taken the job to pay their bills and then used it as an escape from the scary world of artistic rejection. There were chorus boys in their fifties still waiting for their big break and aspiring models too old even to pose for Father's Day ads. A few guys eventually did move on to sell real estate or to open pet-sitting services, but the turnover at the Eton Club was exceptionally low for the bar business. The demographics there made it easy to stay. At Eton, you could be balding with a paunch and still be a boy toy. It was effortless for me to feel good about my body there. I had cut back on working out but never felt guilty since I was still in decent shape from my time as an aerobics instructor. I could gain five pounds (or thirty) and still be hot compared to the customers. This was not the gym crowd. The only muscles they worked were their biceps. Interestingly, a few curls with a heavy cocktail seemed equal to twice as many curls with a cigarette, and no matter how much anyone drank, they smoked enough to counter the tendency to bulk up on only one side.

My job consisted of ensuring that the customers had a good time and that the staff did their jobs. I was the front man who made a good impression in a suit and tie while Denny the general manager, who looked like the slow brother on an ABC After-School Special, tended to affairs in the office.

I found the environment at Eton unsettling. For the first time I was around gay men who weren't in their twenties or thirties, didn't dance shirtless on the weekends, didn't exercise. They drank like fish and smoked like chimneys—a combination that reminded me of lox. They wore navy blazers and bow ties, and every other line they uttered contained a sexual innuendo or double entendre. Drunk and lonely, they grabbed asses and preyed on new waiters who hadn't yet learned to back away after taking their drink orders. That they often paid for sex made me feel contemptuous of most, and sorry for a few who reminded me of old teachers or my dad's friends. Looking back, it's obvious that my contempt was born of fear. The generation of gay men that preceded me had been decimated, and there were few healthy role models. The only future I was getting a good look at didn't look good close-up. But though I viewed the Eton Club, an institution peopled in large part by closet cases and drunks, as a homosexual hall of shame, I did my job and smiled, joked, and listened to the patrons go on about their aches, pains, and disappointments. At Eton I learned how to win over people I wouldn't have wanted to talk to on the street. It was excellent training for stand-up comedy.

The rest of the staff had contempt for the patrons as well—and for me because of my refusal to drink and drug on the job. With the exception of Carl in coat check, a practicing Wiccan who'd just come out of the broom closet, everyone partied during their shifts. Though I was in charge of the waiters and bartenders, and it was part of my responsibility to eradicate such behavior, it seemed hypocritical to enforce the rules too stringently with Denny, my boss, drinking and getting high every night. As long as I didn't actually see anyone indulging—and they didn't get too sloppy—I let it go.

At 4:00 Denny unlocked the oak doors. At 4:01 Wendell's "amateurs" began to arrive. These guys were hardly newbies when it came to drinking, and by early evening each had routinely guzzled down enough booze to hospitalize a college fraternity. But to Wendell, anyone who showed up to take advantage of the happy-hour discount was "common," on par with a Miami Beach retiree at an early-bird special. I nodded in greeting as the regulars filed in.

As usual, the first in the door was Pat Lonergan. Lonergan, a tall puppet-headed queen, was a lawyer, an ambulance chaser of the lowest degree, who I suspected kept a full array of cervical collars in his office to help clients defraud at a moment's notice. That he was an attorney was unusual in that most of the other early birds worked at the Design & Decoration Building around the corner. They were successful men in their field and talked about gingham and tattersall with the gravity of shipping magnates discussing gross tonnage and import tariffs. The other thing that made Lonergan stand out was his complexion. While most of the others were electrically tanned to an artificial shade that looked almost natural in the diffused light of the club, Lonergan, whose pale Irish skin couldn't tolerate UV rays of any wavelength, had managed to color himself a flattering Johnny Walker Red.

I called these early-bird regulars "The Four to Fours." They showed up each day promptly at four in the afternoon and drank steadily until four in the morning, when Steve the doorman would perk them up with a bump of something white and send them home to their duplexes on Beekman Place.

I was a competent manager but an excellent bartender. Not being a drinker myself, my concocting took some guesswork, but I made up for any inexperience by increasing the scotch-to-soda ratio and so was generally acknowledged by the clientele to be a superb mixologist. I also knew every customer's drink by heart, started preparing it the moment he walked through the door, and had it ready before he placed his order. The scotch was waiting for the Four to Fours before their asses hit their stools.

Lonergan set down two packs of Parliaments and a mother-of pearl lighter on the bar, quickly emptied his glass, and pushed it forward for a refill.

"Another, please; I'm parched."

"Want some water too?"

He recoiled in horror from the suggestion, as if he was the Wicked Witch of the West, and I envisioned him shrieking, *"I'm melting! I'm melting!"* while sublimating into a steaming pile of Brooks Brothers.

"Well, maybe just a splash."

I poured the scotch and added a squirt of water from the soda gun, causing him to flinch.

"Not that much!"

I laughed. "Sorry, next time I'll use an atomizer."

"See that you do."

Growing up in a Jewish family where the appeal of booze was eclipsed by the appeal of coffee cake, I never realized how much people actually drank until I started working at the Eton Club. To me it seemed inconceivable that the peaks and valleys of alcoholism could ever compare to the sugar high and hypo-glycemic despair of an Entenmann's binge. And why anyone would willingly take a depressant was beyond my Paxil-drenched brain. In my family we all come with the gloom included and don't need supplements. Although my dad always kept a six-pack in the fridge to buddy up to repairmen in the hope of getting a lower estimate, I rarely saw my parents drink anything stronger than Fresca. The same lonely fifth of vodka has been sitting in their kitchen cabinet since 1972 when my aunt Pearl from Boynton Beach created a scandal by asking for a Harvey Wallbanger. Last New Year's Eve my mom and her friend, Jen Wolfberg, re-discovered the bottle, had two screwdrivers each, and went on for weeks about how wild they'd been.

The owners of the Eton Club had agreed to let Justin, one of the boyish cocktail waiters, hold a fund-raiser for an AIDS support group by exhibiting and selling his artwork that evening. Justin replaced the stuffy hunting prints with his classically in-spired oils of scantily draped, muscular Greeks and Romans wearing stereo headphones and talking on cell phones. I

scanned the exhibit quickly and stopped to contemplate a de-
piction of Mercury typing an e-mail. Justin came up behind me.
"What do you think?"

"Interesting—AOL is putting the messenger of the gods out
of business."

I grinned as I pictured the unemployed deity gaining weight
and getting addicted to Internet porn. "I wonder what his profile would say. 'Former Olympian seeks Adonis for hot Greek
action.'"

Justin pressed, "Seriously, do you think it's too over the top?"

"Well . . ."

Just then Lonergan came up behind us.

"Oh, Justin, your paintings are brilliant! *Sooo* homoerotic!
But not nearly as filthy as this glass! Be a dear and get me a
fresh drinky-poo."

As Justin moved to the bar, Lonergan caught me looking at
him. He offered up an explanation for using his old dirty-glass
routine to secure a free replacement for the gimlet he'd already swigged down.

"Well, I can't drink from a soiled glass! I might catch something!"

I answered confidently, "Vodka is an excellent disinfectant. I
use it to clean my cat's paw prints off my piano's keys."

Lonergan was horrified by such an inappropriate use of
potable alcohol.

"Well, I hope you're not using Stoli Crystal!"

He unhinged his flip-top head, erupted in laughter, and
moved off after one of the dozen or so rent boys working the
crowd.

I turned to Justin. "He's so concerned about dirty glasses,
but an hour from now he'll have his face buried in that hustler's ass."

Justin was oblivious to my comment. "Do you think my paintings are homoerotic?"

"Actually, I think they're homo-*neurotic*. I look at them and think, 'Boy, I need to get to the gym.'"

He wasn't amused. "No really, are they homoerotic? That sounds so cheesy! I want my work to transcend the physical; I don't want to be another 'gay' painter."

I appreciated Justin's desire not to become a cliché. He was an excellent draftsman, and his paintings were flawlessly executed. But his ego was fragile, and I was worried that he might give up and start mass-producing paintings of Cape Cod lighthouses just to pay the bills.

"No, not at all! Not cheesy! Artfully done! And how can a portrait be homoerotic anyway? Wouldn't there need to be *two* men in a painting for it to be gay? The sexual orientation of the art is in the eye of the beholder. And after all, you are showing paintings of nearly nude men here at the Eton Ass Club."

I tried to bolster his confidence and turned to Denny, who was making a rare excursion out of his office to admire Justin's work. "Denny, aren't these fantastic?"

"Excellent work, Justin! Very homoerotic! Keep it up!"

As Denny toddled off in search of the illicit substances that would get him through the night, Justin looked at me despairingly. I was ready to talk him through another round of self-doubt when Jeffrey grabbed me from behind to announce his arrival. I turned around and kissed him. "Hey, baby, thanks for helping me out. Did you punch in?"

"The time clock's jammed."

"Again? Come on, I'll take a look at it."

I turned to Justin. "We'll be back in a few."

"I won't wait up."

He knew I was lying, that sex with Jeffrey in the storeroom would take at least half an hour.

Before we hurried downstairs, as a courtesy I told Denny I was taking a break—even though I knew he'd soon be locked in the office snorting coke with the men's room attendant and would be losing track of time anyway.

As soon as we got past the Employees Only door, Jeffrey pushed me up against the ice machine. Our clothes were off in a flash, and we went at each other like a pair of professional wrestlers. I tried to slow down the action so I could take stock of all my senses and make sure the memory would be indelible. After five years together the sex was still hot, but my neurotic nature made me prematurely anticipate that period of middle coupledom when we'd be recalling romps like this, wishing we'd appreciated them more. I focused on the surroundings while we kissed—the musty smell of the beer-soaked carpet, the clicks and whoosh of the soda system, the biting cold of the ice maker contrasting with the furry warmth of Jeffrey's chest.

I ran my hand up his back, taking in the sensation of razor stubble against my palm. He tensed, pulled his mouth off mine, and looked into my eyes. "Sorry."

I dismissed his apology. "It's okay. We'll shave it tomorrow."

I actually didn't care one way or the other. Jeffrey was sexy—period. He was tall and meaty with thick black hair and icy blue eyes, but in his mind excessive body hair was an affliction of sideshow caliber. His previous boyfriend had been an insensitive jerk who acted as if having sex with Jeffrey was doing him a huge favor, like sympathy fucking Jo-Jo the Dog-Faced Boy.

I had stopped trying to force Jeffrey to put his insecurity into proportion and opted for complicity in doing whatever made him feel more at ease. Once a week, I'd climb into the tub with him and take a razor to his back. It was an exceptionally intimate activity, and it made it clear to me that sometimes loving someone means letting his comfort take precedence over my need to have him accept reality (or my version of it).

The place was in full swing when we emerged from the storeroom. The sun had set, and the only light was the negligible glow from the hunting-horn sconces. The place was so dim that the bartenders mixed and measured by touch and habit. Jeffrey tripped over someone's briefcase and I caught him just in time, before he flew headfirst into a mirrored wall.

"Watch out!"

"Why does it have to be so fucking dark in here?"

"Have you seen these guys in the light?"

I knew it was a cheap remark, but thought it might get a laugh. It didn't.

"They're only trying to get laid."

"Well, it's a good thing they're not procreating. They'd develop adaptations to the dark, like those blind fish in underground pools."

The somewhat smarter comment elicited a chuckle and Jeffrey continued the joke. "They'd be like bats using echolocation to find each other in the night."

"A complex series of high-pitched 'Oh Marys!' and falsetto show tunes!"

As if on cue, the first chords of the score of *The Little Mermaid* rang out from the back room. Jeffrey rolled his eyes. "Oh, no!"

"Afraid so."

"I thought this was Mac's night."

"Brian's covering."

"You couldn't warn me?"

"Would you have come in?"

"Point taken."

Mac had entertained at the club since it opened. He had an encyclopedic knowledge of musicals and was somewhat muscular and appealing in a nerdy way—a semi-hot Marvin Hamlisch. Brian, on the other hand, was everybody's type. Unfortunately, he was much easier on the eyes than the ears. The scratchy, nasal whine that emanated from his throat was evocative of a tubercular coyote, and I wished I could wrap his diseased vocal cords around his neck to put an end to his (and my) misery.

Despite the deluge of complaints, the owners kept Brian on, thrilled that sales more than doubled during his shifts as the customers drank themselves blind in an attempt to achieve a blissful state of tone deafness. Over time, Brian had managed to build up a following of boozy fans. He was a big favorite of the Four to Fours, whose auditory senses were completely compromised by the time the music started each evening. They spent hours crowded around the baby grand as he endlessly recycled the approximately two dozen Broadway numbers he knew by heart. But by far Brian's biggest fans were a pair of sixtysomething Asian identical twins who the staff mockingly referred to as Chang and Eng. Whenever they started singing, I always had an unsettling feeling that Mothra might show up and wreak havoc.

The staff, too, drank more to get through Brian's shifts. I tried to make things easier for them by encouraging him to take frequent breaks—which he was happy to do, since he was constantly taxing his throat to the limit by attempting to make up for his lack of talent with extra volume. Between songs and during his breaks, Brian would sip tea with honey and repeatedly mist his throat. From the effect it had on his voice, I surmised that the spray bottle was filled with bong water.

The surreal air of the Eton Club was enhanced by the overwhelming amount of smoke produced by two hundred men puffing away on Marlboros and Virginia Slims. In the hazy dark, the artistic sweeps of glowing cigarettes reminded me of fireflies in search of mates, and I mused about the poor drunks, lured in by graceful trails of light, who awoke in the morning appalled to get a good look at the insects they'd spent the night with.

Into this dream sequence Wendell Briar made his entrance accompanied by his usual entourage: Buddy Lynch, Richard Rothschild, and Stan Jaworski. Pat Lonergan and the Four to Fours greeted them with air kisses and deferential nods, as if

Wendell were a dowager empress and the others his ladies-in-waiting. The courtiers responded in kind and Buddy raised his hand and wiggled his fingers, showing off a collection of gaudy rings with diamonds the size of rhinestones.

The regulars always accorded Wendell a good deal of esteem. It stemmed from a combination of respect for his genuine blue-blood pedigree and a healthy fear of his razor-sharp tongue. As soon as he saw Wendell's party enter, Justin placed their usual order and the drinks were poured, garnished, and waiting.

Wendell reached for his wallet. "Thank you, Justin."

Justin held up his hand. "They're on the house."

At the Eton Club, Wendell Briar's drinks were always on the house.

Wendell pressed the fifty into Justin's hand. "Then this is for you."

Justin touched the bill to his chest, mouthed a thank-you, and put it into the brandy snifter on his tray. The staff worshipped Wendell. His arrival elicited excitement second only to the nightly visits of their coke dealer. But while the other waiters saw Wendell as a walking ATM, Justin liked him because Wendell recognized his talent and encouraged him. Once the royal party had their cocktails Justin asked with excitement, "Well, have you come to see my paintings?"

Richard Rothschild plucked an olive from his martini and inquired, "Are there any depictions of childbirth or lesbianism?"

"No."

"Then lead on."

Justin escorted them to the back room where the paintings were hanging. Stan quickly looked over the installation and then made straight for the piano, where his piercing warble soon drowned out the twins' hilariously sad rendition of "I Got You Babe." Undoubtedly, an analysis of the register tapes would show a sharp spike in drink sales whenever Stan began to sing.

With Stan's caterwauling in the background, Wendell, Richard, and Buddy moved from picture to picture, spending a polite amount of time before each piece of Justin's work. The artist stood by awkwardly as the queen and her jesters pondered the paintings. Wendell turned to him. "Hmm . . . Is religion harnessing technology or is technology replacing religion? Very interesting!"

Justin smiled, relieved. "Exactly!"

Richard Rothschild interrupted, "Well, which is it?"

Buddy rolled his eyes. "It's for you to decide. It requires some thought."

"Well, either way, the guys are hot."

Buddy threw him a look of disgust and turned to Justin. "The execution is exquisite."

Wendell nodded in agreement. "Yes, it is. I'll take this one."

Buddy one-upped him. "And I'll take these two."

Justin was elated.

Buddy was competitive but was also an artist himself. He'd come to New York from rural Oklahoma and struggled as a starving painter for two years before discovering the huge amount of money to be made converting sketches of spoiled Upper East Side children and pampered family pets into handcrafted needlepoint throw pillows. Justin turned to Richard Rothschild, who responded sheepishly to the expectant look on his face.

"Oh, I'd love to own one, but I really don't have the wall space."

Wendell helpfully suggested, "Perhaps you could take down that Renoir print."

"Now, Wendell, you know that's an original."

"Oh, is it?"

His sardonic tone irritated Richard. "It most certainly is! It was given to my grandfather by the Duchess of Windsor as a token of gratitude for services ren—"

Buddy interrupted, "Oh, shut up and buy a painting, you phony French Jew! It's for a good cause."

His remark pushed his friend's buttons but the AIDS angle hit close to home, and Richard selected a small study of Apollo playing a Yamaha synthesizer. He gave Buddy a sneer, then turned and spoke to Justin maternally. "I think there's an empty wall in my powder room."

These men had lost an army of friends to AIDS in the early years of the epidemic, and many of the Eton crowd had been HIV positive for years. But even with the new drug cocktails available to affluent men like themselves, I don't think they ever felt relieved. Who could? Whenever I was reminded of that, I became less judgmental about their drinking. I figured that to them, the party was an indispensable part of the illness—a way of making the best of a painful reality. It was just the opposite of a lot of younger gay men who viewed HIV as an unavoidable part of the party and were abandoning safer sex.

I complimented Wendell on his choice of painting. "You've selected the best one."

"Of course!"

"I love the way Justin manipulates perspective. And Richard is right, the models are hot."

"His gods are callipygian."

"Well, this crowd does love a nice ass. I'm sure they'll all sell."

I was glad to have met the challenge of Wendell's five-dollar adjective.

Every once in a while Wendell would use a big word, and I'd catch him studying my face to see if it was in my lexicon. I'm an excellent bullshitter and if I didn't know the definition, I easily fooled him ninety-nine percent of the time. But there were still moments when we were both acutely aware of who had gone to boarding school and focused on the lesson, and who'd gone to public school and focused on the clock. Although discovering a hole in my vocabulary might have made Wendell feel superior, to his credit he never used it to make me feel inferior. I think he simply looked for people's shortcomings out of habit—as a way to size them up in a potentially dangerous world.

Wendell liked me despite the occasional vocabulary gap because I was relatively cultured and well-rounded. I'd read Willa Cather and Anthony Trollope and could quote lines from Shakespeare, Walt Whitman, and old MGM musicals. I was a far cry from Denny, who thought that George Eliot and Cyd Charisse were both men. I valued Wendell's appraisal. When you work in a bar, so many people form their opinions based on what you do, and don't bother to see who you are, or what you could be.

As Wendell and the others were writing checks for the paintings, Jeffrey approached. "Wendell, I see you've bought the Poseidon portrait—it's my favorite."

Wendell gestured to the art on the wall. "I was hoping there would be one that you had posed for."

Jeffrey winced. "I don't think they worshipped bears on Olympus."

Justin butted in. "I begged him to sit for me, but he wouldn't do it shirtless. I was going to do a life-size painting of the Minotaur using MapQuest to find his way out of the labyrinth."

Buddy elbowed Richard Rothschild. "I bet you'd be able to find wall space for that!"

Jeffrey changed the subject. "Eddie, may I please have the storeroom key—I think I left my wallet in there."

Wendell peered up at me from his checkbook with his eyebrow arched, then turned to Jeffrey. "Anyway, how are you, my darling?"

"I'm well, thank you. I'm happy to see you!"

He gave Wendell a big bear hug, something Wendell obviously wasn't used to—but also obviously enjoyed.

"Did Eddie tell you about the ballet this Thursday?"

"No, he didn't."

I jumped in quickly. "Sorry, Wendell, I was going to tell him downstairs but we got distracted."

Wendell didn't miss a beat. "I'll bet you did."

Jeffrey blushed and they shared a giggle.

Jeffrey had adored Wendell from the start; he was able to see right into his heart and ignore the Briar facade. That, in turn, softened Wendell and allowed him to be more at ease with Jeffrey than he was with almost anyone else.

I was jealous of their rapport—envious that my cynical New York background made it harder for me to see the good in everyone the way Jeffrey's unassuming Idaho upbringing did. I never quite got past the guilt I felt about the fact that my initial fondness for Wendell was largely due to the fifty-dollar bills he handed out. But I grew to care about him as I started to realize that what my middle-class mind viewed as pretentiousness was simply expected behavior in the patrician world into which he was born. We became good friends, with Jeffrey serving as the catalyst for the bonds we forged. Their friendship was an excellent, if unlikely, fit. They had both lost their mothers as children, and that strengthened their connection. Wendell had a parental affection for Jeffrey who, with a deceased mother and a father who was a born-again asshole, was primed for some mothering. The irony of the situation was that Wendell was probably every Idaho mother's worst nightmare—a biting, affected, *Boys in the Band,* alcoholic homosexual.

Wendell had found his own surrogate mother in the form of his upstairs neighbor, June. She was a ninety-two-year-old former Ziegfeld Girl who'd lived in her spacious rent-controlled apartment for almost sixty years. She had bad hips and wore false eyelashes and a copper-red wig in a *Liza with a "Z"* style. Wendell took her out to dinner every Tuesday and accompanied her to the podiatrist once a month to have her toenails clipped.

Jeffrey was always getting hit on by the patrons at Eton. A lot of men there assumed that because he was young and hand-some, he hustled on the side. We'd both been offered money on several occasions, and though the idea of extra cash made it tempting at times, we never responded to a proposition with anything but an uncomfortable laugh.

The Eton Club was a perfect place for prostitution, although if anyone was seen conducting business, or if a customer com-plained—which they usually did the day *after* the transaction had taken place—the boy for hire was eighty-sixed from the es-tablishment. The smart hustlers soon discovered that all it took to be exempt from eviction was to give a freebie to the cheap-skate owners, a move that hit them right where they lived—somewhere between their dicks and their wallets.

The hustlers weren't the only younger men at the Eton Club. They were actually only a small percentage and were greatly outnumbered by the "archeologists," men in their twenties or thirties with grandpa fixations. For the archeologists, the Eton Club was a treasure trove comparable to Pompeii or King Tut's tomb. The numbers were certainly in their favor, with one Howard Carter for every fifty ancient queens.

Although I'd noticed glances and nods that weren't entirely free of familiarity, Wendell and his attendants never acknowl-edged the working boys, and the working boys knew not to ap-proach them—at least not inside the club. Wendell was very mindful of his family's image and would never tarnish the Briar name. I suspected the same was true for Buddy, and also for Stan, whose aged, immigrant parents still lived on the Upper East Side. Richard's exceptional caution with the Rothschild name was on par with the care one would give to an object on loan from a museum. The majority of the patrons, however, weren't so worried about appearances, and the hustlers flirted openly with Pat Lonergan and the other Four to Fours.

Wendell, Buddy, and Richard Rothschild had joined Stan at the piano. Seeing them all lined up, I was struck by the contrast between Stan and the others. Jeffrey caught me observing them and noted, "You know, for an old guy Stan's kind of sexy."

He was right. As I took in the disparity between Stan's broad shoulders, rumpled blazer, and plain beer bottle and the prim carriage, ostentatious jewelry, and affected gestures of the others, I felt hopeful that maybe I'd mature into a hot daddy and not some eccentric old aunt.

Two days later we attended the ballet at Lincoln Center.

I'd been looking forward to the production of *Sleeping Beauty,* but Jeffrey could barely contain his excitement. He'd loved dancing ever since he was nine years old when his stepmother enrolled him in a Sunday afternoon ballroom class at the Two Right Feet Dance Studio in Idaho Falls. His father reluctantly agreed, but grew uneasy when Jeffrey began to think outside the box step and added tap and ballet to his schedule. He finally pulled the plug on the lessons, concerned by his son's growing obsession with Mitzi Gaynor.

Wendell, Stan, Buddy, and Richard Rothschild arrived for pre-show drinks already well lubricated from their after-work martinis. Then at the performance, Stan snuck out of the first act to grab a cigarette, and had a round of cosmopolitans waiting for everyone at intermission. I stuck to cranberry and seltzer, but Jeffrey tried to match them cosmo for cosmo. It was not a wise move; keeping up with them was impossible. He would have had an easier time playing eighteen holes of golf against Tiger Woods. To the four of them, used to the Big Gulp cocktails served at the Eton Club, the standard shot at Lincoln Center was a child's portion appropriate for a teddy bear tea party. Wendell, Buddy, and Richard Rothschild easily knocked back two rounds. Stan, without pausing, put away four. Wendell thanked us all for coming and made his customary toast, "To health and prosperity!" The sentiment was heartily seconded by all, and a final round was ordered and downed in a race with the intermission bell.

I was excited to be sitting in a private opera box and thrilled to be wearing my old cater-waiter tuxedo without having to pass hors d'oeuvres, but the second act of the ballet dragged and I lost interest. I scrutinized my companions. Jeffrey was intensely focused on the performance, but Wendell and Buddy just stared at the stage with medicated grins. Richard Rothschild had lapsed into a code-blue slumber that not even a kiss from the handsome prince on stage could disturb, and Stan, annoyed by any dancer who wouldn't let you stuff a twenty in his crotch, grew fidgety and ducked out again to chain-smoke. I compared the reality of the experience to the highbrow New York evening I had anticipated and grew angry and sad. Studying these men was like peeking through a keyhole into a room that I swore I'd never enter but was afraid I might end up locked in anyway. Regardless of my familial aversion to alcohol, I vowed that I'd never take up drinking. I also vowed that I'd never wear flashy jewelry, use the word "dahling," or live on the Upper East Side. I slid my hand over Jeffrey's forearm and gave it a squeeze. I was about to suggest that we sneak out and head back to our place in Hell's Kitchen when he leaned over and whispered, *"Isn't this fantastic?"*

As I processed the look of enthusiasm on his face, my heart was suffused with affection, and I realized that this was another situation where I wouldn't try to compel him to accept my reality. I kept my negativity in check, said "Fantastic!" and turned my attention to the stage while attempting to tune out Richard's snoring.

At Café Grisette Jeffrey and I split the bread basket while our companions fawned over the sommelier. To my mind he wasn't particularly sexy, but to them any man with a tastevin around his neck was considered well hung. Wendell looked over the wine list carefully as if he were perusing *The New York Review of Books* and ordered two bottles of cabernet. The sommelier bowed his head, departed, and was replaced by a darkly hand-some waiter. Richard Rothschild fussed over the menu while Stan, emboldened by the drinks at the ballet, said inappropri-ate things to the tall brunette. "Do you recommend the steak tartare?"

"It's very popular, sir."

"Do you like raw meat?"

"Me? No, sir. Not really."

"Are you gay?"

The waiter didn't know what to make of him. Wendell pulled the waiter's attention away from Stan. "Never mind him! Just bring him the tartare. I'll have the carpaccio."

The waiter jotted it down and asked, "And for your entrée?"

Wendell held his hand up. "That's all for now."

Wendell then gestured to Buddy, who was smiling at Jeffrey dreamy eyed. "Buddy? The oysters?"

Buddy sighed contentedly. "That sounds divine!"

With a gesture toward Buddy, Wendell confirmed the order with the waiter. "The oysters."

He then turned to Richard Rothschild. "Richard?"

Richard addressed the waiter directly. "I'll have the oysters as well, thank you."

Buddy snapped out of his trance. "Oysters? Oysters aren't kosher!"

Richard was annoyed. "And your point, Betsy Ross?"

"Real Jews don't eat shellfish! Ask Eddie! I bet he doesn't eat oysters."

"No, he only sucks cock."

I assured Richard, "That's not kosher either," then smiled embarrassedly at the waiter, who looked uncomfortably amused.

Stan motioned for him to lean in and whispered audibly, "Don't mind them. They need to get fucked."

The waiter laughed uneasily and attempted to continue with Richard's order. "Perhaps . . . may I suggest the onion tart?"

Richard stared Buddy down while he addressed the waiter. "The oysters will be fine, thank you."

Jeffrey and I quickly ordered the tart. The waiter marked his pad and asked, "Is there anything else?"

Stan blurted out blankly, "Do you like to get fucked?"

Wendell interrupted. "That will be all, thank you."

The waiter gave Stan the once-over, turned, and walked toward the kitchen.

As obnoxious as he could be when drunk, it was amazing how well Stan did for himself, and I wasn't completely shocked when he stepped outside to smoke a cigarette and returned with the waiter's phone number. Then again, he was the daddy of their group. He was a five-foot-eight, two-hundred-pound fireplug of a man who'd made an X-rated movie back in the seventies before everyone in porn was a "star." His ability to drink so much and look so good at fifty-seven amazed me, and I grew envious as I remembered the glimpse of my own future that confronted me whenever I saw my potbellied uncles at the beach. I was convinced that Stan's ancestors must have possessed a gene that allowed them to survive the harsh Polish winters by synthesizing protein directly from grain alcohol.

After Stan's victory with the waiter, the conversation turned to Justin's paintings, which somehow led to a discussion of Wagner's *Tristan and Isolde,* which then inexplicably morphed into a debate on Eugene O'Neill's protagonists' need for illusion in order to survive (an ironic topic given the company). I had to admit it was refreshing to dine with men who could talk with ease about everything from cock to Cocteau, but the alcohol-infused dialogue was exhausting. By the time we departed Café Grisette at two a.m., we'd gone through four bottles of cabernet and the group's idea of a six-course meal: cocktails, aperitifs, appetizers, wine, dessert, and champagne. I doubt that the waiter had ever seen people drink so much and eat so little. He shot me a look of disbelief when Buddy asked for an Irish coffee to go. When the last round of champagne was poured, Wendell stood up. "To health and prosperity!"

Stan raised his glass and added, "And to more evenings like this!"

As I gingerly clinked my soda glass against their flutes and surveyed the state of the company, I thought, "How many more evenings like this could I survive? *How many could they?*"

Wendell ordered a napoleon and some almond cookies to take home for June the Ziegfeld Girl and then he handed the waiter his Amex. He usually picked up the tab for everything, but I noticed the financial arrangements had changed when Stan handed him a few twenties and then glanced at Richard and Buddy, who took out a money clip and change purse respectively. The significance wouldn't register with me until months later. Jeffrey and I didn't even pretend to reach for our wallets. Wendell had warned us about the worthlessness of our money too many times. After dinner, we all instinctively headed for Eton. Nobody assumed we would go home.

The Eton Club was uncharacteristically dead. Buddy took one look at the slim pickings, tapped Richard Rothschild on the shoulder, and gestured toward the door. "Come on, Jewboy, it's late. I'll escort you home."

"Oh, are you going to protect me with your knitting needles?"

"I don't knit, I do custom needlepoint!"

"Fabulous! If we're attacked you can smother the thug with a throw pillow!"

After they said their good-byes, Stan excused himself to make a call before slipping out to meet our waiter from Café Grisette at an after-hours club in the Meatpacking District.

Jeffrey looked around at the desolate bar and quoted a line from *All About Eve.*

"Where's the body been laid out?"

Wendell caught the reference and responded in a Bette Davis voice, eerily not too different from his own. "It hasn't been laid out; we haven't finished with the embalming. Let's have a nightcap."

Jeffrey and I looked at each other. We'd both reached our limit. I turned to Wendell. "We're done for the night. Come on, Margo Channing, we'll take you home."

He dismissed me with a wave. "That won't be necessary."

I persisted. "It's late, Wendell. You shouldn't walk home alone at this hour. You could get mugged."

He laughed off the thought. "If anyone dared attack me, I'd give them a good tongue-lashing."

There was truth in the statement. Anyone unfortunate enough to assault Wendell Briar would be cut down to size and slink away feeling bad about themselves.

Jeffrey knew Wendell would respond better to a directive from him and took charge. "Wendell, this isn't open for discussion. We're seeing you home."

He grimaced and gave Jeffrey a military salute. "Yessir!"

Wendell nodded to Denny as we headed toward the exit. "Dennis."

"Get home safely."

"How could I not, with such gallant escorts?"

Wendell was the only customer at the Eton Club that anyone ever walked home. Most of the clientele were escorted to the front door and wished good night. Steve the doorman would call a cab for some of the more inebriated ones. Sometimes, if the guy was too fucked up to remember his address, Steve would just tell the taxi driver, "Ninety-third and West End"—and hope for the best.

All the way down East Fifty-sixth Street, Wendell insisted that he was perfectly capable of seeing himself home. Although he lived only a couple of blocks from the Eton Club and the area was basically safe, there had been several muggings in the neighborhood and we weren't going to take any chances. Besides, the staff would never have forgiven me if I'd let anything happen to their cash cow.

When we got to Wendell's building on East Fifty-fourth, we were approached by a muscular Puerto Rican with huge arms and no shortage of tattoos. I recognized him from Eton. Jeffrey instinctively put himself between Wendell and the hustler as I rang for the doorman. As we waited, Wendell peered out from behind Jeffrey's solid torso and waved the guy off. "Come back another time. My chaperones won't permit it."

Jeffrey and I must have looked way more intimidating than we felt because the guy put up his palms in a "no problem" gesture, then turned and headed down the sidewalk. I suspected he'd take a trip around the block and watch from across the street, waiting for Jeffrey and me to leave so that he could make his move. I motioned with my head to the doorman, who'd seen us bring Wendell home before. He was quite used to dealing with the hustlers that Wendell forgot ordering, and he responded with a nod of assurance that he wouldn't admit the guy. I turned to Wendell and apologized. "Sorry, just trying to look out for you."

He laughed. "No matter, I have him on home video being spanked."

As my mind constructed an image of Wendell with his baby-hamster pink body dominating the heavily inked, steroidal hustler, it hit me: no matter how well you know anyone, you never know what they do for sex.

Upstairs, Jeffrey got Wendell into bed while I put the dessert for June in the kitchen. The refrigerator was empty except for a jar of cocktail onions, a bottle of poppers, and an open box of zwiebacks. I took the biscuits into the living room and we waited for Wendell to fall asleep. We lingered awhile after we heard Wendell snoring, in case the hustler made another appearance. Jeffrey sprawled out on the sofa with one leg on the floor while I browsed through the photographs on Wendell's piano. There were dozens of old pictures of Wendell and Stan at the beach with men I didn't recognize. I knew that most of them were dead. I laughed at the sight of Wendell in a fifties sundress, looking like Peggy Guggenheim next to Buddy's corseted drag persona, Minnie Bar, and was touched to discover a framed picture of Wendell, Jeffrey, and me at the Brooklyn Botanic Garden. At Wendell's insistence we had ventured out to Park Slope in May so we could see the peonies in bloom. During our visit Stan had insisted we pose for a snapshot under a trellis of Briar roses. The bower cast a ghostly shadow on Wendell's face. I held the photo out to Jeffrey. "You look great here! I can almost see your abs through your shirt!"

"Really?" He examined the picture closely and made a face.

"What?"

"Wendell looks awful in that light."

"You mean daylight?"

"The roses make it weird."

"It's not just the roses—he looks awful."

"He does, doesn't he?"

The pregnant pause that followed was aborted by a loud, cartoonish hiccup from the bedroom that cracked us up. I held the box of biscuits out to Jeffrey. "Want a zwieback?"

We watched over Wendell a bit longer, then grabbed a cab on Second Avenue and headed home to Hell's Kitchen. Despite Jeffrey's burgeoning hangover, and the fact that we were both exhausted, we hit the sheets running. After a night of inebriated aunts and threatening hustlers, the aggressive sex re-

inforced our bond and made us feel safe. Afterward I wrapped
myself tightly around Jeffrey and stared over his shoulder at the
shelf of photos next to the bed. I wasn't a boozy old cynic, and
I certainly had no plans to become one, but as I scanned the
array of candid shots of friends in Provincetown and Miami, I
thought of all the missing men on Wendell's piano. It jarred
me to realize how unpredictable life can be, and just how possible it was to be blindsided by a catastrophe. It was no wonder
Wendell didn't take his safety seriously. In comparison to the
terror of the plague's early years, the worry about being the victim of a mugging was laughable.

Jeffrey drifted off to sleep, and I held on to him until his
body temperature climbed into the red and drove me to the other
side of the mattress in search of a cooler climate. In the morning we awoke to a messenger with a dozen roses—not Briars
but a similar, commercially available variety in the same salmon
color. In his note Wendell called us princes and thanked us for
keeping him safe. I remember thinking, "If only we could keep
Wendell safe from himself."

The fall, which usually eases the oppressive New York summer into the depressing New York winter, was unpredictably
cold, and by mid-November the interior of the Eton Club was
accented with men in expensive fur coats. For insurance reasons the Eton Club's policy prohibited the coat check from ac-
cepting furs, and the patrons were forced to carry or wear their
pelts while they mingled and drank. There were always men
who didn't want to be encumbered by a full-length chinchilla
while on a manhunt and challenged the policy. I was able to
stand firm most of the time but would bend the rules for some
of the regulars, and gave in to any particularly obdurate customer who was willing to slip me a few extra bucks. I never settled for a bribe of less than twenty dollars, knowing I'd have to

split it with Carl, the Wiccan coat check guy, who'd feign vegan rage at the suggestion that he put aside his "fur is murder" philosophy to violate the regulations.

Hours flowed like scotch at the Eton Club, and I remember thinking how quickly the nights flew by for a place where time stood still. But even though the evenings of drunken affectation ran into one another seamlessly, some minor changes did occur. The staff's coke dealer got busted and was replaced. One of the elder waiters/chorus boys got a big break in an all-male version of Cole Porter's *Can-Can* and fractured his coccyx attempting a move called a cooter slam. Brian added a number from *Sunset Boulevard* to his repertoire, and we all suffered every middle-aged homo in the five boroughs doing a bad Norma Desmond.

For Christmas and Chanukah Jeffrey and I skipped presents and bought a new upholstered chair to replace the one a hideous shelter cat I'd adopted had ripped to shreds. We were invited to a Christmas open house at Wendell's, where Jeffrey received a black velvet smoking jacket lined in paisley silk, and I was given a gift certificate for a fancy Upper East Side men's shop that catered to the madras golf pant crowd.

On the sidewalk in front of Wendell's, Jeffrey held up the jacket, shook his head, and fretfully remarked, "He must be pretty strapped financially if he's regifting."

The choice of the smoking jacket did seem odd given the talent Wendell had always displayed in the past for picking the perfect gift, but it hadn't occurred to me that the inapt selection was the result of recycling. I'd grown to anticipate regifting from my former boyfriend, Doug the Cheapskate, and I'd even done it myself on occasion, but it was not something I ever expected from Wendell Briar.

I pressed Jeffrey. "Are you sure?"

"You've got to be kidding! How much more inappropriate could these presents be? He's obviously cutting corners."

His comments jogged my memory of our night at Café Grisette.

It had never entered my mind that Wendell Briar might be short on cash. In hindsight, I should have been more attuned.

"Well, you can always exchange yours," I said.

"There's no gift receipt."

"Then I guess you're stuck. The only one you could possibly regift a paisley-lined smoking jacket to is Wendell."

After the holidays Wendell came down with a terrible cold, but since it didn't interfere with his drinking and smoking, I didn't really think there was any cause for concern. I did get alarmed, however, when one evening at Eton, I received a call from June. Wendell hadn't shown up to take her out for their weekly dinner, and he hadn't phoned. I assured her that everything would be all right, and then dispatched Jeffrey to her apartment with a plate of lamb chops from the Eton Club's restaurant, the Eatin' Club, next door. When I logged on to the computer to charge the meal to Wendell's account, I was astonished to discover how much he owed. He hadn't paid his tab in over eight months, and there were messages from Denny to the owners asking what to do about it. They said to leave it alone.

The owners of the Eton Club, Dom Pappia and Joe Cigliano, were real penny-pinchers and never missed a chance to collect. They were somehow connected to the mob and tried to act intimidating even though their *Sopranos* personas were closer to Roberta Peters and Beverly Sills. I knew Wendell had done some tax work on their behalf, and it wasn't hard to imagine that he had something incriminating on them. The Eton Club was a cash-only business, and ninety percent of the money never saw the light of day until it was basking on a beach in the Cayman Islands.

Wendell remained out of sight for over a week. When I asked about him, Buddy said Wendell had had minor surgery to have a fatty tumor removed and didn't want anyone making a fuss. His explanation answered my question, but things certainly didn't seem right. When Wendell finally made an appearance, he looked thin and tired, and there was a bandage on his left forearm. Jeffrey, who'd been particularly worried, was over-joyed to see him and threw his arms around Wendell's neck.

"I'm so glad you're okay! You shouldn't have disappeared. Why didn't you return my calls?"

"I didn't want to be a bother."

"Oh, that's silly. I'm your friend; you can ask me for any-thing."

"A drink would be lovely."

"Right away!"

Jeffrey returned from the bar so quickly I wondered if he'd been keeping the drink on ice for the entire week. He pre-sented it to Wendell. "Here you go! It's on me."

"Thank you."

He attempted to slip Jeffrey the customary fifty, but Jeffrey refused. "Wendell, you don't have to do that. I'm buying it for you."

"Buying it for me? Well, well, well . . ."

There was an uncomfortable moment, and I shot a panicked look at Stan, who was standing at the bar. If it were anyone but Jeffrey he'd have received a vicious quip that would have smarted for a week. Even I would have been told, "Don't insult me!" while having the money forced into my hand. But Wen-dell just smiled and said, "Thank you, you're a prince."

Jeffrey lifted the bottled water he always kept on his tray to combat the effect of the smoke on his throat, and gestured with it toward Wendell. "To health and prosperity!"

Wendell answered thoughtfully, "To health and prosperity."

There was a sense of relief in the room, but even Jeffrey sensed that his generosity wouldn't be tolerated a second time. He, and the rest of us, continued to accept Wendell's tips even after it came to light that he and his law partner were dissolving their practice.

Apparently Wendell and his partner, Sam Breyer, had been

delaying the inevitable for over a year. Despite their best efforts, there was no way the firm of Briar and Breyer could survive intact, when after the death of their biggest client, Sam had been unable to convince the deceased's children to refrain from investing their inheritance in a chain of ill-fated Israeli amusement parks.

I'd always had the vague impression that there was a vast Briar fortune moldering away in a dark vault somewhere, but I understood the full reality of Wendell's situation when he accepted an offer to partner with Pat Lonergan. Lonergan was obviously hoping that the addition of the Briar name to his letterhead would give his seedy practice an air of respectability—which it undoubtedly would have, if he hadn't elected to announce the partnership by handing out nail files and pot holders printed with the firm's new name.

Despite his financial problems—and the blow to the Briar mystique from the tacky giveaways and cheesy advertisement that Lonergan placed in every pennysaver and gay bar rag—Wendell did his best to keep up appearances. In the tasteless ad, he retained his dignity seated at a carved mahogany desk, while Lonergan stood behind him, winking at the reader with a fan of hundred-dollar bills in his hand under a headline that read, "Sue Today for a Secure Tomorrow!" I wondered how many Ketel Ones Wendell had knocked back to get through the photo shoot.

Now on the ordinal scale of alcohol consumption, Wendell had always been near the top—just below Stan and above the Munich Oktoberfest. But after each successive blow to his pride, his drinking increased. The pot holders and dubious ad were bad enough, but the four-color business cards that Lonergan printed up specifically for the hustlers at the Eton Club were the worst. He actively solicited their business, should they ever find themselves confronted by the vice squad, and implied that cash wasn't the only way they could pay for his services.

As Wendell edged closer to the top of the drinking scale, he began to mumble and slur, regularly reaching a point of intoxication where he wasn't making sense. Plus, he looked awful. He didn't possess the genes of a Stan Jaworski, and whatever nutrients the vodka contained were going through him like grease through a Grey Goose. The staff, wanting to avoid confrontation and afraid of interrupting the flow of cash, kept pouring.

Usually, cutting drunks off when they had too much was my favorite part of managing the Eton Club. It was the only time when the customer wasn't right. I did feel compassion when the patron in question was a sweet-tempered gentleman who'd tried too hard to drown his problems. But whenever the staff informed me that one of the obnoxious windbags we routinely endured had overindulged and was exhibiting questionable behavior, I practically broke into a little jig at the thought of turning off the tap. It was my compensation for every pretentious boast, every creepy innuendo, and every unwanted hand Jeffrey and I had to brush off our asses. But even though Wendell was obviously way past the "I'm sorry, sir, but I think you've had enough" stage, I just couldn't bring myself to say those words to him.

Pat Lonergan continued to find tacky new ways to exploit his partnership with Wendell. One such attempt at drumming up new business was a low-budget commercial on late-night public access television. I was stunned that Wendell would agree to such a thing, but I guess his situation had worn him down. The commercial for Lonergan-Briar was poorly produced and terribly acted. It featured a middle-aged man in a hospital bed next to a huge stack of medical bills—his wife, in tears, at his side.

"Oh, Bob, that darn asbestos has ruined everything! What are we going to do?"

The melodramatic spot ended with a shot of the two attorneys standing back to back, arms folded, while a voice-over urged viewers to call 1-800-LAWSUIT today.

The night after it aired, Wendell and Stan stumbled into the Eton Club, ordered round after round of sidecars, and spent hours at the piano where Wendell watched quietly while Stan mooed like a cow in time to Brian's spastic attack on the keyboard. After seeing the halfhearted hello with which he returned Jeffrey's exuberant hug, it was obvious that Wendell wanted to be left alone. I kept my distance.

Stan's aural assault went on until almost three in the morning, when the piano stopped for the night. The silence that followed his final number, "Papa, Can You Hear Me?" was absolutely golden but was shattered two minutes later by a terrifying crash when Stan, weaving toward the bar for another cocktail, tumbled face first through a glass coffee table. Jeffrey, Denny, and I all ran back to find him sitting on the carpet dazed, his head a bloody mess. Denny sent Jeffrey to call 911 while I ran to get something to stop the bleeding. Luckily, Stan's injuries looked worse than they were, and a once-over with a wad of damp cocktail napkins revealed only one major cut over his right eye. There was broken glass everywhere, and Stan's shirt was covered with shards. Denny had him remove it while he sent one of the waiters downstairs for a clean T-shirt from the previous night's Goldschläger promotion. Leaning against the wall, shirtless, with a gash over his eye, burly Stan looked like he'd taken a pummeling from the champ in a geriatric prizefight.

The ambulance arrived in minutes. Stan obviously needed stitches, but the paramedics were far more concerned about the possibility of a brain injury. Since it was impossible to know how much of Stan's incoherence was a result of the fall and how much was the result of the sidecars, they couldn't chance not taking him to the hospital. Wendell wanted to accompany them, but the ambulance driver saw instantly how smashed he was and denied the request. Jeffrey went instead. As they were loading Stan into the rig, I could hear him asking the paramedics, "Do you like to get fucked?"

I burst into laughter.

Wendell looked at me suspiciously. "What's so funny?"

"Nothing. Come on, I'm taking you home."

We strolled quietly down East Fifty-fourth Street, and I held Wendell's arm as if I were a Boy Scout and he an old lady. The doorman admitted us, and we took the elevator up to Wendell's apartment. As I helped him undress, I was alarmed at how skinny he'd become. He caught me looking at his body, and I quickly averted my eyes. He grinned, then reached for my hand and brought it to rest on his fragile chest.

"Don't be embarrassed, we all have those feelings."

I couldn't tell if he was serious, drunk, or joking. The ambiguity disarmed me, and I threw my head back with a laugh to escape the awkwardness. When I looked back down at him, Wendell reached up, kissed me lightly on the lips, said, "You're a prince!" and then climbed into bed. I didn't stick around. Once the bedroom light was extinguished, I headed for the door.

That was the last time I saw Wendell Briar.

I called the next day to check on Wendell but only got his answering service. Wendell didn't believe in voice mail or e-mail. If possible, he would have preferred visitors leave their calling cards on a silver tray with a manservant. My message—and the several others that Jeffrey left over the next few days—went unanswered. The service operator said that Wendell hadn't called in for his messages.

Finally, Stan, who'd bounced back from his accident in record time, confided to us that Wendell was in the hospital. We wanted to stop by and see him but were told that the only visitor he'd allow was June. I imagined her sneaking past the nurses' station with a Prohibition-era flask of hooch secreted in her garter. Every morning Stan accompanied her to New York Presbyterian in a taxi but waited outside the room and only got glimpses of her stroking Wendell's hair.

The word "AIDS" was never uttered.

Two nights later, Jeffrey and I were sitting up in bed picking at a falafel platter and watching a six-part documentary on Tudor England. Last-minute preparations were being made for Henry VIII's marriage to Anne of Cleves when the call came from Stan. I couldn't move. Jeffrey buried his face in my shoulder, and I held him tightly while my mind slideshowed through scenes from Eton and the photos on Wendell's piano. We stayed that way for well over an hour. By the time I refocused on the television, Elizabeth was beheading Mary, Queen of Scots.

I thought of Wendell's refusal to seek treatment for, or even acknowledge, his illness. He probably thought AIDS was too common—a malady unbecoming a Briar. After all, it was no longer the disease of beautiful gay men cut down tragically in their prime. In Wendell's mind it had become an affliction of minorities, the poor, and the stupid, and I likened him to a society matron who'd rather go down with a sinking luxury liner than share a lifeboat with the steerage passengers. My realization shed new light on Wendell's reckless behavior. No wonder he'd had no concern for his safety. Having a fatal fall after a few too many or getting bludgeoned in an alley by a hoodlum didn't carry the stigma of AIDS—or suicide.

Wendell's memorial was simple and dignified. His sister Emily read a beautiful poem by Mary Oliver, and his former law partner Sam Breyer announced the creation of a scholarship fund in Wendell's name at the Art Students League. To keep things light, the gay priest peppered his homily with some Ogden Nash and included just enough religion to make the occasion solemn but not hypocritical. Stan delivered an emotional eulogy, and I was struck by the clarity and eloquence he displayed when unencumbered by a cocktail and a cigarette.

Jeffrey and I were invited to ride in a limo with Stan, Buddy, Richard, and June. Appropriately, it had a fully stocked bar. I poured everyone, including myself, a drink. Somehow, given the occasion, it would have seemed disrespectful for me to abstain. We managed to deplete the entire stock en route to the cemetery in Brooklyn.

The gravesite in the Briar family plot was overflowing with flowers. The Four to Fours had outdone each other with their floral tributes, and the mourners whispered and pointed at the wreaths and arrangements like judges at a garden show. Wendell was lowered into the ground next to his mother, and I watched with pressure behind my eyes as the bereaved placed salmon-colored roses on top of the sinking casket. Pat Lonergan kissed his rose, paused a moment, and unhinging his jaw, let out a wail that cut through my flesh. I hoarsely whispered to Jeffrey that perhaps Lonergan and Stan should sing a duet sometime. He smiled and gave my hand a squeeze before releasing it to step forward and toss a rose into the grave. I looked over at Stan, who'd given frail June his elbow for support, and then at Richard Rothschild, who was leaning his head against Buddy's shoulder, and the tears finally came to my eyes.

Afterward, we rode up Briar Avenue in silence.

When we were a short distance from the cemetery, Richard spoke. "I think this is an appropriate time for a toast."

Buddy enthusiastically agreed. "An excellent idea!"

Richard turned to me. "Eddie, will you do the honors?"

"Sure."

He gestured to the bar, which had somehow been restocked while we were graveside. I picked up a bottle and glanced at the label. "Wow!"

Buddy became suspicious. "What? Let me see!"

I held up the wine. When his eyes focused on the Chateau Lafite Rothschild '86, he smirked. "Oh, you've got to be kidding!"

Richard dismissed Buddy's remark and gestured to me with an aristocratic point of his chin. "Just pour, please."

I opened the bottle. Once the wine was poured, Richard made a toast: "To Wendell James Briar!"

"To Wendell James Briar!"

Before anyone could take a sip, Stan raised his glass again and added, "And to health and prosperity!"

"To health and prosperity!"

The irony was lost on no one.

Cheapskate

O n Wednesday, I found an old photograph of the Cheapskate and myself. On Thursday, he called.

I hadn't spoken to Doug since '89, and had seen him only once during the intervening fifteen years—at a friend's Christmas party, where I spied him in a corner preying on a sexy Tunisian boy, whose butchered English made him even sexier. I also saw Ivan, the ex-boyfriend who succeeded me, watching Doug from another corner. As Ivan shook his head in recognition of Doug's unctuous style, he caught sight of me. We laughed simultaneously and shared a congratulatory smile at having dumped the Cheapskate.

Looking at the old Polaroid, I realized that at the time, I'd given Doug too much credit for his looks—and given myself too little. Sure, I knew I could turn a few heads, but I'd convinced myself that the heads I was turning were either too undiscriminating, or too unattractive, to get someone better.

But there, in the snapshot of us at the beach, was irrefutable evidence that I had been a hottie. I got angry with myself remembering the degree to which I'd hated my looks. My head was full of healthy ringlets that I'd finally stopped trying to feather with a hot comb, and though I didn't have a six-pack, my gut was toned and tight. The lack of definition was simply due to genetics. My abs haven't been visible since I was in utero; they never even broke the surface when I was twenty-nine and lost twenty-two pounds on the Gatorade, Ecstasy, and chewing-gum diet.

Hindsight's made me wary of repeating the mistake. I don't want to look back at sixty-five and realize that at forty-one I was a pretty hunky young daddy.

The phone rang just as I was returning from a run in Central Park. Doug got me hooked on running when we were together, even though I had to work my shorter legs double time to keep up with him. Struggling on the heels of his long, elegant strides, I always imagined that I looked like an eggbeater chasing a gazelle. Unfortunately, my love of running is one of the few positive things I got out of our relationship.

Doug's voice took me completely by surprise but the recognition was instantaneous, assisted by the discovery of the photo the day before.

"Hello?"

"Ed?"

"Oh, hi, Doug."

My nonchalance caught him off guard.

"Wow! That was quick! I was all prepared to play *This Is Your Life.*"

"I'd know your voice anywhere."

"That's sweet. Yours is etched in my brain too."

His nauseating attempt at charm only made me mildly sick; apparently two decades after being bitten by the love bug, I was still producing antibodies.

"How are you, Doug?"

"I'm okay. I see you're doing great!"

"I'm hanging in there."

"You're all over the place! I read the piece on you in the *Advocate*. That must've been a nice boost for your career."

I couldn't imagine Doug paying for a subscription and assumed he'd read the magazine at a newsstand or at his gay dentist's office.

"Every bit of publicity helps. So . . . what have you been up to?"

He said he'd been writing for the *National Enquirer* for eight years—the last three covering Martha Stewart exclusively. He spent all day following her into stores—writing down what she bought, what she wore, and whom she talked to. He staked out her home with a camera and sorted through her trash. When she was in prison, he bribed guards for any scrap of information that he could stretch into a viable story. It seemed the perfect job for a cheapskate with honesty issues—getting paid to mangle the truth. As he described the details of his ambush strategies, my mind was searching for possible reasons for his call.

I wondered if he was dying, or if he was in some twelve-step program that required him to make amends. I would have loved it if, in some Dickensian twist of fate, he was calling to borrow money.

He invited me out for dinner, and I immediately thought he must have a two-for-one coupon or a friend who owned a restaurant. I almost declined, but curiosity got the better of me and I agreed to meet him. My shrink, Dr. Ben, was amused.

Although Doug had cheated on me, as well as nickel-and-dimed me, I'd kept insisting to my friends that he had a good side. For a year after we broke up, I attempted to forge a friendship with him. Everyone thought I was crazy, but I would have felt guilty cutting him out of my world completely. I was Doug's only confidant; the friends we had as a couple had been my friends before, and remained my friends after. Sorry that he didn't really have anyone else close to him, I continued to keep him in my life even when his shoplifting escalated and he began to dabble in mail fraud. His egregious behavior, however, eventually wore me down. The final disillusionment came when I ran into him in the company of a beefy Latin boy on Fire Island.

"Hi, Doug, what are you doing here?"

"Oh! Hey, Ed! Arturo, Eddie. Eddie, Arturo."

"Hi, Arturo, nice to meet you."

From his apologetic nod, it was clear that English wasn't Arturo's first language.

"Where's Ivan?"

Doug handed Arturo his towel and pointed toward the ocean.

"I need to *hablar* with Eddie *un momento*."

Arturo smiled, then headed for the beach. As my eyes took in the muscular V of Arturo's dark back, I gestured in his direction.

"Dominican?"

"Guatemalan."

"Ah, Guatemalan! He's humpy—just your type."

"I do love the mud people."

I ignored Doug's racist remark.

"Ivan said you were visiting your mother."

"I just told him that; I needed Arturo time."

His cheating on Ivan hit close to home and brought up a lot of angry memories. My eyes narrowed and panned to the stunted oak over Doug's shoulder.

"I see . . ."

"What's the matter?"

I refocused on his face and, realizing he'd probably never change, let out a sigh of futility.

"That's it. I'm done with you."

"What do you mean?"

"I'm just tired of your bullshit. Have fun with Arturo."

Then I turned and walked away from four years of my life.

* * *

Now, my friends didn't like the Cheapskate from the start—and said so. That should have clued me in. People who love you don't want to rain on your parade; they hold their tongues if they don't like your boyfriend. If they can't, it must be serious. I've dated guys who were beyond horrible and my friends never badmouthed them. Nobody even said anything about Max—the meth-head with dentures who smashed my windshield—other than that they thought he was cute.

I first met the Cheapskate when I was twenty-four and working nights at a no-star seafood restaurant called Squid Roe, where the live display lobsters grossly misrepresented the frozen ones served to the duped customers. Doug would come in on Wednesdays for the chowder, and to marvel at Ur, the one-armed Turkish busboy, shucking oysters. Doug would always ask about, but never order, the special; no surprise since scrod was always the special of the day at Squid Roe. By definition scrod's a young cod or haddock, but at Squid Roe it meant any fish that was overstocked or past its expiration date. The lobsters, scrod, and scrod substitutes were prepared by Bunny, the Chinese cook who wore PETA T-shirts and spent the first ten minutes of every shift apologizing to the raw bar.

Doug and I bonded over our amazement at Ur's dexterity as we watched him effortlessly refill the saltshakers and ketchup bottles. We both had a fascination with carnival acts and human oddities and got into a discussion about the demise of the American sideshow. My nostalgia for the era was peppered with moral questions, but Doug had a strictly economic point of view, stating that banning the exhibition of freaks was robbing them of the opportunity to make a living and guaranteeing that they ended up on welfare—which he, for one, did not want to pay for. Looking back, we each revealed a lot about ourselves in that conversation.

A few weeks later Doug joined my health club, which was running a two-years-for-the-price-of-one promotion. He belonged at the gym. He was a big, boxy guy with a thick neck who played football in high school. His booming basso profundo was perfect for his six-foot-six frame. He took complete advantage of his height, aware from experience and published studies that people are subconsciously deferential to the tall. Next to Doug, my five foot eleven inches felt stunted. Later I'd feel infantilized by his insistence on assigning me diminutive pet names like puglet and fluff-fluff.

We became workout partners and friends but avoided any discussion of his sexuality. Eventually, after more than three months of sidestepping, Doug came out to me, and we traded hand jobs in a locker-room alcove. It was our first cheap date. Afterward we went through the usual gay questions, and I was amazed to discover how deep in the closet he actually was.

"Doug, you're not out at your job?"

"No."

"How come?"

"I don't want to jeopardize my career."

"You work at *Femme Fashion Monthly*!"

"So?"

"Well, they must suspect."

"Why?"

"Because you work at *Femme Fashion Monthly*!"

"I know, but I write about the business side of things, not the faggoty fashion side."

Doug's level of self-delusion shocked me, and I felt sad to think of him hiding in plain sight in the gay-friendly world of ladies' apparel. He hadn't even disclosed his secret to his best friend, who also worked at *FFM*. Her name was Rhonda Fishbine, but we called her the "Infanta" because her mother, Vanda, had scandalized her aristocratic Portuguese family by marrying Bernie Fishbine, a furrier from Rego Park. Rhonda had a pathetic crush on Doug, which he was quick to leverage whenever he wanted a favor.

The coward wasn't out to his family either. When his mother inquired about his new roommate, Doug told her I was a woman named Heloise—which I supposed was to give her a hint about our household. The situation made me determined to be Doug's guide to a positive gay identity; too bad I didn't realize I'd be on the economy tour.

I noticed Doug was frugal right from the beginning, but coming from a family where money had always been tight, I didn't necessarily find it excessive. At the time I was under-employed and happy to eat at cheapo establishments. I even re-member thinking how thoughtful he was to suggest dining options within my reach. Unfortunately, it wasn't until after we were living together that I learned the true extent of his stingi-ness. Looking back, his behavior was abominable. My willing-ness to put up with it in the name of love was pathetic.

Always using his intimidating size to full advantage, the Cheap-skate would haggle with salespeople in department stores as if he were in a Moroccan bazaar. He'd return suits when he was done wearing them. He'd charge furniture, then refuse to pay for it, claiming it had arrived damaged. He'd order stuff from Pottery Barn and Williams-Sonoma and allege he'd never re-ceived it. At the supermarket he'd bully the cashier into ac-cepting expired coupons—even for items he wasn't buying. Sometimes, if the lines were too long, he'd simply walk out with-out paying, rationalizing that the value of the groceries was commensurate with the value of his time. When Doug claimed something was a steal, he meant it.

His most impressive display of chutzpah occurred when, through a series of heart-wrenching letters, Doug convinced the Make a Wish Foundation to pay for his elective jaw surgery. The liar claimed to have a severe case of TMJ (Temporal Mandibular Joint dysfunction), but I later learned the proce-dure had been completely cosmetic because he thought his chin was sagging from Too Much Jowl.

Doug's favorite type of cuisine was complimentary; he'd suffer anyone for a free meal. If Stalin was picking up the check, he was a good guy in Doug's book. The rest of the time we bought day-old bagels and bread, and ate whatever brands were on special. For Easter, Doug would buy broken bunny parts at a discount, and any Christmas gifts he didn't like turned up in someone else's stocking.

My mom always said, "You make allowances for people you love," and in retrospect I think, "Boy, I must have really been head over heels to put up with his shit." I'm not exactly sure why I was so infatuated with Doug. It was probably the same youthful insecurity that had made me hate the way I looked back when the photograph was taken. Loving him was simply another error in perception that would take a lot of time to clear up.

Doug was penny-wise and knew the monetary worth of everything in his place. He'd delight in pointing out expensive items and recounting how much below cost he'd paid for them. By far the most valuable object in his apartment was an authentic Egyptian burial urn that graced the mantel. Doug had inherited it from his father, an amateur archeologist, and used it to house his remains. It made me laugh to think that even the urn was regifted.

To Doug the ancient urn presented a dilemma. He was constantly proclaiming that its sale could secure his financial future, but he couldn't remove the ashes while his mother was alive—and she was as healthy as a horse. She'd won a bronze medal at the '48 London Olympics and at sixty-four still swam every morning and taught Jazzercise at her condo. I'm sure the day after her funeral, the urn will turn up on eBay.

Now, my relationship philosophy's always been: "What's mine is yours and what's yours is mine." Doug's was: "What's mine is mine and what's yours is up for grabs." Luckily, I didn't own much that he was interested in, except for a Queen Anne table I called dibs on when we put my aunt Stella in the home. It's still in his apartment.

We shared the household expenses equally—down to the penny.

Doug would return from the store with coffee, milk, bread, etc., scan the receipt, and say, "You owe me six dollars and fifty-six cents."

"Okay."

"Do you want to pay me now?"

"I'm reading the paper."

"It's okay, I'll get it. Where's your wallet?"

"On the desk."

He'd finger through the bills.

"You don't have any singles, just a ten. I'll bring you change when I come home."

"Whatever."

I'm sure I didn't get any change—I never did. "Whatever," I later realized was a synonym for "I'm a loser, fuck me!" It would be quite some time before I'd use it to mean "You're a loser, fuck you!" The change in connotation occurred when I discovered that the crook had been charging me half the sticker price—even for sale items—and that he'd also been jacking up my share of the gas and electric.

"Hey, Doug, why am I paying two-thirds of the Con Ed bill?"

"You're home more than I am."

"Whatever."

The funny thing is that the difference in our ages led some people to think I must be Doug's rent boy. They didn't know it was because I was paying most of it.

I should have fled under the daily assault of Doug's cheapskatery—but sometimes you need to get kicked in the heart as well as in the head.

Eventually Doug stopped mentioning Heloise to his mom, and told the Infanta that he could just as easily work for the paper's fashion section. But he still told new acquaintances we were just roommates—especially if they were hot. Since he conveniently forgot to paint me into the picture, the Infanta tried to set him up with her friend James. Doug took his number to be polite (and in case he was fuckable) but burst out laughing when he discovered that it was Jaymze with a "Y" and a "Z."

Doug cheated on me and lied about it, even though I told him I valued honesty more than fidelity. I wasn't thrilled that he wanted to sleep with other guys, but I realized that after thirty-something years of self-repression, there was little chance he'd be able to remain monogamous with a *GQ* cover model, let alone me. Doug was particularly happy when cheating and cheapness overlapped. Near the end of our time together he decided to go to Miami—for the "warm weather."

"I'm only going for the sun, Eddie. I can't take the winter anymore."

"Then go."

"I wish you could come along. I'm really gonna miss you."

It was a hollow sentiment. He knew I couldn't afford the trip. I'd lost my job when Squid Roe closed down after the owner was convicted of trading in endangered reptiles. I did suggest that if he was really sincere, there was a way for me to accompany him. I knew proposing that he pick up the tab was pointless, so I said, "Why don't you just lend me the money?"

His response was classic Doug: "Oh, I would, puglet, but I wouldn't want to burden you with any additional debt."

I didn't press the issue. The next day he hopped a flight to Florida, and I went out dancing with friends and did my first line of cocaine.

I'd go clubbing a lot after that—and do a lot of drugs. It was a way to begin distancing myself from him. I'd always been the straitlaced kid in school and found the club scene very exciting. At first I was having a great time but things started to get out of hand when, after an all-night party in Washington, DC, I took a tour of the White House while still high. My friend Ethan's mom worked in Hillary Clinton's office and arranged for us to have lunch with her in the staff dining room. I don't recall much about meeting the first lady, but clearly remember eating six bags of M&M's stamped with the presidential seal on the bus ride home to New York.

Despite the lying, cheating, and stealing, sex with Doug was fantastic—even if I did all the work. He was beautiful; just looking at him could get me off. (I'm sure this is the only one of my observations he'll remember if he ever reads this.) But eventually Doug's cheapness started to affect our sex life too. We were wrestling in bed and Doug was using every bit of his two hundred and thirty pounds to dominate me. I got pissed off.

"Hey, how come you never let me top?"

" 'Cause I'm bigger and older. Did you buy more condoms?"

"No."

"Great! What are we supposed to do now?"

"How come you never buy them?"

"It's your responsibility."

"And it's not yours?"

"I'm the top."

"So?"

"It's the bottom's job to protect himself."

I exploded! I told him that he wasn't going to be the top *or* the bottom unless he chipped in. The next day he swiped some Trojans and lube from a porn store on Eighth Avenue and miraculously declared himself versatile. A few weeks later when he suggested we try a ménage à trois, I found the prospect exciting—until I realized that what he actually wanted was to cheat on me but have me split the cost of taking the guy to dinner first.

Doug's behavior also eventually cost him his job. Losing his position was a shame because *FFM* was the perfect place for someone who loved to work the system.

Whenever the paper did a story on a new clothing line, the manufacturer would send samples over to the office. Technically the garments were supposed to be returned when the illustrators finished their sketches, but nobody really cared if a blouse ended up on a reporter's back as long as a few favorable words were written. Everyone at *FFM* took advantage of this to some degree, except for the Infanta, who covered the fur market and would get splattered with red paint by animal rights activists anytime she made her way through the Garment District in a mink or chinchilla. She was forced to content herself with a macabre red and green rabbit's foot Christmas ornament that she used as a key chain.

Doug, however, took the whole thing to the extreme. After business hours he'd make the rounds of the newsroom collecting samples. If he'd worked for a menswear magazine, he might have been satisfied with an accessory or two for himself, but at *Femme Fashion Monthly* he felt cheated because he didn't wear ladies' clothes. Anyway, even if he'd been into drag, given his size he could hardly buy off the rack.

Once he'd stuffed the samples into his gym bag, Doug would walk around the corner to Lord & Taylor. Claiming he'd lost his receipt, he'd charm the shopgirl or retail fag at the return counter. He'd make similar excursions to Macy's, Saks, and Bloomingdale's, as well as dozens of specialty stores.

Doug was an excellent con man. I once saw him talk a saleswoman at Bergdorf's into crediting his account for a cashmere shawl that the store didn't even carry. To Doug, every swindle was a triumph—validation of his superiority over the smaller people of the world. His sense of victory was dampened only by the fact that most retailers wouldn't give refunds, only store credits. He, however, made the most of it.

Every day for over two years the Cheapskate had lunch at the Lord & Taylor Soup Bar, slowly eating away at the windfall he made returning three Marc Jacobs sweaters and a camisole. He raved about how delicious the split pea was, and could barely contain his excitement each week when his punch card entitled him to a free bowl. Sadly, it wasn't only his charge accounts that Doug was chipping away at. My patience was running out as well. The sex was still good—not great, but not yet bad; I was still tempted by his body even with the contempt in my heart.

Finally an incident occurred that I couldn't deny was the last straw. At a piano bar in the Village, we saw a mockumentary about the life of Nancy Reagan called *Just Say No!* that ironically we saw while high. (I sometimes wonder if my association with first ladies and illegal substances will one day find me shooting up in an alley with Barbara Bush.) The show was hysterical but ran late. Unfortunately, to catch the last direct PATH train home to Jersey City, we had to run out just as Nancy was revealing the intimate details of a three-way she and Ronnie had with Margaret Thatcher.

The PATH is a subway that runs under the Hudson from Manhattan to Jersey City. After midnight there's limited service and the trains are rerouted through Hoboken, where the station stinks like rotten eggs. As we headed down to the station, the ground started rumbling. We flew down the stairs and got there just as the train pulled in. I tried to insert money into the turnstile, but the mechanism wouldn't accept my crumpled dollar.

"Fuck!"

"Ed, come on! I'm not going to Hoboken!"

"It won't take my bill!"

I fished in my pocket for another buck, but all I had was a five. Doug was screaming at me. *"What the hell are you doing? Just go!"*

"I need a single! Do you have any singles?"

"Forget about it! Just go already!"

Doug pushed me through the locked turnstile, and I got a

nasty bruise on my thigh that didn't fade for weeks. He hurdled over the gate after me, and we made it into the last car just in time.

The warning bell chimed, but a man's hand kept the doors from closing. Two transit cops stepped aboard. The short one was unbelievably handsome.

"Step off of the train, please," he said.

Playing the innocent, I put on a confused look and aimed my index finger at my sternum.

"Yes, you!"

As we started to comply, the ugly one turned toward Doug. "Not you, sir. You're fine." (The deference to his height again.)

Doug looked at me sheepishly. He shrugged and pushed out his lower lip as I was handcuffed and read my rights. The train doors shut, and I saw him shaking his head and chuckling to himself as the PATH chugged off to New Jersey.

The short cop frisked me way too quickly while the ugly one searched my Danish book bag. Luckily we'd finished all the pot, and there was only a telltale bag of half-eaten sour cream potato chips. Then, instead of escorting me up to the street, the cops led me to the far end of the platform. There I was made to squat behind a pillar as they tried to catch other ne'er-do-wells attempting to steal a ride. The next guy caught was a junkie, and even though I was still high, I felt superior and thought, "Great! I'm going to spend the entire night with a bunch of whores and drug addicts." I was relieved when the next thief nabbed was dressed in khakis and a blazer.

A muffled announcement came through the PA speaker sounding like an adult in a Charlie Brown cartoon. I assumed it wasn't good news. It was not. We waited over twenty minutes for another train, the three of us handcuffed together—Wilson (the khaki guy) and me on the ends, and Crack Man in the center. Crack Man started yelling incoherently and the ugly cop warned him to be quiet, but he wouldn't calm down.

"Fuckin' cocksuckas won't gimme no dolla! Spend my check on her fat ass? Her momma shouda smacked her harda!"

"Hey buddy, calm it down!"

"Fuckin' mothafucka's playin' me! Ain't my joonya!"

"I told you to shut up!"

"Mothafucka! Gimme my rock!"

"Shut your mouth or I'll shut it for ya!"

Bullying his prisoner, he looked even uglier—but kind of sexy too.

I wasn't sure if the cops' limited patience was because they'd pulled such a stupid assignment, or because Crack Man was turning an easy job into a pain in the ass. Either way, I was amused. At the cop's threat, Crack Man fell silent and stared vacantly at the ceiling for a few minutes. But when the ugly cop turned to answer a call on his radio, he started screaming again. *"I gotta piss! I gotta piss!"*

And somehow, even though Wilson and I were handcuffed to him, he managed to open his fly and proceeded to hose down the platform. I got a terrifying vision of ten thousand volts from the third rail zipping up his stream, into his body, and through the metal handcuffs, frying all three of us.

Too bad Doug wasn't there to get peed on and electrocuted.

The cops were furious. They separated us from Crack Man, and Wilson and I began the bonding that grew into a bona fide friendship when we spent sixty hours together scrubbing train cars as part of our community service.

Eventually more trains arrived and more folks were apprehended. Some were homeless or on drugs, but far more were reputable looking—college types, women in cocktail dresses or with shopping bags, businessmen, and even an elderly lady with a Pomeranian. We were cuffed together like a chain gang and escorted out of the station. To the onlookers on the platform, I tried to convey a sense of amusement about the situation—but would have given my right arm (and the twenty people attached to it) for one of those digitized gray circles that block out the identity of suspects on the evening news.

I pictured Doug at home, eating more than his half of the ice cream while he watched the entire nightmare unfold on CNN.

In the police station downtown, Wilson and I were locked in a small cell with the other male fare jumpers—the women and the Pomeranian were taken elsewhere. We were fingerprinted and photographed. Looking back, I can't help wondering whether I'd find myself surprisingly attractive in my mug shot too. We waited ten hours while the police compared our names to lists of outstanding warrants. There were seventeen of us, two chairs, and a toilet. I spent the entire night praying I wouldn't need to move my bowels.

I thought of Doug on the sofa curled up with Greta, our cat, telling her in baby talk what a little money pit she was.

Once the warrant search was done, we got our court appearance tickets and were released. Wilson and I took the train to New Jersey together and I got home at one in the afternoon. I found Doug lying on the couch, eating Hydrox, with Greta asleep on his chest. I was disgusted.

"Comfortable?"

He jumped up. "Where have you been? I've been worried sick!"

I could tell from the porn video playing on the TV that it was true.

"You're an asshole! I can't believe you just left me there!"

Doug maintained his innocence, saying the doors closed too quickly for him to react. For a moment, I considered that maybe the doors did close too quickly, and that perhaps he did think of me while lying on the couch. After all, the video did have a jailhouse theme—but I knew our relationship was over.

I didn't leave right away—I couldn't. I had to find someplace to go before I could triumphantly march out the door. Defiantly leaving him to go and stay with my parents seemed ridiculous. It took me more than a week to find something affordable and vermin free, but I finally moved in with an anal-retentive guy named Martin who insisted I sterilize the bar soap after every use.

A few days before I moved out, Doug pulled a stunt that could easily have been the last straw—if the PATH incident hadn't already left the camel a quadriplegic.

In the spirit of too little too late, the Cheapskate attempted to make amends. He spent a couple of hours searching through *The Frugal Gourmet,* looking for a recipe that didn't require more than the lonely wok and spatula we used for all our culinary efforts. He set the table with the English bone china he'd taken from his mother's and left an extravagantly wrapped present on my chair. It was over a month before my birthday, but Doug, hoping the display would reverse my decision, insisted we celebrate before I left. With the end of my ordeal in sight, I decided to let go of my anger and enjoy the dinner.

The meal was certainly memorable. Doug had decided on a Gouda, leek, and tuna quiche as the least labor-intensive project. Since attempting to bake in a wok seemed unwise, he further scaled down the time involved by purchasing a ready-made piecrust. The first mouthful of cheese, fish, and graham cracker was unbelievably revolting.

Doug quickly countered the failed entrée with red wine from a gallon jug and then insisted that I open my gift. The small box was expertly wrapped in a Prussian-blue jacquard paper and topped with a gold ribbon. I recognized both from Christmas presents my mother had given him.

I ripped the paper aggressively, and deliberately crumpled it up so that Doug couldn't reuse it another time. Inside the package was a beautiful ostrich-leather box from an upscale specialty shop on East Eighty-third. Immediately I thought, "There's no way that the Doug I know would ever have purchased such a luxury item."

The gift's extravagance was only matched by its thoughtlessness. I was in need of clothing, art supplies, and a new stereo. I was behind on the vet bills and my student loans. My left running shoe was repaired with blue duct tape, and I had to pick dead leaves and cigarette butts off the gummy sole after every mile. Unless it could double as a sneaker, my need for a leather box, no matter how expertly crafted, was nil. But I thanked him politely; given my imminent departure, any other response seemed pointless.

I contemplated pulling a Doug and returning the box, but it seemed like sinking to his level. Just out of curiosity I checked out the store the next day when I was on the Upper East Side to pick up Regina, my other cat, at the vet's. He'd been holding her ashes hostage for two months until his bill was paid off. I laughed out loud when the condescending saleswoman removed the box from the glass case and told me that the price was three hundred and twenty-nine dollars.

The total absurdity of the situation coupled with my impending freedom made me light-headed, and I sang "Getting to Know You" from *The King and I* as I sprinkled Regina over a tree pit filled with marigolds on Lexington Avenue. I headed home thinking how amazingly happy I was to be moving on.

When I got home, Doug, who'd apparently decided to finally put the camel out of its misery, presented me with an envelope.

"What's this?"

"The bill for the car inspection."

Doug wouldn't allow me to drive his car, which was fine. I never wanted to find myself trying to explain what I was doing in possession of a stolen vehicle.

"What am I supposed to do with it?" I asked.

"I'm just showing it to you since you made such a big deal about the utilities."

"But why?"

"So you can see that I'm only charging you half."

"You're charging me half?"

"It seems fair."

"Whattaya mean fair? It's your car!"

"Well, you ride in it too."

A *very* ugly scene ensued, in which I threw every single piece of ammunition I had at him—including my suspicions about the ostrich box—and the box itself.

"Ed, be careful, that's expensive."

"How do you know?"

"Whatdya mean?"

"I mean, where'd you get it?"

"I bought it."

"You bought it?"

"Yes."

"You, Mr. Penny-Pincher, bought me a totally frivolous item from an obscenely overpriced store? Come on . . . Where'd you get it? Was it a gift? Did you find it? Did you steal it?"

"Don't accuse me."

"Okay, sorry! Just tell me how much it cost and I'll believe you."

"I'm not telling you the price of your gift."

"Why? Don't you know how much you paid for it?"

"Of course I do. But why do you need to know?"

I cannot believe I'm having this conversation with an adult. *"Doug, I already know. I went to the store and priced it!"*

"You did what?"

"I priced it. So just tell me what you paid, and I'll drop the whole matter."

There was a vibrating silence as Doug found himself cornered. "All right, look, does it really matter where it came from?"

"Yeah—it does."

It turned out that where it came from was the Infanta's desk. She'd received it as a thank-you gift for a column she'd written about the first company to bring fur jeans to market. Doug felt entitled to the box because he'd researched some sales figures for the article. He swiped it from her desk one Friday when she left early to meet Jaymze for a Lifespring seminar.

It wasn't the last time Doug swiped the box. He slipped it out of one of my cartons when I was moving out. Since I kept procrastinating about unpacking after I got to Martin's, I didn't even know it was missing. Months later, when Doug and I were in our friendship stage, I went to lunch at his apartment. I immediately noticed the box on Aunt Stella's table next to the copy of *Great Expectations* that Doug had never opened— even though I'd given it to him after he'd gotten embarrassed at a party where he was the only one who'd never read it.

"You stole my box, Doug?"

"It's not your box."

"What do you mean it's not my box? You gave it to me."

"You said you didn't want it."

I could tell we were headed for a big blowup but was too tired to pursue it.

"Whatever."

When Doug went into the bathroom with a copy of *People* under his arm, I was tempted to steal the box back. I pictured a tradition where the two of us used increasingly elaborate methods to snatch or protect it from each other—scams, con men, alarms, motion sensors, booby traps, firearms, tear gas.

A lifelong game of that sort would be entertaining with a close friend; we'd end up in our eighties with great stories to share at the assisted living facility. But with Doug the whole thing was too real, too painful, too upsetting. Instead of taking the box, I moistened the velvet lining with runoff from the shrimp salad we had for lunch.

He'll never get the smell out.

*   *   *

After fifteen years of anger, the dinner was more pleasant than expected. Doug looked fine—his eyelift was only slightly obvious—but he seemed less buffed and shorter than I'd remembered. Maybe he was shrinking. Or maybe my emotional growth had put him into perspective.

I'd made up my mind before I arrived to select the most expensive thing on the menu. As the waiter took our order, I watched Doug's eyes for any sign of distress. I wondered if he'd changed. Maybe I'd hoped he'd be miserable, that after years of financial and emotional stinginess, he'd reaped what he'd sown. But when I sat across from him and listened to his account of the intervening years, I heard a calm sadness in his voice that moved me. Isolation is the greatest human fear, and it's not hard to feel compassion—even for an asshole—if he's lonely. I asked about the Infanta, and he told me they'd had a falling-out. When he said that he hadn't had a boyfriend since Ivan and was resigned to a single life, I felt detached from the derision I'd cherished, and a little guilty about the hundreds of jokes and stories I'd repeated about him.

Looking back, I did walk away from Doug with a few improvements. I owe my endurance and big quads to him; I get a lot of compliments on my legs. My stand-up career has been a success in large part because of the material his behavior's provided me with—like his refusal to remove his retainer during oral sex (it was like fucking a mousetrap). Finally, I'm so conscious about not being anything like Doug that I'm always quick to pick up the check and am an extremely generous tipper. I also go way overboard with birthday, Christmas, and Chanukah presents. Sure my credit cards are always maxed out, and I'm usually late with the rent, but while carrying unnecessary debt is overwhelming at times, it's not nearly as upsetting to me as being labeled a cheapskate would be.

I purposely didn't ask for a doggy bag when the waiter was clearing away the uneaten three-quarters of my steak-and-lobster dinner. I checked Doug's face again to see if he was appalled by such a display of waste, but he only winked as he leaned down and reached into his briefcase. The package he pulled out was wrapped in brown shopping-bag paper—a choice I knew he was responsible for.

"I brought you something," he said. "I've wanted to give it to you for a while."

I carefully undid the paper and folded it before I gave it back to him. I took the lid off. Nestled inside was the ostrich-leather box. I enthusiastically exclaimed, "Gee! Thanks!" Meanwhile, in my mind I sighed dismissively, "Gee, thanks."

I picked up the box and opened it, expecting to be assaulted by the stink of fossilized shrimp, but it had a faint aroma of cinnamon. I couldn't hide the expression of surprise on my face when I looked up.

"Wow! How'd you get the smell out?"

"I tried everything, but it just got worse. I had to keep the cover on it all the time."

"What finally worked?"

"Turn it over."

There on the underside was the price tag. In the gift box was the receipt. I noticed Doug had charged the purchase, but stopped myself from guessing how much credit he might still have on account from his days at *FFM*.

"Thanks, Doug."

"I'm glad you agreed to meet me."

"Me too."

I meant it.

We hugged good-bye in front of the restaurant, and then I watched his long, effortless strides carry him across the intersection and down into the PATH station. Although the incident was surprisingly sweet, I still questioned whether he'd really changed—whether people really can. My skepticism made me sad that I was no longer that hopeful boy who'd tried to remain friends.

In my weekly session, I filled Dr. Ben in on the evening. Now, Dr. Ben pretends he has fantastic recall but once, in Starbucks, about fifteen minutes before my appointment, I caught him taking a refresher look at my file. Since the whole Doug chapter happened so long ago, it was amusing to stump him on the facts. He had to ask a lot of questions to jog his memory.

I've been seeing Dr. Ben for almost fifteen years. Most people think that after that long in therapy you should either be cured—or looking for another shrink. But I keep my standing appointment to give structure to my week, and I like knowing Dr. Ben's there when crises erupt from time to time. Over the years we've become more like friends. If there's nothing catastrophic in my life we just talk about politics, or his daughter Madelyn—whom I've never met but have seen grow up in the pictures on his desk. Sometimes I pick up coffee and corn muffins on my way over to his office. I love that he enjoys our sessions and that he likes the filthiest jokes.

"Eddie, how have you been feeling since the dinner?"

"I have to say that I feel really calm—like I've finally emerged from the shadow of the experience in a clear, powerful, adult way."

"It's about time. You've been processing that crap since we first started working together."

"That's a lot of couch time."

"It is."

It was indeed a lot of couch time. Walking home I did the math—once a week for fifteen years, at an average of seventy-five dollars a session, comes to almost sixty grand.

The Cheapskate really should pay half.

Mensch-Hunt

Pretty sure that I won't regret trying something new, and satisfied that at least I'm putting my theater degree to use, I show up dressed in a painter's cap and coveralls. William answers the door in a towel. He's delicious.

"Hey, howya doin'?"

"I'm doin' good. How you doin'?"

A predictable scene ensues. The whole thing seems ridiculous to me, but I go along with it anyway.

William's recently gotten divorced after sixteen years of marriage to the girl he took to the prom at Andover. Due to the sky-high price of New York real estate, he's still living with his ex-wife until they finish the renovations they've started and can sell their swanky Upper East Side condo. He's confided to me, via instant message, his fantasies of having sex with the workmen while his wife's out, and has asked if I'm up for some role-play.

I follow William into the living room, the two of us butching it up, ad-libbing in cartoonish Jersey accents. I figure I'll script things more elaborately if there's a repeat performance. After he points out a few cracks in the plaster, I take measurements, scribble down some figures, and come up with an estimate—which he balks at.

"Hey, man, I don't have dat kinda dough. Ain't dere some way to getcha to come down on da price?"

I swirl my paintbrush across his chest. "I think maybe we could work somethin' out."

After spreading out the drop cloth that William insists we lay down to protect his antique Tibetan carpet, we continue the improv. While manhandling him on the floor, I periodically stop and, pretending to hear a noise, nervously whisper, "I think your wife's home!" The sense of danger heightens the intensity and drives us deeper into the scene; I completely abandon any inhibitions I had when I showed up at William's door. But although the sex is phenomenal, I prevent myself from fully enjoying the encounter because I'm already anticipating the next one. After our romp, we cuddle for a bit and eventually start talking out of character.

"Thanks for inviting me over, William. That was really a lot of fun."

"Sure."

"You up for another round?"

He looks at his watch. "I can't, you have to go. Someone's coming in ten minutes to give me another estimate. I'll call you."

Despite the abrupt ending and my struggle to stay in the moment, I'm ecstatic that my initial hookup on Beef4Beef.com has been so much fun; I feel like I've hit the jackpot my first time playing the slots. On my way to the subway I replay things over and over in my head.

Up until this point I've primarily used my computer for work. As far as recreation goes, I mostly use it to alleviate boredom by looking up trivia. I'm a huge nerd. Finding the answers to questions such as How many teeth does an aardvark have? (twenty) or What's the major export of Zanzibar? (cloves) is fun for me—and a big help when watching *Jeopardy*. Unfortunately, unless you have the hots for Alex Trebec, you'll never find anybody who cares who invented the spinning jenny—or who wants to get sweaty with someone who does.

I've heard Beef4Beef.com mentioned for years. I travel all over the country, and its purple pages are ubiquitous. Every gay guy I know has either scrolled through the profiles or placed his own. If you're queer and don't know about Beef4Beef, you're probably still adjusting the rabbit ears on your TV and dialing your phone with an actual dial.

The Web site has thousands of members in every major metropolis. In my Manhattan ZIP code alone, there are over a hundred pages of men online at any given time—and that's only a fraction of those who have profiles. Beef4Beef's the site that never sleeps. With a few clicks you can make reservations for a lunchtime sex snack or order in to satisfy a four a.m. craving. And B4B isn't limited to big cities like New York, Boston, or LA. There are guys in Topkok, Alaska, manhunting until the wee hours of the morning. Of course, there are only three of them and they've all slept with each other—or aren't speaking to each other—or both. But even there, among the glaciers and the moose, guys are scrolling and trolling, transfixed by the hypnotic violet screen, desperately hoping to find some fresh meat.

In the six years since Jeffrey and I broke up, I've dated a few men, including a Wall Street wunderkind who earned in a month what I've earned since college, a handsome TV reporter who looked even better offscreen, and a blue-eyed veterinarian who broke my heart so completely that I wished he had just put me to sleep.

Sore from the injury inflicted by Chris, the vet, I'm looking for a way to accelerate the healing process. Beef4Beef seems ideal. As a gay Jew I select a two-stage approach: first, soothing my open wound with kvetching, the traditional cure-all of my ancestors, and second, sewing it up by sowing some wild oats, the course of treatment preferred by my peers. In addition to the medicinal (i.e., anesthetic) properties of no-strings sex, having a B4B membership lets me see when Chris is online looking for trouble. That way I can feel like I'm still a part of his world and hold on to being in love in some small way. How pathetic.

Even more pathetic is that I'm taking my cue about cruising the World Wide Web from my mother, who's been chatting with mature gentlemen on JewHunt.net for over two years. My dad passed away almost ten years ago, and apparently her weekly canasta game was no longer filling the void.

When I tell my pal Gary that my mom's Jew hunting, he tries to get me to look up her profile. I never do. Discovering that she has some unorthodox fetish is something I probably wouldn't handle too well. Although I suspect her screen name's something innocuous like MyKidsDontCall247, I'd be genuinely horrified to find out that it's LoxSucker69 and that she's seeking partners for a mahjong à trois. All I know—because she told me—is though she's seventy-three, she's sixty-nine on JewHunt.

"Mom, why are you lying about your age? You look terrific."

"The odds are against me."

"Then why not cast a wider net and join MENthuselah.com or MyWifesinaComa.net? Aren't you already fishing in a limited pool? Why JewHunt?"

"It's easier with a Jew."

"Don't you read *Cosmo*? When you're a single woman in your forties, the chances of finding a guy are bad. At your age, they're horrendous."

"You think I don't know it?"

"So why limit yourself to Jews? You're not religious; you know all the words to 'Away in a Manger'! Besides, you're seventy-three. Are you really so concerned about what religion not to raise the kids in?"

"Trust me, it's just easier."

Who knows? Maybe it is easier. I've never dated another member of the tribe. It's not that I've been avoiding it; it's just never happened. I don't have an issue with the idea, unlike my brother who for years made no secret of his contempt for loud Jewish girls from New York and then moved all the way to Chicago to marry Kimberly Steinberg from Paramus, New Jersey. Unlike some of my friends who won't date outside their religion, their age group, or the Ivy League, my only steadfast rule is that I won't date outside my gender.

Besides, while I identify as a Jew culturally, I don't subscribe to the faith. I've got better things to do than trying to gain acceptance from a religion that doesn't really approve of me. I'm not particularly "spiritual" either; I'm not even sure what that overused word means. Apparently it's got something to do with honoring trees, playing Peruvian panpipes, and assigning excessive profundity to tattoos written in Asian characters. Also, a lot of "spiritual" folks like to point to coincidences to prove the existence of a higher power.

Though I think that coincidences are arbitrary and not the work of some guiding force we're unable to detect with our five senses, I think it's important to be grateful for the opportunities that chance bestows—and to take advantage of them. When the publisher of *Invert* sees my stand-up act and asks me to be the magazine's eligible bachelor for July '06, I agree. Though it seems kind of cheesy, it also seems like a great way to promote my August gig in Provincetown. *Invert* sends a photographer to my apartment, and although he gets me to take off my shirt (and after the shoot, my pants), I have him skillfully crop the picture to exclude my belly, and angle the camera to minimize my bald spot. The shot's flattering enough to make me feel comfortable posting it on Beef4Beef.

SCREEN NAME: **VerbalGuy**
AGE: **41**
HEIGHT: **5'11"**
WEIGHT: **200 lbs.**
HAIR / EYES: **Brown/Brown**
HIV STATUS: **Negative**

Religious, spiritual, or whatever, I'm opposed to anything that narrows down my dating options any further than absolutely necessary; after all, once I rule out everyone I simply can't stand, I'm working from a very short list. So knowing that people in general, and horny guys on the Internet in particular, are not up for reading anything longer than the average penis (although on Beef4Beef average appears to be longer than *War and Peace),* I compose a simple line for my profile that not only doesn't limit the possibilities, but also gives off an air of adventurousness:

Open to any role, position, toy, location, equipment, costume, or fantasy.

I feel good about my post. Despite the strategic cropping, my picture looks like me. My screen name, VerbalGuy, couldn't be more apt; I love to talk—especially in bed. I'm excellent at it; I don't just monotonously bark out orders like some bored porn actor watching the clock. I spin lurid tales full of suspense and conflict. I weave in subplots, flesh out supporting characters, insert unexpected twists, and always end with a killer climax. I love it even more if the guy I'm with talks back—unless of course he uses poor grammar.

Unlike my mom, I'm up-front about my age. Lying about it would be disrespectful to the memory of all the men I knew who never made it to forty. I also think it's important for younger gay guys to see that it's okay to get older. Like a lot of men my age, I'm concerned with the physical changes I'm experiencing and at the same time I'm becoming more accepting of my body. I'm ready to explore things I haven't been brave enough to investigate before. To paraphrase (because I really didn't pay attention in Hebrew school and can't accurately quote) the great Rabbi Hillel, "After all, if not now, when?"

Once I've uploaded my photo and typed in my stats, text, and MasterCard number, I wait for the ding of approval, and I'm off. I'm the new guy in Cybertown, and the "locals," tired of surfing the same old profiles, are quick to roll out the welcome wagon. After opening a dozen or so messages, it becomes crystal clear that though there are boxes to check for dating and friendship, on Beef4Beef.com nobody really cares about much more than finding out if your sexual proclivities match theirs.

In addition to being the leading purveyor of homosex on the World Wide Web with a surfeit of available man-flesh, Beef4Beef sells erotic paraphernalia of every kind—toys, leather, lubricants, etc. The site also links to other sites selling adult DVDs and books, offers helpful hints on sexual safety and postcoital etiquette, and lists warnings about illegal behavior and substances. Everything you could possibly need for any sexual situation is available through its iconic purple pages; it's the one-stop shop for your next tryst or orgy. In addition, anything that isn't specifically advertised can easily be found by reading between the lines—steroids, crystal meth, unprotected sex, low self-esteem.

Luckily, I quickly realize that the anonymity possible on B4B creates an environment that allows men to behave in a variety of dangerous ways. After declining invitations from several members who have no interest in using condoms, I chat for a while with a striking Venezuelan guy whose profile reads, "I'll

take your breath away," only to discover that he's looking for
someone into erotic asphyxiation and thinks "safe words are
for sissies." In order to nip disaster in the bud, I make a simple
modification to my profile.

**Open to any role, position, toy, location, equipment,
costume, or fantasy as long as it's SAFE.**

With my boundaries clarified, I'm able to relax and enjoy the
attention I'm getting.

Before I joined B4B I was a little concerned about competing with guys in their twenties and thirties. My age, it turns out,
is more of an asset than an issue—especially with men twenty
years younger. I get hit on by a lot of barely legal guys wanting
me to be their daddy—until they realize I'm one of those dead-
beat dads who couldn't even afford to send them to a community college. When I politely tell one earnest "proof of age on
file" that I'm looking for someone closer to my own age, he,
obviously not used to rejection, gets nasty:

*"Fuck you, asshole! And who do you think you're fooling with that
crop job? This is Beef4Beef, not Beef4Pork!"*

His remark hurts, but I zing him right back:

"It's not Beef4Chicken either, junior—go do your homework!"

My role-playing encounter with William—despite the abrupt
ending—is a lot of fun. It's also fresh and makes me realize
there's a lot to be learned on B4B. I find myself not only re-
sponding to the guys I find attractive, but also seeking out
those I suspect could teach me a thing or two. I get quite an education on shrimping, docking, and a host of other practices
favored by men who spend long periods at sea.

My "If not now, when?" attitude continues, and I agree to
meet a sinewy blond with light eyes at his midtown hotel.
Tucker, an upstate dairy farmer and a deacon at his Presbyterian church, wants to make me his slave boy. While at forty-one

I'm flattered that anyone still thinks of me as a boy, as a Jew the slave thing conjures up unsettling images of hauling heavy stones up the side of a pyramid or being forced to polish shell casings so the Nazis can win the war. I reason, however, that like my adventure with William, it's possible this could be more fun than I expect.

The session starts off pretty tame, but escalates in weirdness as Tucker removes piece after piece of equipment from an old leather valise. I play along for an hour or so as he shackles, ties, chains, clamps, cuffs, gags, and blindfolds me. While I find the experience interesting in a freshmen-sociology-class-studying-the-bizarre-practices-of-indigenous-peoples kind of way, the scene does very little to fulfill me and I have a hard time feigning excitement. My mind starts to wander. Annoyed, Tucker brings me back to the present by splashing hot wax on my chest. He certainly gets my attention but isn't prepared for the severe case of the giggles I get when I realize he's using a cucumber-and-melon scented candle.

Tucker's not amused. He pulls a steel contraption out of the valise, throws it at me, and yells, "Stop laughing and put this on."

"What's it for?"

"Just do as you're told."

I snap myself into the iron chastity device and Tucker locks it with a little key, which he then slips into the pocket of his leather pants. The heavy contraption's more than a little uncomfortable; it feels like I'm picking up a barbell with my scrotum. Although it's designed to allow urination, rows of tiny spikes lining the inside prevent me from getting an erection—or at least enjoying one. After two more minutes of Tucker touching me, I've had enough.

"This thing hurts."

"You'll get used to it in a day or two."

"What?"

"I want you to wear it while I'm away."

"Oh, no! Absolutely not!"

"It's only for a month or so. I have to make sure you behave."

"You're crazy, give me the key."

"I'll unlock you when I get back; if you want out sooner, you'll have to earn it."

Tucker dangles the key above my head and instructs me on how I might regain my freedom: He'll hide the key in the country, and if I'm very obedient, I'll be given hints as to its location. At first I think that by "in the country" he means for me to come to his place upstate and hunt for the key in his hayloft or garden. I'm flabbergasted to learn that he's referring to the continental United States. The lunatic expects me to travel around the lower forty-eight (by Greyhound, no less) and perform "services" for his Internet buddies in order to accumulate clues. If I'm a clever boy and can decipher his rebuses and cryptic poems, I'll be given a global positioning device to aid me in my search. Idiotically, Tucker won't even guarantee that he'll hide the key somewhere fun like Palm Springs or Miami, and I'm incredulous that he actually thinks I might sit quietly on a motor coach to Altoona while my manhood's ripped to shreds by the barbed doohickey.

"Tucker, I—"

He corrects me. "Sir."

I ignore him. "Tucker, this isn't gonna work for me. I'm far too sensitive down there. I still have phantom pains in my missing foreskin. Give me the key."

"I give the orders here."

"Listen, this mantrap looks expensive. You can unlock me right now and get it back in one piece, or I can call the police and have them mangle it with the Jaws of Life."

He throws the key at me. "Screw it—you're not worth the hassle!"

Later, at home with my perforated dick lubed up with

Neosporin, I sit down at my laptop and amend my profile again.

Open to any role, position, toy, location, equipment, costume, or fantasy as long as it's safe AND PAINLESS.

Beef4Beef's rife with fraud; there's an awful lot of tofu posing as chateaubriand. My mom knocking a few years off her age hardly seems dishonest compared to the blatant misrepresentations that are sometimes revealed when I meet other B4Bers in person. Over the next few weeks I come face to face with sixty-year-olds with screen names like NaughtyBoi and CollegeJock, as well as three-hundred-pound mesomorphs, and even one Asian guy who's checked the Caucasian box. Their deceit's unnecessary and unfortunate, because while I like guys of all ages, sizes, and colors, I'm completely intolerant of old, fat, yellow-bellied liars. When I do meet someone who lives up to his profile, I feel as if I've beaten the odds at the MGM Grand.

I realize that it's partly my fault. I'm an idiot for not insisting on seeing a photo before I venture out to meet someone I've chatted with online. My problem's that if a guy has a way with language, I get lured in by the image I've assigned him in my brain. Also, at first it doesn't occur to me to ask for a picture since Chris is extremely sexy and doesn't have one on his profile. He's afraid it'll harm his business. Apparently if erotic photos of him ever find their way into general circulation, some clients might be reluctant to let him take their shih tzu's temperature.

I come to learn that generally if someone doesn't have a snapshot, it's a good bet he was born before the advent of photography, so I make a steadfast resolution not to meet anyone else whose profile lacks an image. Of course, that's no guarantee that I'll get what I expect; in the age of Photoshop and airbrushing, the deception on B4B isn't limited to the written word. After a few disastrous meetings with men who look nothing like their pics, I develop a critical eye and learn to check what's in the background very carefully. A picture's worth a thousand words and can reveal a thousand truths if you know how to read it. If a guy has a Mondale bumper sticker on his car or a jar of Tang on his kitchen counter, move on. If the furniture's from the seventies, the owner's in his seventies. I don't really understand why someone would bother to post a picture that's twenty years old; I guess some guys never tire of hearing how hot they were in 1987.

After a while, I also learn not to trust anyone who doesn't have his head and his body in the same picture. Now, for some men I guess that's appropriate and necessary. Your ninth-grade math teacher may be open about his sexual orientation, but he doesn't want identifiable pictures of him with his hypotenuse hanging out being text-messaged around the classroom. For a lot of guys on Beef4Beef, however, it's the old bait and switch. They show their face in one photo but "borrow" a pic of someone else's body—as if you're not going to notice that they've gone from George Clooney to Rosemary Clooney in the time it took them to log off and show up at your door. It's important to see the whole package at once; what could be worse than finding yourself intrigued by someone's ass only to discover that you found anything appealing about Richard Simmons?

Although the dishonesty on B4B makes me mental, I play along and keep clicking my mouse compulsively, expecting every click to deliver the next big payout. Of course there will be umpteen losers before another lucky seven (or eight and a half) comes up. But I put up with it and let Beef4Beef both exploit, and erode, my optimism.

At least I am glad to learn from my mom's experiences—that as people age, they're less likely to put up with bullshit. Over a hand of canasta, I hear her gabbing away with Jen, Elaine, and Rita like the *Sex and the City* girls, comparing notes about the aged kosher beef they've been chatting with. I listen with pride as my mom tells her friends how she gave the heave-ho to a fossil named Marv whom she refers to as "Mr. Big." After leading my mom on for over a year, Marv confessed to seeing another widow behind her back and then tried to snake his way out with the old, "I can't make a decision; I don't know what I want" line. For God's sake! If you're seventy-five, have arthritis, gout, cataracts, and your next tumble in the sheets could be on your deathbed, then grow up and make a commitment.

After her girlfriends head home, I help my mom fold up the card table.

"I'm sorry about Marv."

"He's a schmuck. I'm not playing second fiddle to anyone."

"Good for you."

"At least I don't have to get tested."

The statement disarms me. "Why not?"

"Marv couldn't perform."

"I thought he was 'Mr. Big'?"

"He has an enlarged prostate."

"Ah."

By far, the most upsetting thing about Beef4Beef is that some guys are dishonest about having HIV. I know that everyone should be practicing safer sex, and I'm sure it can be difficult to go public with your diagnosis, but I think that lying to your partners is unconscionable. In this particular area we *are* our brothers' keepers. B4B even makes it easy to avoid lying about your status. In addition to selecting "Negative" or "Positive" from the drop-down menu in your profile's HIV status box, you can also select "Don't Know," "Ask Me," or simply leave it blank. It's particularly upsetting when, scrolling through the site, I come across a picture of Doug, the cheapskate I dated years ago. According to his profile, he's not only somehow gone from being seven years my senior to being eight years my junior, but has miraculously been cured of the virus he acquired after we broke up. When I send him a message calling him on it, he writes back, "Eddie, that's the allure of this site—you can pretend to be anything you want to be!"

Yeah, I guess on Beef4Beef it's pretty hard for some people to resist masquerading as decent human beings.

Although I never liked Marv, I did like that dating someone steadily kept my mom from playing the odds online. She loves to gamble; every time I turn around she's in Atlantic City squandering my meager inheritance. I hate to think of her back on JewHunt, instant-messaging into the wee hours with some relic into erotic asphyxiation who's begging her to yank the oxygen tubes out of his nose. I'm relieved when, not too long after she sends Mr. Big packing, she hooks up with Irv, a seventy-three-year-old yeshiva boy and former Eagle Scout.

While I appreciate that my mother and I are apparently both suckers for a man in uniform, and I wish her the best of luck with Scoutmaster Irv, I don't really want to know the details of their relationship—some images are better left unprocessed. I do wonder, however, if the profile that helped her land him reads anything like mine. I have no idea. (I still can't bring myself to look.)

In some ways she's very traditional; her premarital life pre-dated the sexual revolution. She was college age in the early fifties, between the generation of girls who loosened their morals for youths marching to war and the generation of girls who loosened their morals for youths marching for peace. When I was twelve, she and my dad avoided talking to me about sex directly, and instead discreetly left a picture book on my bed about a sperm with a top hat who marries an ovum with a diamond ring. I still get hard thinking about it. A few years later when she found my stash of porn magazines while "tidying up" my room, she simply bundled them up with twine and left a note saying, "Please discard."

But after seventy-three—I mean sixty-nine—years maybe she

too is thinking, "If not now, when?" She's become pretty comfortable *talking* about sex. Having a gay son in the age of AIDS
has made it necessary. We don't exactly sit around comparing
notes, and there's definitely stuff I omit (although I'm sure I
could teach her a few things that would give her a leg up on the
competition—especially among the Jewish girls), but I'm glad I
don't have to censor everything. Whenever she can, she comes
to see my act, which though certainly not all blue, contains
some information I'm sure a mother could live without hearing
about.

While my mom's off earning merit badges and tying knots
with Irv, I continue pressing my luck on Beef4Beef. My revised
profile's working fairly well at keeping the freakazoids at bay,
and I seem to be attracting some men with promise.

When Andrew, with his quarterback good looks, greets me at
the door of his Gramercy Park townhouse, I feel as if I've won
the lottery. When he ushers me into his dining room, I sense
that I may have very well won the grand prize. There on the
Hepplewhite table is a spread fit for a king. For me, nothin' says
lovin' like somethin' from the oven—the stove, the fridge, or
the waffle iron—and the quickest way to my heart (and crotch)
is through my stomach.

Andrew not only insists that I sample everything, but is
adamant that I clean my plate—not a problem, it's all delicious.
Plus, I don't want to be rude; I eat until I'm stuffed. After my
third helping, I pat my lips with my napkin and push my chair
away from the table. "That was unbelievable!"

He's alarmed. *"You're finished?"*

"I am."

"You haven't tried the foie gras."

"I don't think I can eat another bite."

"I bet you can."

As he spreads some of the goose liver on a cracker, Andrew
leans in and whispers something filthy in my ear. The scratch of

his razor stubble and the warmth of his breath against my cheek send tingles to my groin, and I watch the pleasure on his face as he pops the morsel into my mouth.

"Isn't that amazing?" he asks.

"Mmm! Really good!"

"Have some more. There's nothing sexier than a guy with a healthy appetite."

He loads up another cracker and dangles it in front of me, but I push his hand away.

"Enough! I can't eat any more."

"Sure you can."

"No, I really can't—besides, there's something unsettling about being force-fed pâté."

"You're right. It's time for dessert anyway."

"I don't have any room."

He pats my belly. "Oh, there's always room for dessert."

He kisses me and runs his hand down to my crotch before exiting into the kitchen. At this point I'm thinking that if Andrew's a chubby chaser, why me? Why not skip all this work and just start with someone huskier? In any case, he's beautiful, and figuring "How much weight can I gain in one night anyway?" I sit there, stomach distended, with an erection that I can't even see due to the bloating.

Andrew returns from the kitchen, shirtless, with a red velvet cake in one hand and a Mississippi mud pie in the other. Now sex and dessert are my two favorite things. In theory at least, there's nothing hotter than a three-way with Ben and Jerry. I let Andrew feed me a sliver of the red velvet cake, but there's no way I can get myself to even look at the heavy pie. Trying to entice me, he swirls it under my nose. The über-chocolatey smell is too much, and I can feel the entire meal suddenly knocking at my esophagus. Andrew moves in for a kiss, but I turn my head away. "I'm sorry, but I don't feel quite right."

"Queasy?"

"Kind of."

"Perfect!"

"I beg your pardon?"

"Have you ever given someone a Roman shower?"

"Come again?"

Andrew confesses that he's into emetophilia—erotic vomiting—and asks me to follow him into the bathroom so he can lie down in the tub. I jump up abruptly, sending my chair skidding across the floor. *"I have to go."*

"Come on—you know it'll make you'll feel better. Your profile said you were open to anything safe and painless. I'll get you a long-handled spoon."

"*NO!* I'm sorry. Thank you!"

I fly out the door revolted—and a little guilty that he's gone to all that trouble just to have me eat and run. Out on the street my nausea subsides. As I wait for a cab on Irving Place, I can't help thinking how appalled my mom would be by Andrew's behavior, given all the starving children in India. I also think seriously of how we don't choose our preferences and of the rejection Andrew must endure whenever he lets his filthy little secret out of the pantry.

In the taxi I fish my BlackBerry out of my knapsack, connect to the Internet, and revise my ad yet again.

Open to any role, position, toy, location, equipment, costume, or fantasy as long as it's safe, painless, AND NOT TOO MESSY!

I know I should cancel my B4B membership, but I find myself powerless over the one-moused bandit.

Now, Beef4Beef may not always be safe, or painless, or not too messy, but it's almost always funny—at least in hindsight. The site's supplied me with top-shelf material for my stand-up act, and I've scored comic home runs retelling my adventures at cocktail parties and in my weekly sessions with my shrink, Dr. Ben.

By making sure not to take Beef4Beef too seriously, I'm again following my mom's example. I remember very clearly how good-natured she was after her first JewHunt date: coffee and bagels with an eighty-four-year-old haberdasher with a wooden leg. She laughed off the incident, telling her friend Rita, "I don't care so much about the disability, but if I'm going to date a man with one foot in the grave, I'd like him to have another foot." Her second date was even older. When I asked her how the evening went, she mockingly said, "He looks nothing like his daguerreotype, and he wouldn't stop ranting about the Kaiser."

The craziness on B4B demands a sense of humor. I don't know how people surf the site without one. Without laughter, how can you possibly get over the awkwardness of running into your best friend or your boss or your dentist (especially after learning things you don't want to know about a man who puts his hands in your mouth)? If you're able to see the ridiculousness on B4B, you can joke with the cousin who hits you up not realizing who you are and can good-naturedly tease that ninth-grade math teacher for using the screen name Cutieπ.

You'd think that since there are so many gay men who use their finely honed comic skills as social tools and defensive weapons, finding someone on Beef4Beef with a thick, meaty funny bone wouldn't be so difficult. After all, almost every profile that consists of more than a list of inches, pounds, and fetishes is pretty much the same:

"A sense of humor's the most important thing. I want a guy who can make me laugh."

Across the Internet words to this effect appear millions of times—enough to make you think that Jake Gyllenhaal and Brad Pitt are home alone on Saturday night desperately hoping someone will settle for them while Gilbert Gottfried's getting laid 24/7.

Part of the problem is that everyone in the purple haze not only wants a guy with a good sense of humor, but also wants a guy with "no emotional baggage," as if you could have one without other. Let's be clear: if a guy's witty, he's got a Samsonite filled with issues. And if he's a laugh riot, he's got a steamer trunk with decals of where he's been—depression, suicide, addiction. Humor doesn't just come with baggage; it's the matching cosmetics case that completes the set.

My last B4B gamble takes place on a long, lonely night after a casino gig on the outskirts of Albuquerque. My behavior seems appropriate given the obvious parallel to the senior citizens downstairs in the gaming parlor pressing their luck until dawn.

My prize, a tall corn-fed Nebraska boy named Tim with the screen name PumpNPop, tells me he loves that my profile's so open-minded. While we're making out, he whispers, "I have a little fetish that I wonder if you'd indulge me in."

"As long as it's safe, painless, and not too messy."

He pulls me in tight. "Put your hand in my pocket."

His jeans are snug and I'm only able to wriggle my hand partway in. His pocket's filled with condoms—a lot of them, more than I think I've ever used—but they're unwrapped. He looks at me mischievously. "Intrigued?"

"We can't use ones that have been opened. It's unsafe."

"Just pull some out."

I grasp a few between my index and middle fingers and withdraw my hand. He smirks at the puzzled expression on my face as I contemplate the assortment of candy-colored party balloons in my palm.

"What the . . . ?"

"You said you were open to new things. Blow one up."

I oblige.

"Do another."

I feel silly but do it. I have no idea where this is going and joke that he'll want me to twist the sausage-shaped balloons into some kind of animal. "If I fuck a rubber giraffe, do I have to wear protection?"

He looks at me blankly. "No, why?"

"Never mind."

I can't tell if he doesn't think my giraffe line's funny, or if he's too engrossed in his fetish to have heard it. I hope it's the latter. He holds out another balloon. "Here, do a round one."

I puff out my cheeks and inflate the lemon yellow balloon to dirigible size while Tim screams, "*bigger! Bigger! BIGGER!*" and pumps himself into a frenzy. Right when I think he's going to pop, he stops to help me blow up a few more and then starts conducting erotic experiments in static electricity. I find the scene hilarious. "I feel like I'm watching Mr. Wizard," I tell him. "Maybe next you could create a vacuum with a lit match and have your balls miraculously sucked into a milk bottle?"

"Why would I do that?"

"It's a joke."

"Oh."

The fact that Tim's so easy on the eyes would usually be enough for me to look past the weirdness and rise to the occasion. His inability to see the humor in his balloonacy, however, makes it impossible for me to get inflated. Though I have an intense fascination with carnival acts, my attraction to them is far from sexual, and witnessing Tim's sideshowish spectacle is about as arousing as watching the Human Blockhead hammer a nail into his face. I can't wait for the show to be over.

It isn't until the next day that it dawns on me what the appeal of the whole thing must be for Tim. I suspect the possibility that the balloon might burst at any moment heightens his pleasure in the same way that the risk of getting caught by his wife makes sex with a workman exciting for William. All in all, the balloon thing seems a perfectly harmless alternative, though I

do for a moment envision Tim getting arrested for indecent exposure while watching the Macy's parade. I'm sure he wouldn't
find that funny at all.

A few weeks after my hookup with Tim, I head out to Long
Island for dinner and a Blockbuster rental at my mom's. Irv is
there. It's weird seeing them flirt, and I don't want to stare—
partly because it might make them uncomfortable and partly
because I don't want to accidentally catch Irv getting some
over-the-sweater action. But I can't help stealing peeks at them.

I can see that Irv's an excellent communicator and quite
comfortable talking about how he's feeling (though he does
focus far too much on the state of his gastrointestinal tract). He
also gets that humor comes with baggage and understands that
you're very lucky to find someone whose luggage matches yours.
I like him. If he wasn't seventy-five, straight, and the guy I don't
want to imagine touching my mother, I'd probably agree to have
dinner with him.

After the movie, *Dolores Claiborne*, my mom walks Irv out to
his car. I hear them whispering before she laughs and kisses
him good night. It's sweet. My surprise at the pang of jealousy I
feel is nothing compared to my amazement at the thought that
accompanies it: I'm ready for a boyfriend.

I'm further thrown for a loop when, as I replay the scenes
with William, Tucker, Andrew, and Tim in my head, it occurs to
me that they're all WASPs.

When my mom returns she senses something's not quite
right.

"Ed, are you okay?"

"I don't believe it."

"What's wrong?"

"I think I need a Jew."

"It would make things easier."

Still in the Beef4Beef mind-set, my first impulse is to go online and do a Google search for "Hot Gay Jews," but the idea of finding myself addicted to BeefWithoutDairy.com worries me. Just so I won't give in to temptation, I start weaning myself off online cruising, and like a heroin addict switching to methadone, begin cultivating a dependence on Internet Scrabble. Anyway, I don't need a Web site to meet men. I'm a professional comedian. I have excellent social skills—or at least the appearance of them.

Prior to my attempt to get over Chris the vet (also a WASP), I'd never felt the need or desire to go online for sex or dating. My work as a comedian takes me all over the map, and I've always met men easily. On the gay cruises where I perform and in Provincetown where I do my act every summer, I encounter thousands of guys on vacation from every state in the nation. Plus, I live in New York City, where there are homosexuals everywhere. My neighborhood, Hell's Kitchen, couldn't be gayer. In addition to the parade of gym boys on Ninth Avenue and the transsexual hookers on Eleventh, there's a photographer on the fourth floor of my building who shoots gay porn, a therapist on the fifth floor who counsels gay couples, and Dungeon Master Dave in the apartment below mine who hosts S&M parties at a club in the Meatpacking District. My floor alone has seven queer men and one very bitter, frustrated woman.

As for finding a Jew? Easy. There's no need for me to go online to choose one of the Chosen People. I can cruise the Upper West Side, so full of Yids it's like shooting whitefish in a barrel, or I can drag my tuchus to the gay synagogue—Temple Beth Midler—where on Yom Kippur I can scope out the crowd and make a to-do list of things I'd like to atone for.

Having graced me with these bits of clarity, the god of arbitrary coincidence throws into my path a nice Jewish boy with a great laugh and the stocky body of a Polish dockworker. When the hottie tells me his name is Allen Ginsberg, I howl. He's sexy and funny and sweet, and to my delight demonstrates more than a little willingness to open up emotionally over a frozen Sara Lee layer cake. We hit it off at once. Unfortunately, on our second date the mensch breaks the bad news that his company's transferring him to Geneva. God! I feel like Moses, allowed to see the Promised Land but not permitted to set my foot—or any other body part—in it.

After Allen Ginsberg escapes to Switzerland, I'm slightly tempted to log on and go manhunting, but my Scrabble addiction's taken hold and Beef4Beef has lost its allure; now the length of a guy's words is what gets me hard.

I'm grateful that I got off Beef4Beef when I did. I see the effects prolonged exposure has on other guys. Some men become dependent, and even in the most favorable of circumstances, can't function socially without it. I've seen guys browsing the purple pages on gay cruises where there's literally a man (in a Speedo) every ten feet. If you're shelling out seventy-five cents a minute in the ship's overpriced Internet café to hook up with someone on the Lido deck, something's very, very wrong. The same's true for Provincetown. It's not uncommon to see men chatting with each other online across the tiny computer room at Cyber Cove day after day. I'm sure some of them never even make it to the beach and head home from their Cape Cod vacations as pale as ghosts. Friends tell me that in twelve-step meetings for sexual compulsives, it's forbidden to mention "The Purple Site" by name for fear that members will find it too triggering.

Looking back, I wish I'd had some online experience going into my relationship with Chris. I might have known what to expect. When we met, Chris was forty, hadn't had a boyfriend since college, and had had a Beef membership since the site first went online. I would have realized that in some ways I couldn't compete with the men on the purple site. The men you see on Beef4Beef are fantasies—they can be anything you want them to be. And if you meet them, one of two things happens: either the encounter lives up to your expectations or it doesn't. If it does, you fuck the guy, then he leaves, fantasy intact. If it doesn't, you fuck the guy, he leaves, and you forget about it. After twenty years, perhaps Chris didn't know what to do with somebody who fucked and stayed. After all, you never see a guy from Beef4Beef the next day, screaming at his mother on the phone or crying at an episode of *Little House on the Prairie*. The problem with B4B—and the reason for its success—is that the real-life payoff is never as good as the promise of the next click. Beef4Beef exploits the fact that we're all better in theory.

I'll admit that when I look at my mom or think of my own future, I do find some comfort in knowing that the Internet will be there to assist me in a mensch-hunt if I should need it. But until I'm single *and* housebound, I don't foresee that happening. Even then, despite the example of my mom's success, will I, in my dotage, really have the patience to deal with the gay *alter cockers* online? I dread the idea of having to read between the lines of print I can barely make out to catch some octogenarian, not only lying about the size of his equipment, but that it still works at all.

Of course, if I'm still doing stand-up, it's a good bet I'll still be mining the Web for material. I might post a profile just for the jokes. I envision a fantastic response from the assisted-living audience as I tell of the role-playing geezer in a skintight cardigan who shows up at my door suggesting that an hour on my back might get me a better deal on a reverse mortgage. Who knows, mellowed by age I could conceivably find things different the second time around. It's possible I'd discover a willingness to push my boundaries even further than I'd imagined (although it's hard to picture that I'll ever look at erotic vomiting as anything more than a disgusting waste of perfectly good food). Perhaps I'll hook up with Tim again and get off on making his heart literally go pitter-pat as I blow up his angioplasty balloon. Or maybe, despite arthritis preventing me from turning the key that senile Tucker can't recall hiding, I'll gladly hop a Greyhound wearing his chastity device, painfully aware that at that age, "If not now, when?" means "If not now, never."

Supporting Characters

I

"Auschwitz, Buchenwald, Chelmo and . . . Dachau. Eddie, your turn."

"Okay, I'm going on vacation, and I'm going to visit Auschwitz, Buchenwald, Chelmo, Dachau and . . . em . . . em . . . Fuck! 'E' is hard!"

My cousin Elliot gestures with his eyes and head to his daughter Rachel in the backseat. "Hey—watch the language!"

"Sorry."

My new boyfriend Jeffrey, seated next to Rachel, interrupts. "You're subjecting her to the Concentration Camp Alphabet Game, and you're worried about the F-word?"

"Well, you want her to be up to speed, don't you? It's Holocaust Awareness Month at her preschool."

"She's four years old!"

"And?"

Rachel attends prekindergarten at a private Jewish day school in Washington, DC, which, in addition to stressing academics, is committed to instilling in its students an appreciation of Jewish culture and a sense of impending doom.

It's stuffy in the car and I roll down my window to let in some

air. We've hit a lot of traffic on the trip from DC to New York
and have at least another two hours to go on the Jersey Turn-
pike. I continue.

"E . . . E, E, E, E, E . . ."

"Want a hint?"

"No."

The two of us have amused ourselves with ghoulish games
such as this since we were teenagers in the limo on the way to
his sister's funeral. Jeffrey's appalled and tries to block us out
by reading a road map to Rachel. It's his first real encounter
with my family's black sense of humor, and he's not sure how to
react. Eventually, he'll learn what Elliot and I've known since
we were kids—the dark side of funny makes life bearable.

Depression often has a genetic component, and at any given
time at least half of my family is medicated. The resultant
humor is hereditary too. I've had first cousins on both sides
who've offed themselves, and the almost-impossible-to-live-with
loss has been dealt with by a lively exchange of macabre jokes
around the dinner table.

My shrink, Dr. Ben, claims that my ability to laugh things off
enables me to ignore how much they're really bothering me.
He has a point.

Elliot and I finish the game, although as usual we can't think
of a camp that begins with "Z" and have to settle for using Zyk-
lon B, the chemical used in the gas chambers, as a final solution. We finally arrive in NYC after dark, and Elliot drops Jeffrey
and me off at my apartment in Hell's Kitchen before he and
Rachel head off to visit friends on the Upper West Side.

II

I grin at Jeffrey as I turn the key in the lock. We've only been
dating two months, and although I'm not in love with him yet,

I'm a sucker for his blue eyes—plus the sex is fantastic! Jeffrey channels stress into sex the way I channel it into eating. In high school, when I was coping with teenage angst by cramming cookies into my mouth, Jeffrey was dealing with it by cramming varsity tennis players into his.

I'd be lying if I said that sex with Jeffrey doesn't have a strong emotional component; I'm just not saying that it does—at least not out loud. He's well aware of my disastrous relationship with Doug the Cheapskate and understands that I need to take things slowly. He vacillates between patience and frustration as I swing back and forth between rushes of schoolboy exuberance and periods of emotional fatigue where I turn off the phone, take to my bed, and read grim poetry. My bouts of the Edna St. Vincent Malaise serve me well in keeping Jeffrey at a distance without driving him away completely.

Once inside the apartment, I listen to my messages, and then hand the phone to Jeffrey so he can check his machine. I begin ironing my shirt for my shift the next day at the Eton Club where I'm the assistant manager, and Jeffrey reluctantly serves cocktails between acting gigs. He hangs up the phone.

"Paul Almquist called. He's got a job for me."

"Not *A Chorus Line* again?"

Jeffrey's been pursuing his dream of a musical theater career for eight years and works semiregularly. He's performed all over the U.S. and Europe, but every other job has been a tour of *A Chorus Line*. Ironically, he's never been cast as one of the characters who make the final cut.

"*The Phantom of the Opera*. I'd be the dance captain."

"Call him back!"

Jeffrey excitedly dials the phone while I log onto my computer. In among the spam promising me a harder erection and a lower interest rate is a message from Denny, the general manager at the Eton Club. The e-mail informs me that he's going into rehab again and that I'll have to manage the place by my-self for the next ninety days.

"Fuck! I can't believe this!"

Jeffrey cuts his call short—"Okay, Paul, sounds great. I have to go."—and turns to me. "What's wrong?"

"Betty Ford is taking another vacation."

"Again?"

"I wish he'd just overdose."

"Has he told the owners?"

"Not yet. He's afraid they'll fire him if they find out he's a cokehead."

"Please! It's practically a requirement for working there!"

"He's telling them he has to go home to Utica again, to take care of his grandmother."

"The one with heartworms?"

"This time she has tertiary syphilis."

"You're kidding?"

"I'm not. And he must be really serious about getting clean this time—she's in hospice. He wants me to cover for him. I don't know what to do. I can't handle three months of manag-ing that place on my own."

After two years of working at the Eton Club and witnessing the effect the environment had on people, I knew I had to get out soon. Most bars in New York City are staffed by aspiring ac-tors and artists whose careers are in limbo. But the Eton Club is where dreams go to die. The place is a carnival of addictions—booze, coke, smoking, sex—but the most treacherous vice is the staff's dependence on obscene tips. The money's great, so it's easy to let addiction breed addiction and to develop expen-sive and unwholesome habits.

"Well, Eddie, I just might have some good news for you. Paul says that the tour's company manager quit, and they're looking for someone to take over. You'd be perfect."

I know that Paul hasn't suggested me for the job. He has a huge crush on Jeffrey, and I'm sure he's looking forward to time alone on the road with him.

"Where's the gig?"

"Portugal."

"Really? For how long? When does it start?"

"Four months. Auditions start the day after tomorrow. We have two weeks of musical rehearsal here and then two weeks of rehearsal in Lisbon before the show opens."

"Four months! You're gonna be gone for four months?" I'm caught off guard by how upsetting I find the thought. My dread of being left alone is compounded by images of being trapped at the Eton Club 24/7 for three-quarters of that time. Jeffrey rushes on.

"Why don't you come with me? You're a great manager, and Paul loves you."

"No, he loves you."

"Well, you don't want to leave me alone with him for four months, do you?"

"I'm really not worried."

I'm not. Paul's a smart, funny guy, and a very talented director/choreographer, but his refusal to splurge on dental work has left his smile lacking. He's missing more teeth than he possesses, and the four remaining molars he exhibits when he laughs or yawns are evocative of a cartoon hippopotamus.

"Well, then, Eddie, come for me. It'll be a great chance to be together someplace new and exciting. We can take some time after the show closes, and go to Madrid or Barcelona. It'll be like a honeymoon."

"Don't say honeymoon."

"Sorry."

Jeffrey's always two steps in love ahead of me. After only two months, he's ready for us to move in together and gets all gushy looking at the sofas in the Pottery Barn catalogue. I find the prospect stressful. I like things the way they are, with us living a few blocks apart.

"That's a lot of together time."

"When else are you gonna get to Portugal and Spain?"

It does seem tempting—returning to the Iberian Peninsula five hundred years after my Sephardic ancestors fled the Inquisition. I fantasize about sending home a snapshot of me in a yarmulke and prayer shawl, French-kissing Jeffrey in front of Queen Isabella's crypt.

"I guess it couldn't hurt to talk to Paul."

Jeffrey makes the call, and Paul sets up an interview with the producer for the following afternoon.

III

I'm not familiar with the plot of the show, so before my appointment, I hit Coliseum Books on Fifty-seventh Street. Annoyed to discover that *The Phantom of The Opera* is one classic that the CliffsNotes people haven't condescended to condense, I grudgingly purchase a copy of Gaston Leroux's original novel and then head up to Tower Records on Broadway to buy the original cast recording of the Andrew Lloyd Weber musical. I skim the story and listen to the score on my new Sony Discman as I ride the bus downtown. The music, though derivative, is melodic, and the idea of hearing it ad nauseam for the next several months isn't completely unbearable.

I show up for my appointment on the far west end of Twenty-ninth Street dressed in the khaki pants, white oxford cloth shirt, and navy blazer that I wear for work at the Eton Club. The crumbling brick building, a row house without a row, stands between two weedy lots like a tombstone in a neglected cemetery.

I'm buzzed in and walk up three flights to the producer's office. The faded red letters spelling Jolly Jack Productions on the grimy door look anything but jolly.

I'm greeted by an amorphous marshmallow of a man with Einstein hair, dressed in an outfit almost identical to mine.

"Come in, come in. You must be Eddie. Sid Jack—lovely to meet you."

His flabby hand envelops mine, and he shakes his head so vigorously that his hair rattles. Paul Almquist has warned me that Sid's eccentric but appears to be on the up-and-up. Sid looks me over and comments on our matching attire.

"We're twins! That's a good omen."

"I hope so."

"We must've been separated at birth."

He follows up his lame joke with an insane, strident laugh, and I imagine him being whisked away by a wicked midwife to be raised in a sideshow.

I'm not far off. The water-stained office walls are hung with vaudeville memorabilia and pictures featuring Sid's father, Jolly Jack, a Yiddish Will Rogers who riffed on politics and swallowed random items suggested by the audience. Along with the posters and programs are dozens of photos from Sid's childhood, when he and his mother accompanied his dad on tour during the waning days of the Pantages Circuit.

With barely a question about my credentials, he offers me the position of company manager. I proffer the details of my work history, but he cuts me off with a wave of his hand.

"Paul says you're the man for the job. I trust his judgment."

He carelessly outlines my duties, which include acting as a liaison between him and the company and handling problems that the cast and crew might encounter with accommodations, travel, meals, etc. In addition, Paul's apparently guaranteed Sid that I'm qualified to perform the duties of assistant stage manager as well. I neglect to clarify that my stage-managing experience consists of once playing the role of the stage manager in the acclaimed Temple Beth Torah production of *Our Town*.

I quickly look over and sign the contract, and our meeting ends with Sid patting me on the shoulder and insisting I take a hard candy from a grandmotherly china dish.

As I make my way down the filthy stairwell, I contemplate what I'm getting myself into. I consider running back up and reneging on Sid's offer, but I'm haunted by the thought of babysitting the drunks at the Eton Club for the next three months. I exit onto the garbage-strewn street, convincing myself that the theater's full of eccentrics and that sometimes you have to take a risk. I'll revisit this moment over and over during the following weeks, regretting my decision and despairing that time travel isn't possible.

The next morning a FedEx arrives with a copy of the play. I'm opening the envelope when the phone rings. It's Jeffrey.

"Did you get your script?" he asks.

"Just arrived. I haven't looked at it yet."

"It's fucking awful."

"I know it's not the greatest show on earth, but . . ."

"It's not the Lloyd Weber."

"What do you mean?"

"I mean, it's not the Broadway musical. It's a completely different adaptation. And get this—it's written by someone named Jack Sydney."

"You have to be kidding."

I flip open the script. It's not the Tony Award–winning version, but a badly written knockoff, apparently penned by Sid. My ensuing nausea is accompanied by a dull metallic pain in my temple.

"Jeffrey, call Paul!"

"I did. He said he must've forgotten to mention it, but not to worry."

Telling me not to worry is, of course, the surest way to trigger my anxiety. My discomfort escalates as I examine the script and discover that Sid's pseudonym is the cleverest thing in it. The stage directions include pratfalls, a production number with a tap sequence, and the use of a dog act to segue between scenes. It's everything you'd expect from someone who claims to have been born in a vaudeville trunk.

My first thought is that opening night will find us all wearing *Phantom* masks, hiding from an angry mob demanding refunds. But Paul Almquist assures us that even if this guaranteed flop flops, the show's been presold to the promoters in Europe, and Sid isn't relying on success at the box office. Besides, his checks from Jolly Jack Productions have all cleared.

Paul's assurance calms us somewhat, but we're still apprehensive about the situation. To ease our minds further, Jeffrey and I combine our preferred coping mechanisms and indulge in a huge dinner and an extended romp. The combination's foolproof and we drift off to sleep easily. In the morning our anxiety levels start to creep back up, but wary of breaking our contracts, we head over to the studio and production offices on Eighth Avenue that have been rented for the auditions and NYC rehearsals.

IV

When Jeffrey and I arrive for the first day of auditions, Paul's there to greet us. Neither of us has seen him in months, and he looks suspiciously fantastic. His biceps make my calves look spindly, and his abs are visible through his T-shirt. The ironic thing is that I can feel his chemical enhancements affecting me. His shameless flirting with Jeffrey gives me roid-rage, and the botulism in his forehead makes me sick.

Thankfully, our reunion with Paul lasts only a few minutes before the first auditioners arrive. The New York talent pool's overflowing with gifted artists so desperate for work that they'd gladly play to a pile of skulls in the catacombs beneath an opera house. In among the unemployed soap actors and twentysome-things not yet regretting their decisions to major in theater are veterans of Broadway and the Metropolitan Opera. I know work's hard to come by in show business, but the idea of these seasoned professionals wasting their talent in Sid Jack's *Phantom* is as upsetting as seeing Sir John Gielgud's name in the opening credits of *Weekend at Bernie's III*.

The three days of auditions go smoothly and after the final casting cuts are made, contracts are faxed to the agents and managers. Given the tight production schedule, Sid's adamant that all the agreements be signed immediately, and within two days every single contract is safely locked in his desk. First thing the next morning the scripts are messengered out.

Returning from lunch, I fumble with my keys to the production office in an attempt to reach the ringing phone. Regrettably, I pick it up in time. It's the first of a score of irate phone calls. The actors have read the script and discovered Sid's deception. I'm supposed to field the calls, but after being shouted at, called names, and threatened, I start patching them directly through to Sid. He's infuriated and leans out of his office door, shaking the receiver at me.

"I thought I told you to handle these?"

"Sorry, I want too much to be liked."

He snarls at me before speaking sweetly into the receiver.

I listen as Sid charms the angry callers. Although I'm disgusted, I appreciate just how much of the showman is in him. It is, of course, to his advantage that these exchanges aren't taking place face-to-face. In person, he's less like P.T. Barnum and more like one of the human oddities in Barnum's collection.

Sid assures everyone that the show hasn't been misrepresented. After all it's being billed in Lisbon as *The Original Phan-*

tom of the Opera, which apparently is the truth, since he wrote his version when Andrew Lloyd Weber was still an awkward-looking adolescent. In addition, he promises their agents that the cast will be paid each week in advance and that the credit will look impressive on their resumes—plus nobody who is important (back home) will review it in Lisbon.

Finishing a call, he slams down the phone and shoots me a look of contempt. The quivering of his gelatinous eyes causes me to imagine that tadpoles might hatch through the straining membranes at any moment. Then, muttering under his breath, he turns and slams the door to his office. I suspect I might not be going to Europe.

V

Despite being sold the musical theater equivalent of snake oil, the entire cast appears for the first read-through, and I'm struck by just how large many of the actors are. In their attempt to stock the production with big operatic voices, Sid and Paul have cast the show with big operatic bellies. Nine out of the twenty cast members are somewhere in the neighborhood of two hundred and fifty pounds. Four of the men are easily over six foot four, and probably closer to three hundred. Their considerable heft is magnified by the contrast between them and the emaciated ballerinas and wiry chorus boys who comprise the rest of the company.

My immediate favorite in the cast is a wisecracking dancer named Moira Harney, who's also been assigned the part of the wisecracking wardrobe mistress. She's worked with Paul and Jeffrey before on several productions of *A Chorus Line.* A classic beauty, with features part Ivory girl and part Russian grand duchess, Moira's headshot gets her an audition for every ingénue role in New York. Unfortunately, producers' illusions are shattered when she opens her mouth and Buddy Hackett falls out.

After seeing one jumbo cast member after another lumber into the rehearsal studio, Moira leans over to Paul.

"I didn't know you guys held an actual cattle call."

Paul chuckles embarrassedly at her joke. It's obvious that he's struck by the sight of all of the weight watchers together for the first time.

"It's going to be a challenge for the costume designer."

"It would be a challenge for Christo."

Moira dubs the group the Big Belly Club, or the BBC, and Paul remarks that they look more like the Food Network. Their banter seems harmless, and I, a former fatty, laugh along self-consciously but don't call them on it. The fat jokes will continue for weeks.

Paul doesn't work with the actors at all before we leave for Europe. For the entire two weeks in New York, the company works on getting the vocals down pat while he and Jeffrey work out the staging. Dino, the stage manager, writes down the directions in a corner of the rehearsal studio. Dino seems like a nice guy, but I can't quite figure him out. He's in his mid-fifties with hair from the mid-fifties. His pompadour and garish gold jewelry seem incongruous with his peach polo shirt, madras shorts, and canvas loafers. While I can't pin down whether he's guido or gay, I can tell right away that he's meticulous. The papers and office tools on his table are perfectly arranged, and he writes down everything in his script with the seriousness of a senator drafting a bill. He writes very slowly, and Paul has to constantly wait for him to catch up. While his attention to detail seems a little much, I'm grateful for his OCD fussiness. I don't want to be the assistant of a messy stage manager; things are going to be challenging enough dealing with crazy Sid.

Day after day the music grates on my nerves. The performers' voices are impressive, but except for the big tap number, the dreary, atonal score makes Philip Glass seem hummable by comparison. I'd find it maddening that the dissonant chords at the end of every song never resolve, if I wasn't so thankful that the noise had finally ceased. Moira jokes that, "The music is perfect for the plot—if I was forced to listen to this dreck reverberating through the opera house, I'd hide in the cellar too."

Paul lets out a roar so resonant that the entire company looks our way. His guffaw reveals an unexpected set of perfect white teeth. Jeffrey and I, stunned by the sight of his new chompers, exchange looks of astonishment.

When Paul heads to the men's room, Jeffrey whispers to me, "Oh my God, that had to cost a fortune!"

"He must've finally coughed up the thousands in tooth-fairy money he's collected."

"It certainly ups his fuckability."

Not only is Jeffrey's comment unexpected, but I'm surprise by the degree to which it irritates me.

The pang of jealousy makes me glad I've agreed to go along to Europe, where I can foil any designs Paul might have on Jeffrey. Secretly, I'm terrified of finding my way around a foreign country where I don't speak the language. Until this point, my international travel has consisted of a trip with my high school choir to the Pennsylvania Dutch country, where I was beaten up for flirting with an Amish boy selling hex signs and weather vanes from a roadside stand.

I try to cram a course in Portuguese into the few days before our departure, but it is arguably the hardest of the romance languages. It looks like Spanish, but sounds garbled like French to my uneducated American ear. The sample Portuguese dialogues in the textbook are anything but practical, and aside from "hello," "thank you," and "where is the bathroom?" I end up with only a few useless words about my aunt attending the dog races.

The rage I provoked in the Amish was nothing compared to the ill temper I bring out in Sid Jack. My refusal to lie on his behalf and cover for his misrepresentations provokes him to fire me in a fit of screaming that drowns out the finale of the show's first act. My job's saved by Paul, who interferes when Jeffrey threatens to quit if I'm let go. Jeffrey's hardly indispensable to the production, and imagining that the idea of losing him isn't all that upsetting to Sid, I wonder if Paul's also threatened to quit.

Although the likelihood that I'll lose my job is slim, I sense security will come at a price, and feelings of dismay accompany me to work each morning. The constant fear of being fired, though nerve-racking, is actually less stressful than working for someone who hates you but can't give you the axe. Frustrated by his powerlessness, Sid works extra hard to make my life miserable. He's consistently rude to me, assigns me the most menial tasks, interrupts my lunch with pointless errands, ignores my questions, and belittles me in front of the company—all in the hope that I'll quit. I dread the hours I have to spend alone in the cramped production offices with him. The worst part of it all is that he has almost no sense of humor.

Even if I did tender my resignation, I'd have no job and no place to live. I've taken a leave from the Eton Club, convincing the owners that I too had a syphilitic grandmother (using the same bizarre excuse as Denny seemed the only certain way to make my lie seem legitimate). Plus, I've sublet my apartment to a thuggish stockbroker from Elizabeth, New Jersey, who I'd be afraid to evict. To top it all off, when I review my contract, I discover that Sid isn't required to issue my return plane ticket until the end of the show's run.

VI

Two days later, after Sid gives me a particularly severe thrashing, I'm just about to stomp out the door when I catch sight of Paul and Jeffrey embracing in the studio mirror. A squirt of adrenaline whips me around, but by the time my eyes catch up with my body the two of them have disengaged. It takes me a minute to realize that they're choreographing an adage dance sequence for the second-act graveyard dream scene. They're oblivious to me as I watch them rehearse the sexually charged routine from the hallway. In the scene, Christine and Raoul perform a romantic pas de deux that's broken up by the Phantom, who slays Raoul and rips out his heart. The dance involves a series of complicated lifts, but Paul, even with his chemically enhanced physique, has trouble hoisting solid Jeffrey overhead. They make several attempts, but each time Jeffrey ends up cradled in Paul's arms looking like a mermaid caught by a burly fisherman.

"Are you okay, Jeff?"

"I'm fine."

"I was afraid I was going to drop you that time."

"I trust you, you're strong."

"Thanks."

As I spy on them, a voice from behind unnerves me.

"Keep an eye on Paul. He's on the hunt for something to sink those new teeth into."

I turn just in time to see Moira toss a wink and a laugh over her shoulder as she runs out the door.

I'm startled by my own heart's response to their intimacy. Jealousy isn't a familiar emotion for me, but the idea of Jeffrey alone with Paul and his new incisors for four months makes me crazy. I realize that no matter how horrible this job is, I can't quit. Feeling like I have no choice but to stay fills me with rage and makes my previous annoyance with Jeffrey's growing expectations insignificant. I'm livid about being trapped in a job I hate, so I can move forward at a speed I'm not comfortable with, to save a relationship I'm not sure I'm ready for.

For me, feeling like there's no escaping a difficult situation immediately stirs up thoughts of the ultimate way out. I'm well aware that this isn't a normal reaction, but in my family it's an example that's been set. My cousin Elliot and I, to prevent ourselves from actually making a final exit, have employed our grisly sense of humor.

We constantly try to one-up each other with new and inventive ways to end it all. We believe if you're going to go to the trouble of killing yourself, do it with style. Anyone can pick up a gun and shoot himself in the backyard. Where's the fun in that? Make it special! Slap on some clown makeup and blow your head off in front of a blank canvas! It's the perfect way to leave your loved ones with a little piece of yourself. Only an unimaginative bore would jump off a ledge in broad daylight. Be original! Fill your pockets with fireworks, light a match, and go out in a blaze of glory visible throughout the tri-state area!

Elliot jots down all of our ideas in a journal. We know that once it's illustrated it'll make a wonderful children's book. Bipolar kids are horribly underrepresented in preteen literature, and it'll not only let them see people like themselves, but will instill pride by highlighting for them the correlation between depression and creativity. Our plan is to have the stories published before Elliot's daughter Rachel hits puberty and has her first bout of the family illness.

Jeffrey doesn't get black humor at all and is more than a little disturbed at how interwoven it is into our lives. I assure him that, though our suicide game's twisted, it's predicated on a steadfast rule: telling the other player about a new method prohibits you from actually using it. Neither Elliot nor I want to find ourselves on the defensive at the other's memorial saying, "I thought he was joking." Of course, I've assured Elliot that if I ever did follow through on a plan that I've shared with him, I'd leave behind a note absolving him of responsibility.

"Elliot, I want you to know that this wasn't your fault . . . exactly."

And so my anger and jealousy spins into a morbid and quirky daydream. I close my eyes and a silent movie flashes on the inside of my lids. In the warped fantasy, I rabidly bite off my finger and scrawl a suicide poem across the walls with the hemorrhaging nub. The paramedics try in vain to stem the river of blood surging out of my body as they scan my writing and marvel at my innovative use of the double dactyl. The poem is published posthumously in *The New Yorker*.

I call Elliot. He's delighted.

Our sick game aside, I'm not really one to plan a suicide. I'm far too considerate to leave my affairs in disarray. Before shuffling off this mortal coil, I'd feel obliged to settle my debts, make a will, write a note, find a home for my cat, and arrange to have the rug shampooed. The problem is that I'm too much of a procrastinator ever to get everything done; I'm here for the long haul in large part because I find the list of chores overwhelming.

But according to my shrink, Dr. Ben, I might end it all impulsively in a flash of rage that's been brewing undetected or unacknowledged beneath a fragile crust of humor. It's frightening to contemplate that one day I might spontaneously jump in front of the B train, or slam-dunk my Waterpik into the bathtub.

As rehearsals continue, I find myself calling Elliot with increasing frequency. Inventing one absurd method of self-annihilation after another, I laugh off Sid's abuse, Paul's crush on Jeffrey, and a cast worth their weight in problems.

VII

On the day we leave for Portugal, I hail a cab for the airport several hours before our departure time. I need to be there ahead of the rest of the company in case there are any problems with their passports, luggage, or seat assignments. Of course, there are.

Most of the cast makes it to the airport in plenty of time for the flight, but several—including Paul, Moira, and best friends and Big Belly Club members Art Sapienza and Gina Repoli—show up late. Heavy people have heavy luggage, and both Art and Gina are over the weight limit. A scramble to redistribute the excess pounds ensues, and I have to call on the more undernourished members of the company to donate space in their carry-ons for husky clothing from Lane Bryant and Rochester Big & Tall.

The amused ticketing agent gives a nod of approval to my resourcefulness, but there's skepticism on his part that the person in Gina's passport photo is actually her two hundred pounds ago. Indeed, pasty Gina, with her strawberry-blond hair and preteen fondness for pink, bears a closer resemblance to Miss Piggy than the pug-nosed girl in the mug shot. The agent's only convinced when Gina presents him with an intermediate picture on an expired gym ID, apparently taken before she'd let herself go completely. I'm uncomfortable for Gina, who handles the situation with commendable dignity. She's oblivious to Paul and Moira behind her, suppressing giggles and elbowing each other while sharing a bag of rice cakes.

I can see from Art's face that he's aware of their reaction. He chooses not to acknowledge them and rests a protective arm around Gina's shoulder as they head through security.

With everyone accounted for, I breathe a sigh of relief, send my carry-on through the X-ray machine, and walk through the metal detector. I'm reaching for my bag, ready to sprint to the gate, when my hand's intercepted by a security guard.

"Sir, please stand back."

In seconds there are four burly officers surrounding me— one of indeterminate gender. It takes nearly ten minutes to convince the dopes that the bomb squad's unnecessary, that the ticking object they've spotted on the monitor is nothing more than a windup kitchen timer my mother has insisted I take to Europe. Still living in the shadow of the Great Depression, she worries herself sick over every penny and is particularly agonized by the idea of transatlantic phone calls. The timer's supposed to ensure that I don't run up huge bills by preventing me from going over the first three minutes of any long-distance conversation. Although I think it's ridiculous, it proves extremely useful when talking to her.

I'm the last to board the aircraft and hurriedly make my way past the rows of first-class passengers, which include Jeffrey, who's been upgraded so that he and Paul can work on script changes during the trip to Lisbon.

The flight's booked solid, and in my attempt to fulfill the cast's requests for additional legroom, I've settled for a middle seat. I'll spend the next seven hours wedged between Art and Gina, whose leg o' mutton arms violate my seat's air rights, turning my clavicles into de facto armrests.

Travel is stressful, and everyone has their own method of coping with the anxiety. Art closes his eyes and lightly touches his thumbs to his middle fingers. It takes me an hour to realize that the nasal dirge he's chanting is actually the opening of the show. Gina simply pops a couple of Xanax to unwind. Regrettably, they have a particularly relaxing effect on her sphincter.

I can't wait to get up and move around the cabin, but the flight's extremely bumpy, and the captain keeps the seat belt light on almost the entire trip. When we're finally through the turbulence, I squeeze past Gina and make my way toward the front of the plane to visit Jeffrey. I can see him and Paul huddled over the script. Paul laughs and casually moves his muscular arm from the back of Jeffrey's seat to his shoulder. My stride quickens, but my impulse to make three a crowd is abruptly thwarted by the first-class stewardess. With her outstretched arm she bars my progress and defiantly pulls the curtain closed, as if I were trying to get a peek at the great and powerful Oz.

Jeffrey isn't the only one getting hit on. As I shuffle dejectedly back toward my seat, my progress is interrupted by another BBC member, Bud Fu, who Moira mockingly refers to as Buddha, or Bud Food. Bud's taken a shine to me. He's a sweet guy but lacks subtlety, and his crush is as conspicuous as his size. He engulfs me with a sweaty bear hug, which I escape by distracting him with a roll of Necco Wafers I have in my pocket. He takes the whole roll.

"I shouldn't, but I'm starving."

I'm starving too—well, not exactly starving, just stressed. I was planning to use the candy as anti-anxiety medication, but don't have the heart to deny the desperate Bud.

"I put in your request, Bud. They should've had an extra vegetarian meal for you."

"They did, but the portions are kind of stingy, and on my diet I'm supposed to fill up on leafy greens. I wonder if you wouldn't mind asking the stewardess for an additional entrée."

I imagine filling Bud up with leafy greens would involve clear-cutting the Everglades.

"I'll see what I can do."

Bud's request prompts similar demands from the rest of the BBC, who are irritable from the insufficient meals and inadequate seats. I find myself in the plane's galley, begging extra food from a haggard and unsympathetic flight attendant who has logged every mile on her face. Her refusal to issue second

helpings—or even additional peanuts—and make my life easier is rendered moot when service is suspended due to further
turbulence. I'm required to return to my seat and spend the remainder of the flight crunched between chanting Art and fart-
ing Gina.

VIII

It's morning in Lisbon when we arrive. The bus that picks us up
at the airport drops Sid, Paul, and Dino off at their spiffy, first-
class hotel before heading to the Hotel Tareja, which will be
our home for the next few weeks.

Lisbon is sunny and beautiful, though Portugal, one of the
poorest countries in Europe, has a little bit of a third-world feel.
Untouched by either world war, the capital hasn't been mod-
ernized through rebuilding to the degree of Berlin or London,
and its Roman and Moorish influences are in sharp contrast to
the quaint Disneyesque villages of Holland and Scandinavia. It
has also not yet been overrun by American fast-food chains and
retail outlets, although Art does manage to spy a Kentucky Fried
Chicken on a side street near the hotel. As I gape skyward at
the rotating red and white bucket dwarfing the steeple of a
centuries-old church, I can't help but think that the arrival of
Generalissimo Sanders is the first step in the fattening up of
this unsuspecting country. With the BBC and KFC both in my
field of vision, it occurs to me that *Phantom*'s debut will give the
Portuguese a sobering view of the disasters in store for both
their theater and their health-care system.

We arrive at the Hotel Tareja and are pleasantly surprised.
It's a turn-of-the-century jewel box located in the Baixa neighborhood, not far from the Coliseu Lisboa, where the show will
be housed. The hotel staff is extremely friendly, and my fears of

not being understood are allayed by the discovery that most of them speak English. I feel hopeful for the first time since I left the office of Jolly Jack Productions.

The cast is impressed by the Tareja's detailed charm and eagerly queue up to check in. Moira's the first to register and returns to the lobby in minutes. She's wearing a pale ginger sundress, and lights a cigarette as she drapes herself on a chaise. Against the gold damask upholstery, her porcelain features and elegant lines evoke a sepia photograph of Zelda Fitzgerald. Jeffrey and I sit down across from her as we wait for the others to check in and head up to their rooms.

"Finished unpacking?" I ask her.

"Oh, we won't be staying that long."

"What do you mean?"

"You'll see."

As the smoke gently escapes her lips and frames her classic profile, she grins knowingly and gestures with her chin toward the marble stairs.

I glance over as Bud Fu begins his labored ascent. The staircase at the Hotel Tareja is encircled by lacy wrought iron railings, and I briefly speculate on the ability of the dainty filigree to support the weight of the BBC. When the line at the registration desk has dispersed, Jeffrey and I sign in. As we make our way toward the stairs, Jeffrey excitedly points out the elaborate cornice, but Moira's negative assertion has started to eat away at my fragile optimism. As I look back at her chain-smoking on the chaise, she shoots me a self-satisfied smile that seems less sepia aristocrat and more nicotine-stained bitch.

On the second floor, a continental breakfast is being served on a sunny veranda with a mosaic floor. Several of the cast have discovered the free food and are busy stuffing their faces and wrapping baked goods in napkins to take back to their rooms. I notice one of the European guests comment to her companion, and although they're speaking in a tongue I can't decipher, I'm sure her remark has something to do with disgusting Americans.

Our room is sunny with arched windows. The bathroom's adorned with traditional blue and white Portuguese tiles and has a deep tub with a handheld European shower. As I start to unzip my suitcase, Jeffrey reaches around me and starts to unzip my pants. "What are you doing?"

"Nothing."

"Nothing?"

"Nothing."

"Aren't you tired?"

"I can't help it. It's spring, when a young man's fancy turns to thoughts of hot, piggy sex."

"Thank you, Alfred Lord Tennyson."

"Don't mention it."

"Well, we have to break in the mattress sometime."

We pull each other's clothes off and hit the sheets. The room's airy but not air-conditioned and soon we're nice and sweaty. Well, maybe not nice. While the reaction to someone's pheromones is a huge piece of the chemistry between partners, after six hours on a stuffy plane wedged between two large, perspiring people—one of whom is way too stingy with the Arrid Extra Dry—I'm offending myself.

"I'm sorry, I stink."

"Let's take a bath."

"Together?"

"Sure, we'll get clean *and* dirty. It'll be fun."

We're getting worked into a lather when we're interrupted by the phone. I try to ignore it, but it's fire-drill loud and just keeps ringing and ringing and ringing. I jump out of the tub.

"It's driving me crazy. I'll be right back."

I leave a trail of suds on the rug as I run, naked, over to the nightstand and pick up the receiver. I regret it at once.

It's Art calling to complain about the lack of an elevator. I'm about to respond that a little exercise isn't going to kill him, but I can hear him sweating through the receiver and it crosses my mind that it just might. I assure him that he'll get used to the stairs and promise to do my best to get him moved to a lower floor. No sooner do I hang up than I get another call. I spend the next half hour wrapped in a towel, fielding complaints. By the time I return to the bathroom, Jeffrey's drying off.

"Sorry that took so long."

"It's okay, I finished without you."

"I'll make it up to you."

"I'll see that you do."

The rest of the morning is filled with ringing phones. In addition to the stair situation, there are calls about the old-fashioned bathtubs, the lack of variety at breakfast, and the inability to regulate the temperature. The whining continues in person when the cast assembles in the lobby to head to the Coliseu for a brief tour. Art unfolds a tourist map of the city and bemoans the distance between the hotel and the theater. "We were told the Coliseu was within walking distance."

I point to the marquee, visible through a lobby window, less than a mile away. "It's right nearby; you can see it from here."

"I can see the Statue of Liberty from my apartment, but that doesn't mean it's easy to get to."

Behind me, I hear Moira mutter, "If she were holding an ice-cream cone instead of a torch, you'd find a way, fatty."

I blush and Jeffrey struggles to hold back a laugh.

I turn to Art. "It's been a long trip. I'll arrange a taxi for you today if you like."

I know I'm setting a bad precedent; Art and the rest are going to expect taxis every day. Though Sid's going to be furious about the extra expenditure, I'm exhausted and just can't deal with the issue at the moment. All of the BBC except Bud,

admirably electing the exercise, opt to take cabs. I change fifty
dollars for escudos at the hotel desk, and hail four cars from
the queue down the street. Jeffrey and I, along with Bud and
the dancers, head out on foot.

IX

Phantom will be the first show in the historic Coliseu de Lisboa
since its state-of-the-art renovation. It seems a shame.

I have only a few days before I add the duties of assistant
stage manager to the already overwhelming responsibilities of
company manager, and so, after touring the venue, I set out to
get as many things organized as possible. Jeffrey offers to accompany me, but I assure him that I'll be fine on my own. As he
and the others head off to explore the Castle of Sao Jorge that
overlooks the city, I set out to address the cast's issues. In addition to moving all of the BBC to a lower floor and having the
breakfast expanded to include ham, eggs, and fruit, I arrange
for dry-cleaning services, find a nearby chiropractor for the
dancers, contract with the restaurant adjoining the hotel to serve
family-style suppers, and stock the cast's rooms with menus
from KFC. I even spend two hours, at a company member's request, checking out gay bars and inquiring about hustlers in
the area known as the Barrio Alto. By early evening, when I return to the Tareja, I'm worn out.

After fielding an assortment of complaints, including one
from Bud Fu about the periodic power outages that are preventing him from steaming a cabbage on a hot plate, I'm ready
to hit the hay big-time. Jeffrey has other ideas. All of Paul's at-
tentions have him horned up, and he makes his move before
my head hits the pillow. I need to sleep but feel guilty about
abandoning him in the tub earlier. For the first few minutes

I'm just going through the motions, but then his razor stubble grazes my nipple and I get a second wind. Of course the phone rings, and although I try, there's no ignoring it.

It's the hotel manager. Something's causing a dangerous power surge that the Tareja's antiquated wiring cannot tolerate. I throw on a T-shirt and a pair of boxers, wait for my erection to subside, and head down to Bud's.

He's slow to answer and finally opens the door wearing a sleepy shar-pei face and a pair of briefs barely visible beneath the folds of his belly.

"What's up?"

"Bud, you gotta turn off the hot plate."

"It's off."

"You sure?"

"See for yourself."

He steps back to admit me, and I'm almost knocked off my feet by the stink of boiled cabbage and its aftereffects. Bud holds up the disconnected plug of the cold hot plate, but next to it on the nightstand is another appliance—a white box with a small water tank. The apparatus, connected to wires, tubes, and an oxygen mask, is making a wheezing sound.

"What is that?"

"It's my VPAP machine."

"Come again?"

"I have sleep apnea."

"Maybe that's the trouble."

It turns out that Bud's device isn't the problem—only part of it. Gina, Art, and three other members of the BBC are also using breathing aids. Apparently, obese people are especially prone to sleep apnea. Breathing is made difficult by the excess weight compressing their chests when they're lying down. Unfortunately, the hotel's outmoded electrical system just can't handle the demands of modern medical equipment, and to avoid a fire, everyone has to unplug and sleep sitting upright. I lie awake until dawn prepared to call an ambulance and dreading the impending search for a new hotel.

Jeffrey's pouring me a fourth cup of morning coffee when Moira, in a floral kimono, flows through the French doors onto the veranda.

"Jesus, Eddie! You look like pig shit!" she says.

"And a gracious good morning to you too."

Jeffrey explains the electrical situation. "He was afraid someone might not make it through the night."

Moira laughs. "Be serious! Those chowhounds would make it through a nuclear war, if there were a free breakfast at the end."

Sure enough, minutes later the double doors swing open and the race to the muffins is on. Within fifteen minutes, everyone's accounted for.

A half hour later, I break the news to Sid. He has no problem with the "kill the messenger" approach to problem solving and screams at me, sclera swelling, for a full ten minutes. I hate him so much at that moment that I'd gladly observe him stroke out if I wasn't apprehensive of the complications that his dropping dead would cause. Thankfully, his tirade dissipates, and an aneurysm is avoided when he stops to gasp for breath. He grumbles "Just handle it!" and sprinkles me with sweat as he dismisses me with a flourish of the monogrammed handkerchief he uses to mop his brow.

Finding new accommodations for an entire bus and truck company in Cleveland on such short notice would be difficult. Locating a hotel near the Coliseu, with modern wiring, an elevator, and an all-you-can-eat breakfast buffet is a Herculean task. A simple solution doesn't exist. But after ten hours of dragging my sleep-deprived ass up and down the Lisbon hills under the blistering sun, I somehow manage to patch together a collection of suitable rooms for all of the breathless. I return triumphantly to the Hotel Tareja as fetid and fatigued as if I'd spent the day mucking out the Augean stables.

The company's enjoying the cool breeze on the veranda where the BBC, still ravenous and cranky from a night of battling suffocation, is raiding the cereal and plastic-wrapped pastries that have been preset for the following morning's breakfast. They're relieved to hear that they'll be able to sleep horizontally again, but go completely mental when they learn their weight is to be evenly distributed throughout the Baixa. I apologize. "I'm sorry, folks. It's the best I could do."

Art, beside himself at the prospect of being separated from Gina, lashes out.

"They should've hired a company manager with more experience."

Bud Fu comes to my defense. "Hey, it's not his fault we have all this optional equipment."

"Oh excuse me! I didn't know that breathing was optional!"

Moira's unable to resist butting in. *"Buddha's right. You're lucky Eddie found you a room and that you won't be spending the night in an alley with your iron lung hooked up to a car battery!"*

"It's not an iron lung, it's a VPAP machine!"

"Either way, if you can't breathe, go to a hospital! And for God's sake put down that brioche!"

Everyone is stunned. Moira stares him down, and Art, mortified, slams the roll into his cereal bowl and thumps away with a box of Cap'n Crunch tucked under his arm. I turn to Moira. "Thanks."

She winks at me, her Buddy Hackett softened. "Don't let 'em walk all over you, honey. With this crew, the pounds per square inch'll kill you."

Five new hotels to deal with (Bud remains at the Tareja), and the problems are overwhelming. Everything has to be researched, negotiated, and arranged over and over and over again and I fall into bed each night too exhausted to return Jeffrey's advances, forcing him to attend to his own needs. In the mornings, when I can detect a vestige of my libido, the sex is unfailingly interrupted by calls about low water pressure, expensive laundry, thin walls, and ugly furniture. One morning after a ringing phone pulls my focus from Jeffrey just as he's about to come, he snaps. *"Jesus Fucking Christ!"*

"Sorry, I gotta answer it."

"Of course you do."

"Oh please, don't give me grief." I pick up the phone. "Hello? Hi, Gina . . ."

Jeffrey rolls his eyes and slams his head down into the pillow with a puffy thud.

". . . Okay . . . Calm down . . . Yeah . . . Did you call the desk? All right, I'll go over and check on him. I'll call you from there."

"What does she want now Eddie?"

"She's in a panic. They have fried dough at her hotel, and she's been unable to reach Art all morning. I'm going over and make sure he's all right."

"Tell her to go herself."

"I thought of that, but he's at the top of that hill. I'm not sure she could make it. I'll be back in a little while."

Jeffrey, gestures to his crotch. "Well, what am I supposed to do?"

I half joke that he should get Paul to lend him a hand. It appears I've hit a nerve. He jumps up and heads for the bathroom. *"You're an asshole."*

"Go fuck yourself."

"I practically have to." And he slams the door.

It's not the only slam of the morning. Art's fine. Actually, he's more than fine and has found a way to get his breath going without his apnea machine. I only get a quick glimpse of the guest on his bed before Art shuts the door in my face, but judging from the trick's age and appearance, I'm sure there's money (or maybe candy) involved. I head down the hall pissed off and pent up, certain that after he pays the young man, Art will be calling me to whine about his hotel's crappy exchange rate.

As I stomp through the lobby of Art's hotel, a *Phantom* poster next to the concierge desk catches my eye. I involuntarily gnash my teeth, dreading opening night when the shit hits the fans.

X

I practically tear the door off the hinges as I exit Art's hotel, but outside my spirits are lifted by the sun bathing the Avenida's patterned sidewalks in a butterscotch glow. I take a circuitous route back to the Tareja to enjoy the rays, and by the time I return to our room, Jeffrey's at breakfast. Alone, I prolong the therapeutic effects of my stroll by nesting myself in denial. I ignore the stack of petty problems the cast has slid under the door and lie on the cast-iron bed, anticipating the start of my stage management duties with self-deluding naïveté.

In addition to relying on my dark sense of humor to help me through life's unpleasantness, I also I have a terrible habit of suffering through a difficult situation by daydreaming about the next one. So, blinding myself to the glaring fact that adding the tedious duties of assistant stage manager to my busy schedule is going to suck, I embrace the illusion that the start of my backstage commitment will bring an end to my current difficulties. I romanticize my new responsibilities, convinced that the old-world charm of Lisbon will somehow add cachet to my position and elevate my sense of worth. I'll find myself, a common gofer, suddenly a species of interest in an exotic habitat. Sauntering along Lisbon's light-drenched streets with the importance of a cultural attaché, I'll uncomplainingly fetch coffee and perform other menial tasks I'd be unable to tolerate at home.

Of course my projection's overly optimistic, but somehow I

convince myself that the cast, once engrossed in the intense rehearsal schedule, will focus less on their petty problems and acclimate to the food, lodgings, language, and currency. The BBC will find clever ways of procuring after-hours snacks and of hoisting themselves out of antique bathtubs. On top of that, the show's bad writing will go undetected by an audience whose primary language isn't English, the hoodwinked promoters won't notice the Andrew Lloyd Fibber score, and Sid will be so enraptured seeing his script on the stage instead of in a drawer that he'll barely notice any extra expenditures. In that environment I'll be able to focus on Jeffrey. Once the chinks in our relationship are spackled, Paul will lose interest and entertain himself with one of the sinewy stagehands.

Of course, the fantasy that the weather, people, and novelty of Portugal are going to save me from becoming a common grunt is about as realistic as Gina's assertion that she can slim down by eating dietetic fudge, or Sid's belief that ending every song in a loud, angry chord makes him an avant-garde genius.

I procrastinate, watching the numerals on the digital clock from the seventies flip over, but eventually I get up and head to the Coliseu. It's my responsibility to arrive before anyone else and get everything set up for rehearsal.

I enter the empty venue and am jolted into the here and now by the Alcatraz echo of the metal door slamming shut behind me. Just inside, I'm assaulted by my name scrawled in red ink on a batch of notes pinned to a corkboard. As I shuffle through the daunting stack of things requiring my attention, it dawns on me that "The Theater," the masses' reprieve from reality, will hold no merciful illusions for me. This is going to blow bigtime.

Most of the messages are from Dino the stage manager and deal with odd details, such as adding fragrance to the artificial fog and which brand of tea should be used to give the Phantom's sheet music an aged appearance. I try to convince myself that the specificity of his requests is indicative of his exceptional organizational skills, but the degree of minutiae worries me.

Unfortunately, the other communiqués have nothing reassuring about them either. The most important two, in sealed envelopes, are from Sid. The first notifies me that from now on I'm to be the only point of contact between him and the producers. They're not to be told at which hotel he's registered, or even that he's in Lisbon. I'm forbidden from sharing his phone number with anyone, and under no circumstance is it to be made known that Sid Jack, the producer, and Jack Sydney, the playwright, are one and the same. I'm appalled by Sid's contempt for the Portuguese's intelligence—as if the people who discovered the trade route to India are going to be incapable of deciphering his ridiculous nom de plume.

Sid drops the bomb in his second message. Since sleep-apnea-induced budget constraints have forced him to eliminate the position of prop master, those duties now full under my purview. The news is jarring. There's no way I can daydream this information into something good, and my mind turns once again to thoughts of escape through self-annihilation. I turn the note over, and on the back doodle a clever Rube Goldberg type of Kevorkian device with which to dispatch myself and escape the situation. My fantasies are interrupted by the groan of the heavy door and the voices of the company members as they enter the Coliseu. I save the sketch and mail it to Elliot in DC. It'll make a great cover for our children's suicide book.

XI

After unlocking the orchestra room for the musicians and setting up chairs for Paul and Dino behind the production table in front of the stage, I sit down in the first row of theater seats, and going through my script, begin making a list of the props needed for the show. As the squeals of strings and woodwinds drift in from the hall, I dread having to shield Sid from the producers' wrath when they discover the cacophony they assumed was the orchestra tuning up is, in fact, the entr'acte.

From a blue canvas tote, Dino removes a roll of paper towels and a spray bottle of Formula 409. He proceeds to wipe down the table and then, satisfied that all is clean, carefully sets the Formica top with his script, pencils, sharpener, stapler, ruler, pads, paperweight, coffee mug, Kleenex, and a small basket of cough drops, Lifesavers, chewing gum, antacids, and breath mints.

I find his behavior disturbing, but help myself to some gum.

"Wow, Dino, you're so organized!"

"I hate disarray."

Throughout the morning I glance up from compiling my prop list and observe Dino painstakingly making notes in the prompt book as Paul explains the blocking to the actors. When we take five, I step up to the table and Dino snaps the binder shut.

"Eddie, I need to use the restroom. Keep an eye on this."

"Okay."

"Don't let anyone look at it. It's a mess!"

"No problem."

Of course my interest is piqued. When he heads backstage to use the toilet, I flip the book open.

"Holy cow!"

Paul and Jeffrey look my way. I hold up the open book for them to see. Dino has not only written Paul's stage directions in excruciating detail, he's set them down in an ornate calligraphy worthy of a medieval monk, making the terrible libretto look more like the Book of Kells than a cheesy knockoff of an overrated Broadway musical.

Paul shakes his head. *"What the hell's he doing?"*

"Apparently, preserving this piece of 'literature' for posterity."

"Don't be funny."

"I'm serious—at this very moment there could be marauding Visigoths breaking through the city gates."

Jeffrey chimes in. "We're more likely to be attacked by a disgruntled audience. I'd rather fight the Huns than face a horde of angry matinee ladies."

I scan the script. *"Listen to these stage directions: 'Christine coquettishly tosses her hair back as she glides down stage left under Raoul's lustful gaze.'"*

"My God, it sounds like a Harlequin Romance."

Paul pulls the book from my hands. *"This is insane!"*

"I'm just being thorough!" We all turn to see Dino, standing arms akimbo, on the apron of the stage.

Paul lets him have it. *"Are you kidding? No wonder you're always telling me to slow down. 'Christine crosses down left—C X DL!' How hard is that? C X DL! Just write it down! We don't have time for this nonsense!"*

"Whatever you say."

With the disappointed face of a child told to put away his crayons, Dino shuffles back to his seat behind the production table.

I can see that he's miserable, and I feel guilty. I try to get back in his favor by polishing his Murano paperweight, but from his venomous stare I know I won't be forgiven.

XII

Over the next week Dino and I clash continuously, making my days in the theater unbearable. The tension infects my muscles and causes my jaw, and ass, to constantly clench. Although the addition of my new responsibilities is overwhelming, I can't wait to flee the dark Coliseu and begin shopping for the odd assortment of props that Jack Sydney's *Phantom* requires. I know that some items, like a china teapot and skeleton keys, will be relatively easy to procure, but locating others, like the ear trumpet used by the character of Madame Valerius in the second act, will require extensive hunting. Despite the fact that Sid's decision to give a solo to a character he's written as deaf is idiotic (although the audience will certainly envy her disability), I'm hopeful that scavenging for the antique hearing aid will keep me away from rehearsals for several days.

It's not to be. Unfortunately, Dino's illuminated manuscript is only the first problem brought to light. Once we start running the show, it becomes obvious that he's embellished his resume as well. While his academic knowledge of Leroux's gothic tale is impressive, and he's undoubtedly done his best to read up on the specifics of stage management, book learning is no substitute for hard theatrical experience. Under the glare of the spotlights his inadequacies are magnified, and I'm forced to pick up the slack. Each morning I find at least one sealed envelope from Sid tacked to the corkboard. At first he assigns me relatively minor tasks that would normally fall under the stage manager's job description, but as Dino's incompetence snowballs, Sid shifts more and more responsibilities to me. It's just assumed I'll find gentle ways to inform Dino of these changes— a practical impossibility given his level of animosity toward me. While I'm grateful that Sid's sealed these documents, Dino's knowing looks cause me to imagine that he's already coaxed the envelopes open with the steam shooting out of his ears. So, with the same regularity with which Art reaches for the last cruller on the breakfast buffet, I enter morning rehearsals with the trepidation of a page sent to inform a puppet king of the most recent blow to his once-sizable empire.

All of this breeds more hostility in Dino, and his palpable enmity toward me discomfits anyone within twenty feet. Whenever company members see us together they keep their distance behind unseen ropes, as if they're spectators waiting for the bell at a heavyweight fight. I have no personal beef with Dino, and I'd choose sex with a porcupine over his job, but painfully aware of my own inexperience as a stage manager, and still feeling guilty for messing up his calligraphy, I put up with his increasing nastiness.

My new duties tighten my schedule, and I'm forced to cram my anticipated weeks of leisurely prop shopping into hellish lunch hours. I madly dash around the broiling streets, overspending on items that only somewhat approximate what the script calls for. In the afternoons I return to the Coliseu, sweat drenched and prickly heated, where I continue my crash course in backstagecraft. Even though I have a theater degree (that I'm still paying for), I have no idea what I'm doing and rue my clever scheme to dodge my college stage crew requirements by working in the box office.

Dreading the idea of going over budget and having to ask Sid for additional funds, I hastily improvise whatever props I'm unable to locate easily. My first shortcut proves disastrous. I nix Madame Valerius's silver ear trumpet in favor of a plastic funnel I swipe from a gas station. Unfortunately, the metallic spray paint I use to decorate it triggers a severe allergic reaction, and the actress ironically suffers a partial hearing loss. After a smug Dino informs me of her decision to file a lawsuit against Jolly Jack Productions, I expectantly check the bulletin board for a pink slip from Sid. I'm shocked when Jack Sydney risks detection by the Portuguese and appears that evening in the flesh, sitting in the third row at a run-through of the second act.

XIII

It's the first rehearsal Sid's seen since New York. I watch him from behind the scenes through a small tear in one of the flats.

Reflecting the stage lights, his eyes look like deep-sea jellyfish floating in the dark of the Coliseu.

His presence rattles Dino and causes him to fuck up big-time. The errors would be Keystone Cop hilarious if it wasn't so close to opening night. Set pieces enter mid-scene, the masquerade ball is plunged into darkness, and the graveyard fog starts rolling into Madame Valerius's bedroom, rendering her blind as well as deaf. As the mistakes mount, Sid's eyes bulge frighteningly and sweat cascades down his chins. He finally loses it when the free-falling sandbag that the Phantom uses to scare the impresarios drops in unexpectedly, almost killing Moira and another ballerina. Sid jumps to his feet, and charges the stage, bellowing like a bull in a slaughterhouse. "STOP! STOP, STOP, STOP, STOP, STOHHHHHHHHHHP!"

Sweating and snorting, he hoists his fat ass onto the apron and plants himself like an explorer center stage. "EVERYONE OUT HERE NOW!"

The actors and crew file on from the wings and form a semicircle around Sid at a distance appropriate for the revulsion and fear he elicits. Physically he's not intimidating—most of the cast easily outweigh him, and the rest could easily outrun him—but the precarious bulge of his aspic eyeballs and his Queen of Hearts "Off-with-their-Heads!" volatility inspire wariness. And so we stand, chins into necks into shoulders, as Sid showers us with insults and spit in a sweeping arc like a lawn sprinkler.

Working his way from left to right, Sid tears into the musicians, stagehands, and each of the actors. By the time he gets to the far end where Dino and I are standing, the two of us have withdrawn into ourselves as far as possible. With our heads poking timidly out of our collars, we resemble nothing so much as a pair of skittish prairie dogs afraid to leave their burrows.

I brace myself for my turn at humiliation, but Sid passes over me and rips full force into Dino.

"*And you, you idiot! I cannot believe your level of incompetence! This is an Equity production! Do you have any idea what the hell you're doing? Have you ever even seen a Broadway show? It's bad enough I'm paying you a fortune to make my beautiful musical look like crap, but do I have to worry about you killing someone? Isn't one lawsuit enough?*"

Madame Valerius shoots me a death-ray stare as she fingers her bandaged ear. I respond with the best look of contrition I can muster and focus ashamedly on a patch of floor. I'm aware that everyone notices the exchange, and I fight my urge to check the stage for expressions of sympathy.

Sid eviscerates Dino with a barrage of cutting epithets that would reduce a truck-driving crack whore to tears. Dino, humiliated (and with no legitimate defense for his incompetence), jumps off the stage and flies out of the Coliseu in a pastel blur. With a wave of his hand, Sid abruptly dismisses everyone for the night before waddling furiously out the stage door. Apparently, I'm not even worth acknowledging.

The rest of the company stands in shock, their expressions appropriate for a crowd who've just witnessed the Wild Man of Borneo cannibalize an infant. The painful silence is broken by Moira, apparently no worse for the sandbagging.

"It'd be so much easier if those two just admitted their attraction to each other."

A smattering of laughter ripples through the group and everyone disperses. Jeffrey, sharing my relief that I've avoided a public thrashing, sneaks up behind me and whispers, "You realize this means we have the evening free."

"You don't miss an opportunity."

"We never have any. Let's go play."

"You go; I have to finish up here."

He pulls my head back and kisses me before heading off. "Hurry!"

As I turn around, my eyes meet Paul's. He flashes me a smile.

The light reflecting off the imitation enamel illuminates strands of silky spittle stretched between his lips, and I can almost believe some hideous arachnid has taken up residence in his throat, ready to paralyze and devour Jeffrey if he ever gets too close.

"Good night, Paul."

"Have fun."

He winks at me and smiles again, his jealousy visible through his porcelain veneer.

"I intend to."

Although I'm exhausted, I can't wait go back to the room and have sex with Jeffrey—just to piss off Paul.

I hurriedly clear the stage and am presetting things for the morning rehearsal when Dino unexpectedly enters from backstage and grabs a parasol out of my hand. *I'll put that away. You've got better things to do.*

"What do you mean?"

He flings a crumpled-up piece of paper down on the property table. *"You're in charge."*

I open the note. Sid must have scrawled it before he left the building. There's a pinhole where it's been tacked to the corkboard: "Eddie, effective immediately, you'll be taking over backstage. Dino will handle props."

I look up from the paper into Dino's dejected face. I'm not surprised he's been canned but I'm shocked that I've been put in charge. I guess temporarily ruining someone's hearing is preferable to killing them with a fifty-pound bag of sand. I want to tell Dino that I'm surprised by his demotion, but the lie can't find its way to my mouth. All I can manage is an unintelligible gurgle and a guilty look. He screams at me to get out, slams the parasol down, and braces himself against the table. I leave him there, convulsing emotionally, as if there's an alien pupating in his thorax.

Balancing my sense of superiority at being put in charge with the knowledge that there will be no escape from the impossible demands of the situation is difficult. I wander around the Baixa trying to center myself and return to the Hotel Tareja much later than expected. Back in our room, I find Jeffrey, naked on the bed, asleep from the waist up. He's covered the dresser, sills, and nightstands with dozens of the elegant tapers used to illuminate the Phantom's subterranean lair. The smoky paraffin gives the air a waxy, Catholic feel, and face up on the embroidered bedspread, framed by the candle-shadowed drapes, he resembles a cardinal lying in state. I stand quietly for a moment, but when an involuntary twitch of his dick shatters the funereal tableau, I erupt in a spray of laughter and snot. His spastic boner and dreamy half grin change my perspective, and as I work a rubbery booger into a ball between my palms, I envision a hypocritical memorial attended by scores of former altar boys contemplating sodomy charges.

The sex is religious—in the opiate of the masses sense—and provides a few moments of escape. But my orgasm immediately gives way to crushing despair as the reality of my new situation comes into focus.

XIV

With opening night approaching like a tsunami, I hardly have to rely on my imagination to manufacture a sense of imminent disaster. The next ten days are difficult beyond belief. From the old grammar-school desk backstage that serves as my base of operation, I struggle to synchronize the lights, sound, scenery, curtains, artificial fog, and crashing chandelier. I'm terrified that I'm going to screw up worse than Dino. The stress is so great, I start to age visibly. My eyes get puffy, and trenches line my pasty forehead. I really do feel like pig shit. To top it all off, Dino looks fabulous. Sid, not wanting to buy him out of his contract, hasn't fired him, and Dino, despite the humiliation of being demoted, hasn't quit. Like me, his financial circumstances won't allow it. But his new, lighter duties agree with him, and he seems well rested. I resent his suntan, which gets deeper each time he goes out prop shopping, while my ghostly skin qualifies me to haunt an opera house.

Solicitous Bud Fu, alarmed by my appearance, begins a tradition of bringing me a bakery box of Portuguese suspiros each morning.

"Bud, you're very sweet, but this isn't necessary."

"It certainly is necessary—you need to keep up your strength. Have one."

"For breakfast?"

"Oh come on, it won't kill you."

Feeling obliged to afford the dieting Bud some vicarious satisfaction, I pop one of the meringues into my mouth. As he watches me with the look of a forlorn puppy seeking supper scraps, feelings of pity and contempt well up in me. Hoping he'll go away, I thank him and turn my attention to some lighting plots. He doesn't take the hint and thrusts the box between my face and the blueprints.

"Have some more! I like a man with a little meat on his bones."

As I crunch down on another of the sickeningly sweet treats, he smacks his lips, transforming the puppy into a hyena menacing a lion with a kill. His look is so disconcerting that I fear if I let my guard down, he'll devour the suspiros and me—bones and all. It occurs to me, I could escape all my problems once and for all by simply rolling in sugar and throwing myself to the BBC.

Now, I'm a little long in the sweet tooth and, even without Bud's encouragement, have trouble saying no to desserts. By a quarter past nine two-thirds of the box is gone, and I'm on the jittery cusp of hyperglycemic shock. Luckily, Art helps himself to "just a tiny taste" and finishes off the suspiros. It's too late, though. The damage is done, and my yo-yoing blood sugar exacerbates my stress.

Obviously in a cast of such heavy hitters, the connection between food and feelings isn't limited to my glucose level or to Bud's jealousy. The looming premiere has everyone on edge, and eating is the preferred method of coping. The BBC's voraciousness reaches livestock levels, and as in a herd, they nudge out the smaller individuals in the competition for food. By the time the lunch platters reach Madame Valerius and the dancers, they've been licked Jack Sprat clean. Moira leads the rebellion as the featherweights try to assert themselves, but her ensuing tug o' war with Gina over a crab leg results in bloodshed. As the doctor's stitching up her hand she remarks, "I should know better than to try and wrest food from a hungry animal."

I do my best to secure larger portions, but the restaurant's struggling under the burden of feeding the BBC and can't afford to increase the amount served. My food budget is stretched to the limit, and Sid won't part with one additional cent.

"Eddie, it's your job; negotiate a solution."

"How? I have nothing good to negotiate with."

"Then use something bad."

Another appeal to the restaurant is met by a definite no. And so, like a trapped man forced into collecting protection money for the mob, I thuggishly trash my morals to save my skin. I "imply" to the owner that if we take our business elsewhere, it "might" generate negative publicity—a shame, since the eatery's proximity to the Coliseu makes it the ideal place for pre-theater dinning. I don't even let myself think how furious he'll be when the dreadful reviews reduce his anticipated stream of theatergoers to a trickle.

My strategy doesn't work. The owner isn't intimidated at all and responds by lowering the overall quality of the food served.

The cast is in an uproar, and Sid won't budge. To keep the peace, I spend my own money to supplement the cast's diet with pre-dinner meals from Kentucky Fried Chicken. It takes a lot to satisfy Art, Gina, and the rest, and the delivery guy needs an assistant just to carry the coleslaw.

Unfortunately, though he's been unwavering in his allegiance to cabbage, Bud can no longer white-knuckle it. Like a shark drawn from miles away by a single drop of blood, he can detect the aroma of a biscuit two floors below, and a mere whiff of KFC's eleven herbs and spices sends him charging down the Tareja's stairs to man the bucket brigade. It's disturbing to pass Bud's room and see the pile of red and white cardboard pails outside his door. It isn't so much the evidence of gluttony that freaks me out, as the fact that the debris has been picked clean. There's not a piece of skin or gristle anywhere. I shudder thinking of the ravenous beast that's been unleashed—even a Grimm ogre would leave a few bones on the welcome mat. To top it all off, poor Bud regains the few meager pounds he's lost, plus a lot more, and has to be hastily duct taped into his costume after he splits his trousers in the opening number.

Gorging himself on fast food unleashes Bud's sexual appetite as well. His sweet nature vanishes, leaving behind a sexual predator of the first degree, and I hypothesize that the Colonel's secret recipe includes Spanish fly and powdered rhino horn. He ambushes me with bear hugs and slobbery kisses that leave me feeling as if I've been beaten about the face with a raw flank steak. Dodging his advances is one more challenge I don't need, and after one particularly aggressive mauling, I contemplate sprinkling saltpeter on his mashed potatoes.

Bud isn't the only one whose appetites are in high gear. Opening night's approaching fast, and everyone needs an outlet for their stress. The rest of the company are eating like pigs and fucking like bunnies. Art's penchant for chicken can't be satisfied by wings and drumsticks, and I receive more than a few complaints from the Tareja's manager about the parade of young street hustlers passing through the lobby on their way to brave Art's fleshy chasms.

Gina, too, gives in to her primal urges. In an estrogen blast of Hiroshima magnitude, her libido is unleashed like Godzilla, freed from the ocean depths. The Portuguese stagehands quake whenever they hear her seismic tread echoing through the Coliseu. Moira, amused by the panic in their faces, mocks them. *"Oh my God! It's the snatch that ate Lisbon! Run, fellas, run!"* They scamper into the flies while Moira calmly puffs away on a Salem Light. Gina passes by her without notice, a hunting tyrannosaurus oblivious to the tiny shrew in the grass.

Tobacco is Moira's vice of choice; she's never without a cigarette. Backstage, with the stench of smoke clinging to the long black skirt and white apron of her wardrobe mistress costume, she reminds me of one of the few lucky girls who survived the Triangle Shirtwaist fire.

Unfortunately, aside from overindulging in Bud's baked goods, my schedule allows no time for vices. It's a huge problem. Our sexcapade after Sid's outburst has opened the floodgates of Jeffrey's libido. I do my best to keep up with him, but I'm exhausted, and he doesn't know when to stop. It would be so much easier if I could just set my mom's egg timer and tell Jeffrey he's got three minutes to get to the boiling point.

In order to take the edge off and get to sleep, Jeffrey's forced to take care of his own business. He tries synchronizing his strokes with the rhythm of my snoring, but alas, my breathing isn't controlled by the consistent pulse of a VPAP machine. The natural fluctuations in my airflow keep pulling him back from the brink, and night after night of exasperating starts and stops make him unbelievably irritable. I begin to believe he might smother me with a pillow while I sleep. I pray it'll happen before opening night.

XV

The few remaining eighteen-hour days fly by in an exhausting blur as Paul tries everything he can think of to compensate for the show's flaws—bolder staging, flashier costumes, sexier choreography. The problem is that attempting to dress up this mess is akin to putting whipped cream and sprinkles on a bowl of raw fish heads and thinking nobody's going to notice it stinks. Paul doesn't seem to care, since each change of choreography requires late-night rehearsals and offers new opportunities to get his paws on sex-starved Jeffrey. His modifications to the script are so numerous that I have to use colored markers to keep track of them. Eventually, Dino's beautiful pages have the look of a Gutenberg Bible used as a coloring book by a four-year-old.

On the eve of the opening, there are still a ton of problems to be solved (although I can't help thinking that not opening would solve most of them), and Paul and Jeffrey continue working down to the last minute, fine-tuning the dance numbers. That night I observe them, unnoticed, from the mezzanine.

Their movements are infused with an increased sexual tension, which at first I attribute to the new choreography. But something's different and I literally start shaking as I watch Paul bare his fake fangs. My agitation increases when I sense Jeffrey might allow him to strike, and I go into full panic mode when Paul moves in for the kill. I leap up from my seat applauding furiously.

"Terrific! That's great! Perfect family entertainment! Will we be observing the stage decencies, or will the fucking take place in view of the audience?"

Startled, Jeffrey flushes red, but Paul, quick on his feet, lobs my sarcasm back at me.

"I think somebody should do some fucking around here. Don't you think so, Jeffrey?"

Jeffrey looks at me sheepishly. He knows I'm furious.

I can barely hold myself together. "Well then . . . carry on."

My words sting my ears as they leave my lips, and I manage as quick an exit as possible.

My head's so clouded with the idea of Jeffrey and Paul together that I'm not aware of my surroundings until I'm accosted on the sidewalk by a Gypsy kid playing a Barry Manilow medley on a concertina. I toss the urchin the loose change and Necco Wafers from my pocket and stomp down the street summoning up pictures of Jeffrey and Paul in every Kama Sutra position. I know I've pushed Jeffrey too far away and am sure a breakup is imminent. I'm terrified. Even though we've only been together for two months in addition to our time in Portugal, and I've been dragging my feet, our shaky relationship's the only thing that I feel anchored to at all. Despite my ambivalence, I can't handle losing the feeling of control that comes with being the one who's less in love.

Jeffrey never comes home, and I spend the night on the bed alone staring into the dark. My racing thoughts contrast sharply with the slow, lugubrious hours and the starless silence, broken only by the screams of some hapless stagehand as Gina fucks the lifeblood out of him in the room below.

The loneliness is crushing. Suddenly it occurs to me that DC is seven hours behind Lisbon, so I pick up the phone and ask the switchboard operator to give me an outside line. I set the egg timer for three minutes and then purposely ignore it as Elliot and I play another version of our alphabet game—this time starting off with, "I'm going to therapy and I'm going to discuss Abandonment, Bulimia, Codependence, Death . . ." We then try to one-up each other, inventing more novel ways we can do ourselves in. We finish off the call discussing creative ways to permanently fuck up his kid and listing all of the things we'll never accomplish.

None of this makes me feel any better.

XVI

The sky eventually lightens and I realize there are only twelve hours until opening night. I've missed my last chance to escape under cover of darkness. Paul calls for one last dress rehearsal that afternoon to implement the latest round of changes. Even though the newest updates make the prompt book illegible—and I'm more concerned with avoiding eye contact with Jeffrey than focusing on the stage and lighting cues—I miraculously manage to make it through the run-through without a major mistake. I'm more than skeptical of the power of prayer, but pray anyway that the old theatrical superstition that says a bad dress rehearsal means a good show, isn't true in reverse.

Finally the moment I've been dreading arrives. The premiere's sold out, and as the eager audience files in they marvel at the beautifully renovated Coliseu. Little do they suspect it will be the highlight of their evening.

Amazingly, the complicated opening goes off without a hitch, and Act I is met with polite applause. I foolishly begin to calm down. Then, during the second act's first number, the audience's discontent becomes audible. Even though they're grumbling in another language, I don't need a Portuguese-to-Profanity dictionary to figure out what they're saying.

I can't wait to get the hell out of the Coliseu, so I deafen myself to the agitation in the house and refocus every bit of my being into just getting through the show. I call the cues with robotic precision and keep everything under control. Then, BOOM! The first chords of the graveyard dance number reach my eardrums and a hundred billion neurons fire at once. My brain bombards me with so many memories and emotions that I can't move. I stand frozen for over five minutes as I watch Jeffrey and his dance partner repeating the sexy moves I witnessed him and Paul working on from the mezzanine.

I remain transfixed by Jeffrey as he and the other dancers

hold their final pose. Somehow he's aware of me and throws his
eyes in my direction before exiting to the opposite wing. The
moment of connection discombobulates me, and too fuzzy to
focus, I lose my place in the script and call for a blackout half a
page early. I quickly try to fix my mistake, but the set pieces are
already in motion. The lights come up on a bunch of confused
actors and a dozen stagehands scrambling to get out of sight.
Dino, standing near me, laughs with satisfaction.

"Not so easy, is it?"

"Fuck you, prop boy."

Our exchange escalates and I miss another important cue,
which screws up a third—and then a fourth. The crowd gets
hostile. Those that aren't booing and throwing things are walking out. The insults overwhelm the actors' dialogue, and I can't
hear where they are in the scene. I grab the ear trumpet from
the prop table, stick it in, and aim it toward the stage. It magni-
fies the voices but distorts them, causing me to misjudge horribly and call the cue that releases the chandelier. In a split
second, the heavy fixture swings down, and terrified actors dive
out of its path and scatter like roaches as it crashes with a terrifying thud into a grand piano that isn't supposed to be there.

Everyone goes crazy. The yells of the audience, bouncing
around the acoustically designed Coliseu, are deafening but hypnotic. They collide with the roar in my head, the way the screech
of the subway smashes against the music on my earphones. I
hear both, but hear nothing, and I'm immobilized. My eyes dis-
connect from my brain, and I watch, detached from the disaster-
film soundtrack, as Dino, a smirk on his face, quickly pulls the
grand drape closed.

Paul runs onstage from the audience and ducks under the
curtain just before it hits the stage floor. The thick velvet blocks
out the crowd, but backstage everyone's panicking. Actors are
running around, Dino's calling me names, and a crew member

with a bloody hand is cursing me in Portuguese. Paul's furious.
He backs me up against the wall. *"WHAT THE HELL ARE YOU
DOING? ARE YOU A MORON? WE'VE REHEARSED THIS PART
A HUNDRED TIMES!"*

"I'm sorry."

*"YOU'RE SORRY? THE SHOW DOESN'T SUCK ENOUGH
THAT YOU HAVE TO SCREW IT UP EVEN MORE?"*

Dino butts in. "I knew he'd mess things up."

Paul cuts him off. *"SHUT UP!"* and turns back to me. *"JESUS!
YOU'RE SO GODDAMN INCOMPETENT!"*

As he's screaming, the finger he's waving in my face turns
into a fist, and his hand trembles as he struggles to keep from
punching me in the nose. With a yell he pounds his fist into the
wall to the left of my head. I jerk to the right in response, my
face reddens, and the pressure builds up behind my eyes.

He leans into me with his finger again, the sweat dripping off
his creaseless forehead. *"Don't you start crying."*

Over Paul's shoulder I spot Sid huffing and puffing toward
me. His rage is in the danger zone. If he had a gun, I'd be dead.
My body instinctively braces itself against the wall. *"YOU FUCK-
ING PIECE OF SHIT! I'M GONNA BEAT THE LIVING CRAP
OUT OF YOU! YOU RUINED THE WHOLE GODDAMN THING. I
SHOULD'VE FIRED YOUR ASS RIGHT AT THE BEGINNING."*

He turns to Paul. *"AND YOU! HOW DID I LET YOU TALK ME
INTO KEEPING HIM?"*

"DON'T PUT THIS ON ME."

*"OH NO? NO! 'OH, KEEP HIM, SID, HE'S JUST OFF TO A
ROUGH START' BULLSHIT! ALL YOU WERE WORRIED
ABOUT WAS GETTING INTO THE OTHER ONE'S PANTS."*

*"FUCK YOU! FUCK YOU AND YOUR CRAPPY SHOW, YOU
SON OF A BITCH. I SHOULD HAVE MY HEAD EXAMINED FOR
TAKING THIS JOB."*

They're shouting inches from my face. I'm trapped against

the wall, and I can't breathe. The rest of the company is standing around, their faces indistinguishable. All that my brain registers is Dino's satisfied smirk. There's no escape. I lose it.

Without warning I let out a scream that could demolish a
city, grab a bottle from the prop table, and smash it over my
head. My explosion stuns the company who watch, terrified, as
I repeatedly jam the jagged glass into my scalp. It takes a moment for their minds to register what they're seeing, and I'm
able to inflict several deep wounds before Paul wrestles the bottle out of my hand.

I scream, *"GET OFFA ME! GET OFFA ME!"* break free of Paul's
grip, and bulldoze through the crowd. Jeffrey tries to stop me, but
I push him to the floor, yelling, *"STAY THE FUCK AWAY FROM
ME!"* and run backstage, my vision blurred. I lock myself in the
men's room and drop to the floor. Holding my face as the blood
splatters on the blue tiles, I sob uncontrollably for what seems
like forever, my body in spasms.

Though my cries are echoing around the empty bathroom, I
become peripherally aware of the commotion outside. Jeffrey's
talking to me through the door. I can hear that he's freaked out
but trying to maintain a soothing tone.

"Eddie, please open up."

"LEAVE ME ALONE!"

"I need to see that you're okay."

"I DON'T WANT TO TALK TO YOU!"

There's murmuring, then a light tapping.

"Eddie, it's Moira. Can I please come in?"

I don't answer and she asks again. "Sweetie, please?"

"Just you."

"Just me."

"Okay."

Turning the lock cracks the dried blood and snot between
my fingers. I open the door just enough and Moira squeezes

through. She looks me over and says in a June Cleaver mixture of scolding and concern, "Oh, sweetie, you look like pig shit."

XVII

Moira holds me as I cry out every drop of the anger and anxiety I've been pushing down since I first read Sid's script. She tries to fix me up, but the men's room isn't stocked for this kind of emergency; the commercial hand soap stings, and there's a limited amount of first aid you can administer with toilet paper. Jeffrey calls to her through the door. "Moira, is he okay?"

"We're going to need an ambulance."

I protest, *"NO!"*

"You have to go to the hospital. You're going to need stitches."

"I don't want an ambulance."

"You're seriously hurt."

"NO AMBULANCE!"

"Okay, okay. Will you go in a cab?"

"Yes."

"All right, let's go."

"Tell everyone to go away first."

"I'll be right back."

I can't make out the conversation in the hallway, but a few seconds later I hear the slam of the heavy metal door as people exit the Coliseu. Moira comes back in. "Everybody's gone. Bud's getting us a taxi."

The three of us—Bud, Moira, and I—stuff ourselves into the backseat of the compact European car and sit quietly en route to the hospital. I'm much calmer now. My flash of rage has released a lot, and though there are still tears falling from my eyes, I feel my body relaxing like a deflating balloon. Suddenly the car makes a sharp left, we're thrown to the right, and I burst out laughing at the sight of us in the rearview mirror. It alarms Moira.

"What's wrong?"

I point to our reflection and she cracks up too—and not just because I look ridiculous applying direct pressure to my temple with a roll of Charmin. Bud Fu, still dressed in the slashed doublet he wears as Faust from the opera within the play, could pass for a Chinese Henry VIII, and Moira, in her blood-soaked apron, now resembles an actual casualty of the Triangle fire. Wedged between the two of them, I look like the victim of a horrific time-travel accident.

The hospital's anything but modern and has the feel of a turn-of-the-century sanatorium. Luckily, my lacerations look worse than they are and require only a couple of stitches. Unfortunately, in an emergency room, patients are seen in order of the seriousness of their complaints, and those with lesser injuries are continually moved to the bottom of the list. We're there for hours.

Finally I'm called into an exam room. Bud goes to find a pay phone, and Moira sits with me while the nurse buzzes away sections of my hair. After the attending physician sews up the biggest wounds, he excuses himself. We're left alone for a few minutes.

Moira looks over the doctor's handiwork.

"Wow!"

"What?"

"He did a really good job. I bet you'll hardly have any scars."

"Well, the Portuguese are good with head injuries—they invented the frontal lobotomy."

"Really?"

"Their only Nobel Prize so far."

"That's creepy."

"But kind of fun."

"I hope this won't take too much longer."

"They probably want their psychiatrist to talk to me."

"You think? You only carved your head up in front of a hundred people. It's not like you're some kind of sexual deviant."

I love that Moira's mocking me. It makes me feel less ashamed.

"Thanks for staying with me. I'm so sorry—I don't even know how it happened. I just snapped."

"Oh please, you were the best thing to happen on that stage all evening. You should do it every performance."

"They all must think I'm completely mental."

"Don't sweat it, sweetie. Everybody's got their fucked-up shit."

I'll never forget the truth in that line.

Bud Fu pokes his head in the door. "Okay in here?"

"I'm fine."

"I bought you some jelly beans. They're good if you've lost blood. I used to get them at the Red Cross when gay people were still allowed to donate."

"Thanks, Bud."

"I'll be in the waiting room if you need me. Jeffrey's here."

He exits, and I turn to Moira. "He's a good-hearted guy."

"Free candy at the blood bank? He must've been anemic."

"You're awful."

"I am. He is sweet. You should talk to Jeffrey; he's very worried."

"About?"

"Don't be an asshole. I was up until four trying to calm him down after your incident with Paul last night."

"He was with you?"

"Why do you think Paul was so angry with you before? He doesn't care about the show. He's just frustrated 'cause he's not getting any."

"He will. Jeffrey's been flirting with him."

"Well, what's he supposed to do? Paul's the only thing keeping Sid from firing you."

"So nothing happened?"

"I tried to seduce him, but apparently Jeffrey prefers someone with bigger tits—with hair on them."

"I'm a schmuck."

"You need to talk to him."

XVIII

Moira heads out to the waiting room when the psychiatrist shows up. He asks me a few simple questions, his attitude inappropriately nonchalant, considering that my scalp is sewn up like a softball. I guess he determines I'm no longer a danger to myself, because after he leaves, the nurse returns with my discharge papers and a box of tranquilizers. I exit the examination room to discover that Moira and Bud have gone and Jeffrey's waiting there by himself. It's awkward.

"Nice haircut," he says.

"Thanks."

He hands me a folded newspaper.

"What's this?"

"The review."

"I open the paper. "*O Fraud de Broadway!*—Nice."

"I asked the guy at the Tareja to translate it. It says that the biggest applause goes to whoever released the chandelier and brought the train wreck to a halt."

"That'd be me."

"Are you ready to go home?"

"I guess I'll have to face everyone sometime."

"Not the hotel, I mean New York. I got our tickets."

"How?"

"Paul got them for me. Bud's meeting us at the airport with our stuff."

"And Sid?"

"Fuck him."

"I have to pay my bill."

"Do you need money?"

"I have some from petty cash. Sid can pay it."

"All right, I'll go hail us a cab."

At the cashier's, I can't help but find it ironic that the escudos I'm using to pay for the stitches in my head are imprinted with the likeness of Dr. Egas Moniz, the father of the modern lobotomy.

Out on the sidewalk, Jeffrey hands me a can of ginger ale. "I was going to get you a bottle, but I figured you'd hate trying to hurt yourself the same way twice."

"Thoughtful."

"But, here, I saved you the plastic rings from the six-pack. Maybe you can swallow them and fatally clog your intestines."

"Not bad."

"Or wrap them around your ankles and drown yourself off the coast like a tangled sea lion—after calling Greenpeace, of course, so they don't waste a photo op that'll help fight ocean dumping."

"I'll write that down."

"Okay, but if you include that method in your children's suicide book, I want credit."

"Maybe if I actually kill myself that way, my cousin Elliot will feel obliged to put you in the dedication."

"Maybe we could check out together! I bet that would sell a lot of copies."

"Absolutely not! That would ruin everything! You have to stay around. Half the fun of killing yourself is imagining the person you love reliving the horror day after day."

"Point taken."

"Exactly."

"Okay?"

"I feel a little better."

"That'll change."

Acknowledgments

I'd like to acknowledge my gratitude to the following people for providing me with information, inspiration, advice, criticism, cash, quiet places to write, warm places to sleep, much appreciated pats on the back, and much needed kicks in the ass: Mickey Abbate, Peter Antony, Matt Brewer, Christopher Broughton, Joe Cigliano, Jaffe Cohen, Mark Dempsey, Amy Engelberg, Wendy Engelberg, Martha Ertman, Lauren Essex, Victor Flatt, Charles Flowers, Terry Gatewood, Alan Ginsberg, Hilary Goldmann, Penina Graubart, Shira Graubart, Steve Graubart, Will Guilliams, Michael Hart, Gary Kahn, Mariko Kaonohi, Eric Kornfeld, Mike Krsul, Gregory Marro, Phil Mause, Bill McDermott, Sarah McGraw, Danny McWilliams, Thomas Palatucci, Ian Phillips, Maureen Phillips, Arn Prince, Mark Roberts, Joe Robertson, Glenn Rosenblum, Patrick Ryan, Amy Saidman, Anthony Santelmo Jr., Jack Sarfaty, Ella Sarfaty, Sonny Sarfaty, Andrew Scharf, Cathy Sembert, Rick Shupper, Mark Solan, Jack Sprague, Bernie Stote, Mehul Tank, Chris Tittel, Robert Trachtenberg, Don Weise, Mark Williams, Garth Wingfield, and Michael Zam.

For all their patience and support, I'd like to express my appreciation to my editor, John Scognamiglio, and to my agent, Alice Martell.

I'd also like to thank Maggie Cadman for being so generous with her time and for her enthusiasm.

And I'd especially like to thank my good friend Bob Smith for insisting that I put pen to paper, and for his assistance and encouragement throughout this entire process.

FYI—The spinning jenny was invented in Stanhill, England, by William Hargreaves and patented in 1770.